T0005767

Play to Win

Also by Jodie Slaughter

Bet on It

All Things Burn

White Whiskey Bargain

Just One More

To Be Alone with You

Play to Win

A NOVEL

JODIE SLAUGHTER

ST. MARTIN'S GRIFFIN
NEW YORK

This is a work of fiction. All of the characters, organizations, and events portrayed in this novel are either products of the author's imagination or are used fictitiously.

First published in the United States by St. Martin's Griffin, an imprint of St. Martin's Publishing Group

PLAY TO WIN. Copyright © 2023 by Jodie Slaughter. All rights reserved. Printed in the United States of America. For information, address St. Martin's Publishing Group, 120 Broadway, New York, NY 10271.

www.stmartins.com

Designed by Meryl Sussman Levavi

Library of Congress Cataloging-in-Publication Data

Names: Slaughter, Jodie, author.
Title: Play to win: a novel / Jodie Slaughter.
Description: First edition. | New York: St. Martin's Griffin, 2023.
Identifiers: LCCN 2023009388 | ISBN 9781250821843 (trade paperback) | ISBN 9781250821850 (ebook)
Subjects: LCGFT: Romance fiction. | Novels.
Classification: LCC PS3619.L3776 P53 2023 | DDC 813/.6—dc23/eng/20230227
LC record available at https://lccn.loc.gov/2023009388

Our books may be purchased in bulk for promotional, educational, or business use. Please contact your local bookseller or the Macmillan Corporate and Premium Sales Department at 1-800-221-7945, extension 5442, or by email at MacmillanSpecialMarkets@macmillan.com.

First Edition: 2023

10 9 8 7 6 5 4 3 2 1

*This is to my mother and her
scratch-offs and penny slots
and anything else that ever
felt like it might have the
ability to save us*

1

MIRI

Digging a hole was not nearly as easy as it looked on TV. First off, shovels were heavy. Second, South Carolina dirt seemed to be as hard as her mama always said her head was. Miri had thought that breaking the tough topsoil would have been the easiest part. The very same dirt that bubbled up any time it rained, sticking to the bottom of her shoes and releasing slimy worms onto the concrete. It hadn't been, though. She'd been forced to bang the head of the shovel against the earth so many times her shoulders ached. Once it finally cracked enough for her to bury the tip of the shovel in the ground and pull from it, she felt like she'd already done an entire day's work.

It had only been two hours. Two long, torturous hours of labor that left her cursing under her breath. Always under her breath. With enough force that the words felt satisfying to say but not loud enough that Ms. Candice could hear. Though the woman was eighty-two and more than twenty feet away, sitting on the back porch with her feet up on the railing, Miri had no doubt the woman still had ears like a bat. And enough stamina to call Miri over for a pop in the mouth if she heard her cussing.

Ms. Candice wanted the hole three feet deep exactly. And she would know if it wasn't too—she could tell just by eyeballing if Miri missed the mark by even a few inches. The last time Miri had done this for her, it had taken three hours. But she'd been younger then, with a body that didn't ache because of a shitty mattress and much less hopeless resignation about where she was in life.

She was thirty-two now. Her muscles were softer and her patience was much, much thinner.

Miri paused to wipe the back of her hand across her forehead. She had on an old, rough pair of work gloves that she'd borrowed from her cousin Jay. When the material brushed against her skin, she grimaced. It was hot out. The sun was well hidden behind the clouds, so her skin didn't burn, but the humidity rolled in from the coast, making the temperatures feel even more suffocating. She hadn't even been able to dress in her coolest clothes. Not unless she'd wanted to hear from Ms. Candice how she didn't need to be "showin' all her stuff" around town. So she wore her cheapest leggings, a pair from the Family Dollar that were so thin they showed her panties when she bent over, and a long, loose tank top. Sweat pooled at the small of her back and dripped down her collarbones. Every time she pushed the shovel deeper, dirt flew into the air, coating her skin and clothes and hair. She felt disgusting, especially knowing that she had multiple errands to run once she left but before she'd be able to go home and shower. Fantastic. She couldn't wait for the rumors to roll through Greenbelt letting everybody know that she'd walked around town stinking like outside and looking like she'd been rolling around in filth.

She knew she was too old to still get embarrassed about something as ridiculous as a small-town rumor mill, but fuck . . . the whispers were just gasoline on the garbage fire that her life had turned into.

"You need some more water, baby?" Ms. Candice may have been closer to a century than anyone else in town but she still had a voice that could carry like nothing else.

Years of being the lead—and loudest—soprano in the church choir would do that, she guessed.

"No, ma'am," Miri called, pausing to make eye contact with the woman. "I'm almost done actually, if you want to go ahead and get your box."

Ms. Candice's lips straightened, and she groaned low as she stood up out of her chair and disappeared behind the black screen door.

Miri kept shoveling, moving faster the nearer she got to being finished with her task. She had dinner plans with her friends tonight, and the only thing getting her through this job was the promise of losing herself in the love of her best girls and a giant pile of lemon pepper wings.

Ms. Candice had switched her house shoes for a pair

of thick-soled clogs when she returned. Miri kept her back to her but she could hear them clacking on the dirt.

Miri paused when the other woman stopped next to her. She held her breath as Ms. Candice turned her eyes to the hole. A little milky around the centers but still alert.

"That's three feet," Ms. Candice said.

Miri released a breath of relief. "You want me to put it down there for you?"

They both looked down at the box Ms. Candice was holding. A shoebox, wrapped in multiple layers of newspaper, taped shut around the edges, then secured with multiple thick rubber bands for good measure.

"Yeah, all right." She handed the box to her, not fully allowing Miri to take it for a few seconds. "Make sure you get it all the way down in there. Right at the bottom of the hole."

Miri had to get down on her knees to reach. She handled the box gently, like it was the most precious thing she'd ever touched. Shit, it actually might have been. It was certainly the most expensive.

"Hurry up and get it covered, will ya?" Instead of walking away, Ms. Candice stood right next to her as Miri shoveled dirt back into the hole. The older woman kept her eyes glued to the box, even after it disappeared beneath the soil.

Miri's voice was breathless when she spoke. "You know, Ms. Candice, there's a Black-owned bank over in Beaufort. One of my best friends and her boyfriend bank with them. She says it's owned by a local family and that they take real good care of the folks that bank there.

Maybe . . ." She paused, considering her next words. She knew she was overstepping and that she might have had an easier time getting the CEO of an evil tech giant to give away his billions than she would convincing an older Black woman to stop doing something she'd been doing for sixty years.

When Ms. Candice turned her milky eyes to her again, Miri had no choice but to look into them. They hadn't turned unkind, but they were more serious than she'd ever seen them.

"I used to help my daddy do this when I was just a girl. Any money he got that didn't have to be spent on feeding and housing us was bundled up and shoved into a burlap sack and buried somewhere on our land. Daddy always said that money was dangerous. That it made you a target and turned you into somethin' . . ." She paused, turning her face to the side. "Somethin' nasty. Daddy always wanted to keep his money close to the earth. Make sure he didn't give himself the chance to flash it around and let everybody know he had it. Whenever we got in a bind, needed somethin' fixed on the house or faced a rough winter, he would get to diggin'. And when I left his house to go be with my husband, Lord rest his soul, Daddy made me dig up the money he'd put aside for me, told me to bury it in my backyard along with all my other money and that if James ever did anything untoward, I'd have the means to slip away without him knowin'."

"That's . . . real smart," Miri said quietly. "Your daddy seemed like a smart man."

"Smartest man I ever knew." Ms. Candice snorted.

"Which ain't sayin' much, but if he knew enough not to trust nobody with his money but this South Carolina soil, I sure can't say I know any better. I taught the same thing to my boy and both my girls. Not that they listened to me, mind you, but at least they'll know how to get what I left behind for them when I'm dead and gone from this earth."

Miri tossed the last of the dirt back into the hole, patting the shovel down on it to pack the dirt in tight.

"Do you want me to put some kind of marker here? Maybe I can arrange some rocks in a shape or somethin'."

"I know where it is," Ms. Candice said. "I'll have my boy around here tomorrow to lay some new grass down. Come on in and get your money."

She took the shovel with her as she followed the older woman into her house. She left the tool next to the bottom step, leaning against the back of the house.

Ms. Candice handed her a wad of cash silently, and Miri took it without looking at her. It didn't matter how many times she did something like this, it always felt weird to accept money from someone she knew. Even if she'd worked for it. She didn't bother to count it as she shoved the cash into her bra with a quiet thank-you.

"Here." A foil-covered plate was shoved into her hands. "Take these salmon croquettes to your mama. I know she's cleanin' Della Jones's place today and that old bat don't even got the manners to offer somebody a cold drink when they come in her house, let alone a plate."

Miri snorted. Her mama had cleaned houses for nearly every Black family in town at one point or another and the only one she'd ever actively complained about was Della Jones's. Apparently, she was just as filthy as she was ornery.

"Speaking of, let me go ahead and get out of here. Mama wanted me to pick up a few things for her before I go home. She wants me to go to the corner store near the house because that's the only place she'll play her numbers."

Ms. Candice nodded like she understood exactly. "I won five hundred dollars with a ticket from that store in 1976. May Abbott won a couple thousand sometime about twenty years back too. It's lucky."

Miri raised a brow. "Two winning tickets and it's lucky?"

She dodged a swat to the back of her head. "That's more winnin' tickets than the Sunoco's got, ain't it?"

There was no denying that, she supposed. But she still thought it was ridiculous. She thought all gambling was ridiculous. From penny slots to bingo to the lottery. It all seemed like the perfect way to throw your money down the toilet. How was winning a thousand dollars worth it when you'd spent twice or even three times that in your effort to win big? Especially when you barely had anything to begin with.

Both her mama and her aunt played their numbers every day, without fail. There had been times, ones when they were truly on their last, when Mama would still manage to scrounge enough change to play the Mega Millions. Searching through the couch and the car for two dollars so she could get her ticket.

As ridiculous as she found it, Miri figured she couldn't

judge too much. When you were broke, there was nothing you could do but try to find joy in the little things. For Miri, it was spending four dollars on fancy gelato from the Piggly Wiggly. For her mama, it was playing her numbers. At least her mama's thing filled her with some kind of hope. Hope that one day she'd win and be freed from the poverty that had affected every part of their lives for so long. Playing the lottery gave the woman something to look forward to, a reason to get to the end of each day.

All Miri's gelato gave her was the crunch of Oreo chunks and one night of bland satisfaction. Hell, she could have gotten the same things raiding the cabinets of one of the former Greenbelt High School football players she'd slept with.

"I'll see you later, Ms. Candice." She paused with her hand on the doorknob. "Let me know if you need anything else, okay?"

The woman nodded, a small smile across her weathered lips. "You be safe getting home now, Miriam. And don't forget to play your mama's numbers ... maybe play your own too."

"Yeah," Miri laughed. "And if I win I'll make sure to cut you a check."

"Don't turn your nose up at it, little girl. You don't know what this world has in store for you."

2

MIRI

There was only one real corner store in her neighborhood. The place was older than she was, so old that the sign reading the name had completely faded away from the building. The owners, the Adomos family, hadn't bothered to replace it. Not that anyone in the neighborhood cared. It was likely that they'd still just call it "the corner store" either way.

The teenage son, whose name Miri couldn't immediately recall even though she knew his high school basketball stats to a T, greeted her with a distracted smile when she came in. Miri wandered aimlessly for a bit, slightly dead-eyed as she grabbed a few items off the shelves. A can of Arizona Iced Tea—the original flavor—a bag of Takis, and a roll of Mentos for her mama. Briefly, she eyed the display of individually wrapped Little Debbie cakes.

When she'd been young, you could buy a two-pack of Swiss Rolls for twenty-five cents in this very store. Now, they were a dollar. Her bank account was probably pennies away from overdrafting and she barely had enough cash to get what she'd actually come in the store for, so she left them where they were.

"I'm also gonna get a Mega Millions ticket, please," she told the kid at the counter as she set her items down and dug around in her purse for her wallet.

"What are your numbers?"

Her mama, Patrice, played the exact same numbers every time. Each Mega Millions ticket required five numbers to play. The numbers could be between one and seventy, which meant that the possibilities felt damn near endless. Miri knew the significance of some of the numbers her mama played; others, she was completely ignorant to.

Three, because it was Patrice's lucky number. Seventeen, because it was the date of her granny's birthday. Nine, because it was Miri's birth month. Sixty-seven and twenty-two she was clueless about.

She gave the kid the numbers in their proper order.

"Is that it?" he asked. "Biggest jackpot in years, don't want to miss out. Gotta play to win, yadda yadda yadda."

She admired how the kid didn't even bother trying to hide that the store made bank on selling dreams when the jackpots got this large. It was ridiculous. The entire fucking thing. A waste of time, a waste of money. Giving false hope to people who needed something to cling to.

The "what if" stopped her from grabbing her mother's ticket and walking off. It was a tiny thing that she probably would have been able to stave off easier if she'd ended up grabbing a second bag of chips or a Little Debbie. But she hadn't.

She already felt like a damn fool, why not act like one too?

"Fuck it." She dug into the back pocket of her jeans, looking for the small bills she had stashed away, handing him a couple. "I'll do another one."

The kid didn't even react. "What are your numbers?"

For a second, Miri's mind went blank. She wasn't like her mama; she didn't have any lucky numbers or superstitions. Jade had been mentioning something called "angel numbers" a lot recently, and while Miri was already wasting money by buying a lottery ticket in the first place, she wasn't about to completely screw it up by just putting down a bunch of threes.

Then, things started coming to her . . .

"Six."

The age she was when she met Leo Vaughn.

"Thirty-one."

Like the day in July she'd kissed him for the first time.

"Fourteen."

The number of wildflowers he always brought her, two more than a dozen to make up for the fact that he couldn't get her store-bought ones.

"Twenty-one."

The most times he'd told her he loved her in one day.

"Fifty-eight."

The number of days it had taken her to leave the house again after he'd left.

The kid repeated the numbers back to her. Suddenly her brain was so fuzzy from memories that all she could do was nod, grab the tickets when they printed out, and shuffle back to her car. She took a few minutes to try to gather herself. Head against the worn leather-covered steering wheel, she bit back tears, tearing into the skin of her lips until she could bring herself to turn the ignition over.

She tucked her mama's ticket into her wallet in her purse to keep it safe. Hers, she clutched half-crumpled between her fingers the entire drive home.

As soon as she opened the front door she knew her mama had dug the big cast iron out from underneath all the other pans they kept in what was supposed to be the broiler. She could hear the loud sizzling of grease and smell pork chops frying in the cast iron. She hadn't eaten much besides a bowl of oatmeal and a peanut butter sandwich all day, and she hadn't been very hungry either. Not until she stepped into the warmth and smelled the food she knew her mother was putting her foot deep in.

Patrice Butler didn't tend to cook on Friday nights. Normally, that was a night both of them fended for themselves. Sometimes, Miri would eat ramen and others she'd smash a burger at Minnie's, it all depended on how tiring her week had been. Patrice was never one to leave leftovers uneaten, and they always had something left over. So if she wasn't eating her meal during a Friday-evening Bible study, she was likely digging something out of the back of the fridge to eat. In dire times, she'd eat a fried bologna sandwich with two slices of white bread and a whole lot of mustard. Miri always considered it a treat when she got a home-cooked meal on a Friday night, especially since she sure as hell never lifted a finger to cook on those days.

"Hey, Mama." She tried to kiss Patrice on the cheek, but the older woman screwed up her nose and moved her head back.

"Girl, you stink."

"I was outside all day. Ms. Candice worked me like a dog, dang near."

She heard her mother say something, but the words refused to stick anywhere in her head. Miri's eyes couldn't help but stray to the piece of pork frying in the pan. Mama was convinced that the first chop was always a dud, so she took the smallest piece out of the pack, coated it in flour like normal, and let it fry up. They always picked at it together before the rest of the meal was done. It was a ritual of sorts, one that always ensured their meal turned out well.

The edges sizzled and bubbled, slowly turning the outside of the pork chop to a gorgeous golden-brown color.

She should have been hungry—starving, really. She'd spent all day moving her body, working in the hot sun. Nothing should have sounded better to her than a nice hot meal made by her mama's hands. But her body couldn't muster up even so much as a stomach growl.

Exhaustion had settled comfortably in her bones but her head was anxious.

She almost felt like she'd forgotten something, but couldn't remember what that something was. Something, not butterflies, fluttered around in her stomach. Part of her felt like she wanted to be sick. The other part just wanted to go crawl under her covers.

The second she'd put those numbers on that ticket, her entire mood had changed. Something had shifted and she couldn't quite let it go, whatever it was.

"Miri!"

Patrice put a hand on her upper arm and shook her a little bit.

"Girl." Her tone was annoyed but her eyes were concerned. "Where are you at?"

Miri shook her head. "Sorry, Mama, I'm just a little tired."

She could tell Patrice didn't believe her.

"I'm serious." She put her hand over her mother's. "I just need to eat, I think."

Patrice pursed her lips. "Well, supper will be ready in a little bit. Go wash up first . . . Did Ms. Candice pay you good?"

Miri nodded, pulling the cash out of her bra, finally counting it. Ten crisp twenties, smelling fresh and new. The scent of future bills to be paid loosened some of the tension between her shoulders. She separated five of the bills, handing them over to her mother.

"Uh-uh." Patrice shook her head. "That's your money, girl. You worked for it."

"I worked for it so *both* of us could have a little change. I know we're short this month after all the bills but we still need some walking-around money, you know . . . just in case."

Patrice sighed. "I'm not supposed to be taking money from you like this. I'm the mama, not you."

She used her mother's lowered guard to press a kiss to her forehead. Miri was taller than Patrice by almost five inches. Had been since she'd turned thirteen. Even when her mother swatted at her in retaliation for her insolence, it wasn't painful.

"Doesn't matter what's supposed to be, Mama, this is what is. We help each other. That's how it's always been. It's how we survive."

"It ain't right."

They'd had this conversation countless times before. Miri had gotten her first job at thirteen on her own accord to help out with their ever-worsening money situation. Mama had hated it then just as much as she did now. But as much as she complained about it, she remained resigned to the reality. It was necessary if they wanted to stay afloat. Miri just didn't know how it was going to be sustainable the older they both got.

She pulled the small printed square out of the center of her rectangular wallet and handed that over alongside the cash. "Maybe this'll make you feel better."

Patrice clicked her tongue, used the tongs to flip the meat over in the skillet, then grabbed the ticket. "And you went to the corner store like I said?"

"Yes," Miri groaned. "Of course, Mama."

"Good. That's the lucky one, you know?"

Miri refrained from rolling her eyes. "That's what Ms. Candice told me. Look." She held up the second ticket, the one she'd bought with her own money. "I even got myself one. Maybe I'll win a little something-something as a tip for running your errands."

"Go on and take a shower, you little smartass. I don't want you sittin' at my table smellin' like outside."

"Yes, ma'am."

"And hurry up, too," Patrice yelled at her back. "I don't want this food getting cold. The last thing we need is to waste it because your finicky behind let it sit too long."

The Mega Millions numbers weren't drawn until eleven. By that time, Miri had already canceled her plans with the girls and tucked her body deep into the twin bed in the room she'd lived in since she was a little girl.

She was in her bed by nine, having completely forgotten that her lottery ticket sat on top of her dresser, right next to the solid-gold bracelet her granny had given her before she'd died and her one bottle of good perfume.

Sleep refused to come easy. Crickets chirped loud next to her window. These weren't the romantic, summer sounds that lulled softly. They were loud and grating, keeping her on edge. There was a full moon waning, glaring through her sheer curtains, making it impossible to stay on her left side with her face toward the window for long.

Their little old house didn't have central air and they kept the one window air-conditioner in the living room. The little box fan whirred fast but provided little relief. The backs of her knees were sticky, chafing her skin every time she rolled over between the sheets.

Her mind was flooded with memories. Things she'd rather walk across a bed of coals than remember. The smell of wildflowers and rain. Soft kisses in too-small beds. Warm arms wrapped around her waist from below. A wide smile and eyes warm enough to keep the cold away in winter.

He was on her mind heavy, and it set her on edge so much her teeth ached.

She gave up her quest for sleep around 3:00 A.M. Hauling her sore body out of bed in search of a glass of water and some unrecycled cool air. The ceilings in the living room weren't much higher than they were in the rest of the house, but they were vaulted. Which meant that on hot days, the heat rose more, making the space down below more bearable. Miri tucked her body into the couch, folding her thick legs under her and pressing the cool water-sweat of the glass against the back of her neck.

She turned the TV on, not wanting to sit in the dark but not wanting to be bathed in the bright overhead light either. Channel surfing was exactly the mind-numbing activity she needed. Her brain was still hazy and unfocused and she had no space left to consume any real media. Not even old episodes of *227* she loved so dearly. She was sure she could spend hours flipping through the same hundred channels with her eyes glazed over until the sun came up.

Channel 5 was playing a commercial about some birth control she'd been considering switching to but hadn't had enough money to cover the copay for. The second it was over, a replay of the night's lottery drawing appeared. Since she hadn't heard Patrice yelling the house down the way she would have if she had won, Miri assumed the ticket she'd bought her mother was somewhere in the garbage along with the scraps from their dinner.

She kept watching, though, partly to give her thumb a break from scrolling and partly out of morbid curiosity to see what would happen. It was a bizarre scene to watch. A white woman who looked like she'd stepped right out of a newscast from 1985, all hair spray and shoulder pads, stood alone on the set. The little metal basket that held the balls rotated on its own. Once it stopped, she reached in and pulled one out, turning the ball to face the screen before saying the number aloud. "Six."

The number then appeared on the black bar on the bottom of the screen.

It was an incredibly monotonous process. One that involved way too much fanfare for Miri's liking. There had to be a way to streamline this kind of thing, didn't there?

The metal cage spun on, and every time the host slid her wrist through the door Miri had to fight off intrusive thoughts of the woman accidentally getting her hand chopped off by rogue mechanics. It would be horrific, sure, but at least it would be something.

"Thirty-one."
"Fourteen."
"Twenty-one."
"Fifty-eight."

Just like that, in what seemed like an hour since it had started, the balls were finished being called. The winning numbers were lined up in a neat row along the bottom of the screen. But Miri's brain was practically a soggy wet ball of nothing. It wasn't until the woman spoke them out loud that they actually registered.

"One last time, the winning numbers of the Mega Millions jackpot are: six, thirty-one, fourteen, twenty-one, fifty-eight."

Miri blinked, suddenly more alert than she had been in hours. The fog that had settled in her brain turned into a mist, then disappeared completely. She seemed aware of everything all at once. The rough feeling of the sofa material against the backs of her thighs. The sports bra that dug into her ribs. The loud sound of the refrigerator running. The world felt tiny and huge at the same time. Her head started to hurt.

All five of those numbers had been embedded in her brain for years, for better or worse. Her entire history with a man she wished she could forget.

It wasn't just the history that shocked her, though.

It was that when she'd been standing in front of the cashier earlier that afternoon, making the rash decision to buy her very first lottery ticket, those were the only numbers she could think to tell the boy to print on the paper.

Six, thirty-one, fourteen, twenty-one, fifty-eight. In that exact order.

She jumped up, feet pounding against the old carpet as she bounded down the short hallway to grab the little slip of paper sitting on her dresser. She rushed back into the living room, finally turning on the ceiling light so she could make out the numbers clearly.

They were there, just like she thought they'd be, in a perfect little row, eerily similar to the way they'd appeared on the screen minutes before.

The channel had already switched over to an episode of some incredibly unfunny sitcom, but it didn't matter, Miri had the numbers embedded in her brain. The very brain that buzzed so fast she felt light-headed.

Nausea rose along with the faint feeling. It was too much. Way too much. What was she supposed to do with this information? How was she supposed to go on knowing that she . . . that she'd . . . that she had apparently won the motherfucking lottery?

Her body was rigid as she stood in the middle of the living room. Knees locked and knuckles clenched tight as she clutched at the damning, lifesaving slip of paper she'd spent two dollars on, for nothing more than a whim.

Doing what she always did when she had something valuable, she tucked the paper into her bra and rushed back to her room to grab her phone off the nightstand.

Google was her best friend—her ride or die. But even it couldn't provide her with much comfort.

Her search for "What do you do when you win the lottery?" revealed very little. She didn't need lists about how she should pay off her debt first, then buy a home, then set up college funds for her children that would never exist.

She didn't need advice on what to do with the money, she needed to know what to do in the immediate. When it was almost four in the morning and her head was about to explode. How was she supposed to calm down enough to claim her winnings? How was she supposed to wrap her head around this? Was this even real? Was she dreaming?

She slapped a hand against her cheek. The sting sure felt real. She wiggled her toes and counted all ten of her fingers. Those felt real too. So why did she feel so . . . removed? Like she was there but not there at the same time. Like she could feel every single cell in her body buzzing even though her heart felt like it had completely stopped pumping.

It was like she was a child again. Standing alone, confused about what she was supposed to be doing at any given moment. Just like back then, there was only one way she knew of to find comfort—she went to find her mama.

Patrice was bundled up under her covers, the old box TV that sat on top of her dresser playing an episode of *Forensic Files*.

"Ma . . ." Miri's voice shook. "Ma . . ." She reached out

and shook her mother around her left hip. Patrice sniffled, but didn't stir.

"Mommy!" Her volume went higher, shrill as she trembled at her mother's bedside.

Patrice sat up in a fright, her eyes wide and her wrap scarf askew. "What, Miriam?"

Miri couldn't find it in herself to feel the admonishment. She'd spent her life trying her level best not to wake her mama up out of her sleep, but it couldn't be avoided now.

Her hand shook as she handed the slip of paper to the other woman. The light wasn't on, and the TV provided very little, so she knew the writing wouldn't be legible. She still felt the need to hand it over, though. Partly as proof. Partly because doing so took some of the weight off her own shoulders. Like the responsibility of handling all that this would bring didn't solely fall on her. Patrice could handle it. Patrice could handle anything, she always had.

"Mama, I . . ." She swallowed. "I think we won the lottery."

Patrice went stock-still, her eyes turned to saucers. "What?"

Miri nodded. "The numbers . . . the ones I picked . . . they . . . the lady called them, I just saw."

"In order?"

Miri nodded.

They were both silent for a while. Both of their eyes stuck to the little red-and-white square that had, inexplicably, changed their lives. All of it felt real. None of it felt real. This wasn't how Miri had imagined winning the lottery might feel. She'd always assumed it would involve less tight throats and clenched bellies and more straight-up joy.

"How much did you win?" When Patrice broke the silence, it was with the backdrop of a murderer finally being identified on the TV.

"I . . . I don't know . . . I didn't look."

3

MIRI

Corey Whittaker worked in an office in Old Charleston that had been converted from a house. There was a heavy swinging sign hanging from the front porch that identified the place as "Whittaker & Son Wealth Management." Miri stood next to her mother on the immaculate sidewalk outside of the building, both of them looking up at it as if it loomed over them at forty stories high rather than two floors.

"Which Whittaker are we comin' to see again?" Patrice asked, clutching at the purse on her shoulder.

"The son," she responded. "You remember my friend Aja, right? The one who lives in Beaufort?" Patrice nodded. "Corey Whittaker is her boyfriend's best friend."

"He's a Black man?"

"Yeah." Miri watched as her mother's shoulders

visibly loosened. "Aja says he's good people and I trust her not to lead me into some mess. Besides, we don't have to sign with him if we don't like him. We just have to hear him out."

"You." Patrice curled her lips around the end of the word.

"Huh?" Any other time, her mother would have scolded her for answering a question so disrespectfully, but Miri figured the situation was stressful enough as it was.

"You don't have to sign him, Miri. You just have to hear what he has to say. Ain't no *we*. Your money bought that ticket. Your numbers won. This is your win, girl."

Miri shook her head. "No, it's not. It's ours. I can't do this without you, Mama. I can't even imagine what I would do if you weren't here with me. That alone makes this win ours. You . . . you know I'm going to take care of you, right?"

Patrice cackled. "Oh, trust me, I know that full well. I'm just sayin' these decisions are yours to make in the end. Can't nobody but you tell you what to do now."

Miri shuddered. "I used to think that was a good thing. Now it's just scary. I don't even know the first place to start."

Patrice reached out and took her hand, squeezing it. Her mother's palms were roughened from a lifetime of manual labor, but they were warm and comforting in their firmness. The feeling of them steadied her.

"Let's start by seeing what this man has to say about your money, huh?"

They walked up the steps onto the porch together. A small bell jingled as they opened the glass front door. A cute Black receptionist sat at a desk in what must have been the foyer in the past.

"Hi." Miri cleared her throat. "I'm Miriam Butler and this is my mother, Patrice. We're here for an appointment with Mr. Whittaker . . . uhm . . . Corey."

"Of course." She stood up out of her seat and straightened out her skirt. "I'll go let him know you're here. Y'all can have a seat while you wait."

Both she and Patrice chose to remain standing. It had been a week since Miri had claimed her lottery winnings from the state. South Carolina was one of the only states in the country that allowed lottery winners to claim their money anonymously. When she'd read that little fact online, she'd damn near cried from the joy of it. The last thing she wanted was for everyone to know about this before she could even properly figure out how she was feeling.

Still, she knew that she couldn't just chuck all the money in her little savings account and live life like she normally did. She knew exactly how to manage money when she had none. All that scratch she had now? She had no fucking clue.

So, aside from her mama, the only other people that knew about her newfound wealth were Walker and Aja. Largely because she'd heard Walker talk about his money-manager friend before and wanted the hookup. And, well, everyone knew that Walker wasn't going to keep anything from Aja.

She'd felt guilty when she begged them not to tell anyone until she was ready. Asking people to hold on to your secrets was always a little shady, but she'd felt like her options were basically nil.

It had been a week since she'd managed to let herself truly relax. Her nights were restless, she spent most of her time in the house, and the world still felt suffocating. She didn't have it in her to put up the facade of relaxation. Not when her body felt like it was resting at the business end of a live wire.

When the receptionist returned, there was a man behind her. Average height, medium brown skin, a bald head, and a full, plush beard. He wore a well-tailored navy-blue suit that was just nice enough without being too showy.

"Miriam Butler?" he asked as he approached, holding a hand out for her to shake.

She managed a farce of a smile long enough to be polite. "Yes. You can call me Miri, though. This is my mama, Patrice."

He shook her hand too and then led them toward the back of the building into a medium-sized office. Two chairs sat opposite a large wooden desk and a gorgeous back bay window filtering in sunlight and shadows of the greenery from the large tree, covered in Spanish moss outside.

"So." Corey cleared his throat. "You won the lottery?"

It was a question with an incredibly obvious answer, but it loosened her up a little bit anyway. She knew that Walker had informed him of her circumstances when he'd connected them. She'd reiterated her reason for in-quiring about his services in an email. Still, hearing him say it out loud felt wild as hell.

"Yes." She nodded. "Two-hundred-and-twenty-million-dollar jackpot."

She watched as his eyes went comically wide at the number she presented.

She got it. It didn't seem real.

"Walker told me that you've worked with lottery winners before?"

"Yes, we have. But, I'll admit, never for anybody who's won that much. The most a client of ours has won is a little over five million."

Patrice, who had been uncharacteristically quiet, spoke up then. "But you work with other wealthy people, right?"

"Yes, ma'am." Corey turned his kind brown eyes to the older woman. "I'm not at liberty to disclose exact amounts or clients, but we do work with people who have considerable wealth. I can say that if Miriam were to sign with us, she would be our highest-earning client."

Patrice flashed her a look, and Miri knew instantly that her mama was well on her way to being convinced that they should go with Whittaker & Son to help her manage her money.

"I like that this is a smaller company," Patrice said. "And Black owned. Makes it easier to trust you with somethin' so big . . . and . . ." She leaned forward in her seat, making sure to keep her eyes on Cory's. "Makes it easier to find out who your people are too . . . just in case."

"Mama!"

Patrice ignored her. "I don't play about my baby, Mr. Whittaker."

Miri expected him to politely ask them to see themselves out. She clasped her hand tighter around her purse strap and braced her thighs. Instead, Corey's smile widened and he leaned forward, elbows on his desk so he could look even more deeply into her mother's eyes.

"Ma'am, I'm looking you in your eyes right now so you can see the honesty in mine. I'm not going to give you the runaround and feed you lines about how I only want to help out of the kindness of my heart. We both know that working with your daughter would mean big things for me and my family's firm. But I'm an honest man. So is my mother, the woman who started this business. We're not interested in screwing you over, because we're interested in building a long, mutually beneficial relationship with you."

He turned to Miri, and the smirk on his lips might have been the least slimy one she'd ever seen. "Plus, Walker already told me that he'll be the first one to beat my ass should I mess around here. And I believe him, too," he chuckled. "That big white boy may look nice but he's got some fight in him."

Miri looked at Patrice, and Patrice looked right back at her. They'd spent a lot of time together. Hell, Miri had lived in the same tiny two-bedroom house with her for most of her life. They knew each other inside and out.

And Miri knew exactly what her mama looked like when she approved of somebody.

And she approved of Corey Whittaker.

It may not have been the smartest way to think, but that was all Miri needed to trust him. Patrice was the most discerning person she knew. The hardest to please and the most impossible to impress. Especially to strangers. Her mama rarely steered her wrong, and with the stakes this high, Miri didn't think she was about to break her winning streak.

"What's the process, Mr. Whittaker? Where do we start?"

He leaned back in his chair, not smug but certainly confident in the knowledge that he'd successfully gotten her business.

"Well, first I'll take a look at your finances, see where you currently are. With this amount, I'm sure there are people in your life you want to break off a little something to. We'll discuss reasonable amounts for that. And we'll make sure to pair you with one of the accountants we work with regularly to get your taxes squared away. In my opinion, setting up trusts would likely be the best course of action. That way, you get a monthly or yearly sum. It can be whatever you want but I'm here to advise you on how to make wise decisions so that you don't blow through your money and wind up down and out in five years. That means investments, that means savings. I'm not saying you can't splurge, that you can't live well. But it's important to think about your future. If you do this right, this wealth will last you the rest of your life."

A long, heavy breath released from her diaphragm. It was so strong it nearly made her chest tremble. It was an incredible relief to speak to someone who actually knew what to do. He'd said a lot and he'd said it fast but she could tell he knew what the hell he was talking about. Nothing had been set in stone yet, but it still felt incredible not to have it all on her shoulders.

Whatever extreme happiness she knew she was supposed to feel about winning the lottery still hadn't set in. But the stress was waning more with every minute.

"So there won't be any . . . legal issues when it comes to finally getting the money?"

There was a ton of red tape with winning the lottery. Technically, she had won $220 million before taxes two weeks ago. But all she currently had in the bank was the same $600 in her checking account she'd had at the beginning of the month.

It was a bizarre thing—to somehow be rich but too poor to pay all your bills at the same time. There had been all kinds of paperwork she'd had to sign at the lottery office, but they had required that she hire a financial advisor before her funds were turned over to her. They'd told her that they couldn't force her to keep one in the long run, but that it was the safest way to move. They'd recommended their own, of course, but she hadn't been interested in that. She'd never have trusted them, not fully.

"There shouldn't be," Corey answered. "Not unless there's anyone else who has a claim to your money. Someone who went in with you in buying the ticket, someone you made a legally binding agreement with to split the winnings. Even a spouse. According to the state of South Carolina, you wouldn't be legally required to split the winnings with them, but they could take you to civil court and sue you for a portion of your winnings, up to fifty percent, in theory. There's precedent for things like that happening. That shouldn't be an issue, though, since—"

Patrice audibly sucked in a breath while Miri felt her throat closing. Her vision blurred around the edges, tunneling.

Corey raised an eyebrow, his eyes peeping at her left hand—the one that held a bare ring finger.

"That . . . won't be an issue, right?" he asked. "Walker didn't say anything about you being . . . divorced?"

"Because I'm not," she choked out. "I mean . . . he doesn't know. I . . . I'm still married but we're . . . we're . . . estranged, I guess . . . We have been for a long time. About . . . eight years." Her eyes strayed to the window behind Corey. Suddenly, she felt the urge to leap through it and leave all this behind. Being poor was awful. It was stressful and exhausting and traumatizing, but those were things she'd gotten used to over the years. She'd never quite managed to get used to the feeling of being apart from Leo Vaughn. No matter how desperately she'd tried. And God, had she been desperate.

Corey framed the right side of his face with his thumb and index finger. One of his ankles folded over his knee.

"So, you're estranged?"

Miri nodded.

"No contact?"

"None. I don't . . . I don't even know where he is right now."

Nor did she want to, thank you very much. She'd gone to great pains to get herself out of the habit of finding covert ways to check up on her husband. The process had somehow been worse than pulling teeth with a pair of rusty pliers. But instead of a broken smile and dry socket, she was left with the sweet ignorance of not knowing if Leo was all over Instagram with some other fine-ass woman on his arm.

"Maybe it's finally time to reach out," Corey said. "Get to him before he finds out from somebody else. Make sure there's no bad blood."

Patrice released a wry snort. "Oh, there's plenty o' bad blood. You don't go eight years with no divorce and no contact if there was no bad blood there."

Corey paused. "Maybe we can find a way around that."

"How?" Miri asked.

She knew she had a tendency to be fatalistic, but the only outcome she saw here was one that allowed Leo Vaughn to lay claim to half her money. And that was infuriating, especially when he'd walked away from her so easily.

"The way I see it, you can approach him first and put an offer right on the table. Offer him a lump-sum settlement if he agrees to a quick and easy divorce where he signs over any right to claim your winnings. We have a lawyer on retainer who can draw up a contract for that, no problem."

"How much of a lump sum?" Patrice's tone had an edge to it. Miri could tell she liked the idea of giving Leo any of her money about as much as she liked the man himself, which was basically not at all.

"That's up to Miriam. But, if we want to lessen the risk of him fighting, it would probably be best to offer a hefty one."

Miri pressed her back against the chair, the wooden notches that held it up digging into her muscles. She shifted as her brain fumbled its way through a million different scenarios.

It was a good idea, she knew that. Probably the best shot she had at avoiding some kind of drawn-out legal battle. But she couldn't honestly say that she felt confident her husband would take the offer.

A man she'd known since she was six years old. One she'd chased down ice-cream trucks with, one she'd shared her first kiss with, one who she'd ultimately promised to spend her entire life with. She knew that boy-turned-man better than she knew herself. But whoever Leo was now, eight years removed from the last time she'd laid eyes on him, she had no idea who that man was.

All she knew was how much she'd changed in that same amount of time. The softness that had existed around her edges was barbed, with the inside saved only for the few people in the world she cared about. There was something jaded in her, something that kept her from opening up fully. That, combined with the exhaustion that had settled in her bones, made her very different from the twenty-four-year-old he had left behind.

If Leo had changed even a fraction as much as she had over the years, he was completely unpredictable now, and that . . . well, it scared the hell out of her.

There was also the fact that this little plan would force her to face him again. And not only face him, but be the first to reach out. Something she'd sworn she'd never do the second the sight of his back disappeared from her doorway. No matter how much she'd wanted to at various times over the years.

She felt like she was stuck between two boulders. Crushing her from both sides, constricting her movement. Part of her wanted to pick the animal's way out, to find a way around both options by gnawing her own arm off to free herself.

She let out a string of curses in her head, trying to keep her face impassive so neither her mama nor Corey saw the internal struggle she was facing.

"All right," she sighed. "I don't really see any other option, so . . . have your lawyer draw up the contract and . . . I'll get him to come sign it."

"How are you goin' to get in contact with him?" Patrice asked, her eyebrows raised.

Miri bit the inside of her left cheek to keep herself from groaning like a toddler. She knew exactly how to find him, but the sacrifice she'd have to make in order to do so might have been worse than whatever she encountered when she did find him. "I'll ask his sister."

Patrice grimaced, looking away.

This entire plan was rotten—top to fucking bottom. It stunk like the unthawed chicken breasts she'd forgotten in the back of the fridge for a week and made her stomach gurgle just as bad as it would have had she managed to eat them.

More money, more goddamn problems.

4

LEO

Jacksonville was a swelter. All wet heat that made his lungs feel soggy and air that smelled like hot asphalt. When he'd gotten word of a job opportunity in the city—under-the-table contracting work on some fancy new high-rise downtown—he'd pictured blue skies and pretty beaches. There were those, sure, but the perpetual sawdust in his ears made the waves crashing against the shore sound muffled. The old shag carpet in his motel room felt like sand in the worst way and every single blue-sky day seemed to be followed by a rainstorm so thunderous it made him feel like he was moments away from being struck by lightning.

When she called the first time, he was suspended from a wire, the strap from his hard hat digging into his chin as he secured the newly installed windows with a drill. He'd missed the call completely and when lunch came around and he could get his hands on his phone, he hadn't recognized the number on the screen.

The second time she called, he purposely ignored the ringing. His boss had shorted him a hundred dollars on his pay. And since working under the table meant getting paid under the table, he'd had no recourse to fight it. Not unless he wanted to use his fists and either end up in jail for putting hands on some white man or stuck stranded in fucking Florida without a job, or some combination of both. He'd taken it on the chin with gritted teeth and a clenched jaw, too pissed to deal with whatever debt collector or scammer was inevitably on the other line.

It wasn't until the third time she called that he finally answered. He'd been pumping gas into his little hooptie, despairing, cursing every single choice he'd ever made.

He hadn't even looked at the screen before he answered, all gruff tone and short words. When he heard her voice, he had to press a foot back against his tire to keep from falling over. Years and years of no contact, of not seeing her face or being engulfed in her scent. Blood so bad he wasn't sure it could ever be clean and a history so long and deep it was embedded in him as deep as his own heart. None of that shit mattered. He could have been dead and buried and still recognized the sound of her voice. Blood rushed to his ears instantly and the ten dollars he'd been meaning to put into his tank quickly turned into fifteen, then twenty as his body tried and failed to fight off impending shock.

He couldn't make out much of what she said but his

brain picked out the words and phrases that it perceived to be most important.

"I need . . ."

"You . . ."

"Come back to Greenbelt."

"Somethin' we need to talk about."

"Need . . ."

"In person . . ."

"Please, Leo."

Before he knew what he was doing he'd agreed. By the time he was pulling into his motel room to gather his things, he'd already figured out the quickest route from Jacksonville to Greenbelt. A place he'd barely been back to in eight years. A life he'd left behind for reasons that seemed nonexistent now that Miri was asking him to return.

He was on the road in an hour without so much as a courtesy call to his piece-of-shit boss to let him know he wouldn't be returning to the job site tomorrow.

Fuck him. He didn't matter.

Nothing mattered nearly as much as Miri did. Miriam. His wife. His . . .

It was bold of him to assume that the reason she'd called had been because of her desire to reconcile. But what else could it have been?

Every week, his sister, Thea, called him to keep him updated on all the shit going on in Greenbelt. It always went in the same order. Anecdotes about her life, whatever was going down at church, a voiced wish that he would come back and join her on their ancestral land.

Then, before they hung up, she'd grant him what he was always hungry for but too cowardly to ask after—an update on Miri.

The two women were far from close these days, so it wasn't like Thea had all the inside details on her life. But Greenbelt was so small you had to damn near try not to know everybody's business. He never asked Thea explicitly to tell him. Never used sly words to dig for information or updates, but he didn't need to. His sister knew him well enough to see what he needed. Even if it was just a little story about the fact that somebody in town had seen Miri buying condoms at the Piggly Wiggly.

Anything was better than nothing when it came to her. Which was exactly why he made the three-and-a-half-hour trip home in a little over two.

He'd been back to Greenbelt a handful of times since he and Miri had split up. Almost every time, he did it the coward's way. Arriving in the dead of night, going straight to his sister's house, parking his car in her little backyard garage. He never stayed more than a few days at a time, and spent most of his time indoors, hiding from the mere possibility of running into his wife.

He'd never considered himself a coward before he'd left her. In fact, he'd thought himself to be the exact opposite. The brave hero she could count on to fix all of her problems, slay her demons, be there for whatever she needed. When all three of those things proved to be false, whatever he'd previously thought was bravery had shriveled up and died, leaving him something sad and unrecognizable even to himself. A small, shameful shell of the man he'd been before.

He knew that she'd moved back in with her mama after he'd left. And he knew that Ms. Patrice still rented the little two-bedroom bungalow she'd been in his entire life. He knew exactly where it was too. All these years later and he probably could have gotten there with his eyes closed. Every traffic light, every stop sign, every turn. He'd learned to drive by memorizing the way to Miri's house from just about every location in Greenbelt.

When he pulled up in front of it, very little had changed. The front door was still the same burgundy red, only more faded. The three concrete steps that led up to the door were cracked and haggard. The roof sagged and the vinyl siding on the house desperately needed to be replaced.

Still, a wave of comfort settled over him. The familiarity of the home, even if it was fraught, calmed his nerves enough to get him out of the car.

Before he rang the doorbell, he wondered who was cutting their grass. It was perfectly level, and if the clear lines on the lawn were any indication, freshly done. That had been his job what seemed like a lifetime ago. First, when he'd been thirteen and trying hard as his little bird chest could manage to get Miri to fall in love with him. And then, when he was twenty and trying to keep her.

The doors and walls on the house were old and thin, like they'd always been. And he could hear the sound of footsteps beating against the floor. The Butler women were hard walkers. The thought gave him a small chuckle before it was wiped out completely by the sound of the locks undoing.

Leo didn't know who to expect on the other side of the door. Either outcome was scary as all fuck.

He'd come all this way for Miri. Just for the promise of seeing her, being near her again. And with the full hope that the reason she'd called him was because she still missed him the way he missed her. It was a ridiculous thing to hope for, but that hadn't stopped him.

Ms. Patrice, on the other hand, had always liked him. She'd told him countless times that she thought he was a good match for her baby. But that had been before he'd broken that same baby's heart. He had no idea how the woman felt about him now. Any fond memories she might have had of him as a kid had probably been completely washed away. And he'd seen the way Ms. Patrice could get with people she wasn't very fond of. The last thing he wanted was to be on the receiving end of a bitching out from a woman he'd once viewed as a mother.

It was Miri who opened the door. Her eyes went wide as soon as she saw him. Dark and endless and full of a thousand things he loved and a thousand things he hated.

She had her afro out, the large puff of it taking up the majority of the doorframe.

Jesus fucking Christ. It didn't matter how long he'd tried to prepare himself, being in her presence again was an overwhelming experience. Looking at her hurt, he felt like his chest was caving in, and his lungs seemed to have shriveled in his chest, refusing to filter air. Everything about her was familiar yet strange at the same time.

She had the same oval face and high cheekbones. Her chin still had the barely noticeable dimple in the center. Her skin was still dark like the color of rich carob. She was a little rounder in parts of her body. Belly, hips, thighs— she'd always been thick, full of curves that he'd used to revel in traveling. Now she was even more lush, and it made his mouth wet.

Even with all these familiarities, though, there was something about her that almost made him question whether or not she was a complete stranger. There was a look in her eyes he didn't recognize. Something in the way she held her shoulders and curled her lips that he'd never seen before.

Leo hadn't come here expecting to learn something new. He'd come expecting to rekindle something old. And seeing the changes in her, no matter how small, reminded him that, truthfully, he didn't actually know why the fuck he was here.

"Miriam," he breathed, biting his tongue to keep his body from moving forward toward her. It was hard not to be overly familiar with someone when you knew what every part of their body tasted like.

"Leonard." Her tone was terse. Cold.

"How—" He cut himself off. Asking how she was didn't seem sufficient. It wasn't like they'd run into each other at the gas station after not seeing each other for a couple weeks. It had been eight whole years that felt like a lifetime. There was no way she could fit everything he was dying to know about that time into an answer for one shitty, loaded question. "I came," he said instead.

She crossed her arms over her chest and he spotted a dark tattoo on the back of her forearm. That was new too. "I didn't think you'd get here so soon."

"I was in Jacksonville."

"Still, I figured you'd need some time to square things away with work . . . let your girlfriend or whoever know what you were doin'."

"No girlfriend." He found it important to address that part first. "And work is . . . it ain't no big deal."

"Hmmmm."

"Are you goin' to invite me in?"

She leaned her shoulder against one side of the doorway, hip cocked so she practically took up the entire space. Her eyes ran up and down the length of him. For a beat, she looked like she was about to deny him, then she took a step back, allowing him to pass by.

The house smelled like a mix of Fabuloso and lemon-scented candles. Familiar, and not unpleasant. The scent drew him to sit on the same couch where he'd waited for Miri on prom night, the same couch he'd once been close to losing his virginity on.

Instead of sitting down next to him, Miri stood, leaning against the arm on the left side of the couch nearest the door.

"Your mama here?" he asked.

"Nah, she's out."

"Right."

They found themselves stuck. Him, half scared to broach any topic that came to mind, and the other half desperate to say something—anything. Her reasoning, he still wasn't sure of—no matter how high his hopes were.

"Look, Leo, I—" She ground her teeth together, her jaw pulsing as it clenched. "Thanks for coming, and for gettin' here so fast."

"Well, you said it was important, and you know I'd do anything for you."

The line didn't hit her like he thought it would. She didn't flash him the girlish smile she used to when he said things like that. Instead, her mouth straightened into a hard line, lips tucked in, shoulders tighter than they'd been when she'd answered the door.

The last thing he wanted was to make her angry. As much as he'd missed her, he hadn't missed the way she looked at him when he'd fucked up. He had enough images of that in his head to last a goddamn lifetime.

"Miri . . . look." He sat forward, putting his elbows on his knees. "I know it's been a long time. I know . . . I know I'm the one who got us all fucked up . . . but . . . you askin' me back here means a whole lot to me."

Her thick brows furrowed and she shook her head a little. "Leo . . . I don't know what you think I called you here for, but . . ."

She trailed off and he filled the silence. "I'm not saying I expect anything from you but I figured . . . I figured you called me because you missed me. I mean, I hope you did."

She took a long breath, coming around the love seat

to sit, pushing herself back into the cushion like she wanted to disappear. She caught his eyes then, and from the look of them, he wasn't going to like what she was about to say.

"I didn't ask you to come back because I wanted to see you, Leo . . . I asked you because . . ." She closed her eyes. "Because I want a divorce."

The words were like a sledgehammer against his chest. Knocking the breath out of him, making his body feel like it was caving in on itself.

The humiliation of being so thoroughly wrong compounded with the devastation of what she was asking him to do. Put the final nail in the coffin of their lives together. Even after what felt like a lifetime of separation, knowing they were still bound to each other in some way was the only thing that had him keeping it together sometimes.

Talk about hope. Leo could have gone twenty years without seeing her. As long as he had that marriage certificate tucked away in his duffel bag, there was still a permanency to the thing that lived between them. Without it . . . there was nothing but two people and a relationship broken beyond repair.

Hearing her asking him to give that up made him want to jump up and leave. To take his ass right back to Jacksonville and hammer away at a concrete wall until his shoulders hurt more than his heart.

But he couldn't move. He couldn't do anything. Not when his mouth opened to speak and no words came out. Not when his palms started to sweat and he felt like he was seconds away from a heart attack.

All he could do was sit there like a damn fool in front of her. Watching as she retreated further and further into herself. Seeing that the further she burrowed, the farther she got from him. He'd been hundreds of miles from Greenbelt and he'd never felt farther from his wife than he did at this moment.

"Why?" he rasped, the word repeating in his head on a loop. "Why now?"

"I . . ." She turned her back to him for a moment. Her shoulders drew in as tight as the fist in his stomach felt. When she turned to face him, her jaw was trembling. "It's been a long time, Leo. I figured . . . I figured it was time we finally did this so we could move on with our lives."

Move on with their lives. He wanted to curse and spit. What had they been doing for the past eight years if not getting on with their fucking lives? He'd been doing a sorry-assed version of it, he knew, but still.

Miri rubbed the space between her eyebrows.

"Bullshit," he ground out.

"Excuse me?" She straightened up, a sneer appearing across her thick lips.

"Bullshit," he repeated. "You're doin' that thing you do when you're lying through your teeth. I'm callin' bullshit on that bullshit-ass reason, Miriam."

Fire sparked in her eyes, and she took her hands off her face, securing them behind her back. "I am not bullshitting."

"Of course you are. The last time I saw you, you told me you'd rather set yourself on fire than be in the same room as me again. And I know you meant that shit. You didn't have a change of heart, you want this now for a reason . . ." He swallowed so hard and fast it made his throat hurt. "Did you . . . is there . . ."

Miri scoffed, taking a deep breath. "No, Leo, I promise you I'm not doin' this because I'm trying to tie myself to yet another disappointing spouse."

The dig hurt. Cutting deep and hard like he'd taken a stab to the kidneys. The only thing that soothed it was the relief that came with her admitting her request for a divorce wasn't because she'd found someone else.

Fucking ridiculous. What sense did that make, anyway? Eight years they'd spent apart. He would be delusional to think that a woman like her would have gone so long without finding someone else to love her far better than he'd been able to.

"Fuck," she cursed. "I shoulda known better than to try to lie to you, of all people." The words were mumbled, and he realized that they weren't for him, but for her. "Fine, Leo . . . I won the lottery."

He blinked, unable to take his eyes off her, but not for the usual reasons. She wasn't showing any of her telltale signs of lying. No rubbing between her eyes or licking her lips too often. She was straight-faced, her mouth pressed in a tight line. Her eyes were boring right into his, too. She was dead-ass serious and he didn't know what to do with that revelation.

When he didn't say anything, she took it as her cue to keep talking.

"A few weeks ago I got this . . . urge to play some numbers when I ran Mama's for her. And I . . . I won."

"How much?"

All his life he'd been told that it was rude to ask people how much money they made. It went against every southern-boy sensibility to ask Miri the question, but he couldn't stop himself.

"A lot . . ." she said.

He raised an eyebrow.

Miri groaned like he was pulling off her fingernails one by one. Like the burden she found herself under was literally crushing her. "Two hundred and twenty million dollars."

He had to grip the fat arm of the couch to keep from falling over.

That was not a real number. It couldn't be.

"Are you fuckin' serious?"

"As a heart attack."

"Jesus, Miri . . ." He clutched his chest, his mind rushing. Two hundred and twenty million things ran through his mind and not a single one would pause long enough for him to grasp on and process it. "What the hell does this have to do with me?"

"We're married, Leo."

"So?"

She threw her head back so hard even he felt the pain of it. "So . . . because of some ridiculous fuckin' law some old white man made up before either of us was born, because we're married, you could . . . you could probably sue me and claim half my money. You see how that's a problem, right? This shit might be more trouble than it's worth but I'll be good goddamned if I let you—"

"I would never do that, Miriam, I lo—" He stopped himself, biting down on his tongue to keep it from speaking words he knew wouldn't be welcome. "I don't need your money."

"Of course you do," she scoffed. "You're just as broke as me. Hell, that car you've got out there looks worse than mine. I know your sister and Ahmir are both workin' two jobs right now to stay afloat. Plus"—her eyes turned real soft for a second, warm enough to melt butter, before the guardrails locked right back into place—"I know Auntie Roberta's house is . . ."

He made a stopping motion with his hand. "No."

"Sorry, but . . . Leo, those are all reasons why I know you need my money."

He couldn't look at her then. Everything about that face and what was currently coming out of it made him seethe. He wanted to run. He wanted to rage. He wanted to turn back time. None of which he could do.

"I thought you knew me better than that." His voice was low, colored with his anger and disappointment. "I would never take what's yours unless you chose to give it to me."

She shook her head. "It's been a long time. I don't know anything about you anymore."

"Shit like that doesn't change."

The face she made was sharp, a hair off from being a sneer. "Everything changes, Leo. Everything."

"Fine, Miri." He stood up. "Fine. I'm sittin' here, tellin' you that I'm not goin' to take your money. You can either believe it or not, but it ain't goin' to change what's happenin' here."

"And what's happenin' here?" She crossed her arms.

"I'm leavin' here the way I came." It pained him to say it, especially when she looked so unfazed hearing those words. "Broke."

. "And divorced?" Her voice was almost timid, but not quite. She'd never been that a day in her life. See, he thought, some things never did change.

He'd have been lying if he said he didn't think about saying no, about booking out the door and running back to Jacksonville so he didn't have to comply with her request. Even for a split second. And it made him just about the biggest piece of shit in existence. Tying her to him when she had no desire to be tied.

Truth was, he didn't know who he was if he wasn't hers in some way. When they were little, her mama had taken to watching some of the neighborhood kids for extra cash on the weekends. He'd been one of them. Playing on Mrs. Butler's porch with Vaseline-covered knees and store-brand Dr Pepper on his tongue. Miri had always been two steps ahead of him with her bright smile and inability to be anybody but herself. He'd loved her when he was six, he'd loved her when he was fifteen, and even now, growing closer and closer to thirty-two, he loved her. And now they were barely speaking, but that certificate declaring them husband and wife was the only thing he had tethering his heart to the earth. He'd had eight years to try and figure out who he was. And he'd learned a lot. He'd learned how to properly take his whiskeys and to build something with his hands from the ground. But he still hadn't managed to figure out how to stop loving her. Not by a long shot. He wasn't sure he ever would.

He also didn't know how he was supposed to live with himself if he just walked away from her for a second time without some kind of fight.

He didn't have much, and he had even less to give Miri. But there was something he had.

Her doubt.

And maybe that was enough to buy him time to do what he'd thought he was doing by coming to Greenbelt in the first place—winning her back.

"I'll give you your divorce." His heart thundered. "But I want somethin' too."

She rolled her eyes, those arms crossed even tighter across her chest, like she was holding her organs inside her body. "What do you want?"

"Two million." He said the words immediately, without even putting much thought into the number he was throwing out into the air. "Like you said, my sister and her family could use the money. This way, they could buy their house outright and give the boys a chance at getting through college without goin' into debt for the rest of their lives."

"And you? How much do you want, Leo?"

"I don't want your money, Miriam."

"That's—"

"But." He cut her off. "You're right. I would like to fix up Auntie Roberta's house."

She squinted. "How much would that cost?"

"I don't know. I'd like to do most of it myself. But I'll need to outsource a few things. I can give you a quote but I'm thinkin' somewhere around three hundred thousand."

"You're goin' to fix it yourself?" She looked skeptical. He understood; the last time she'd seen him, he could barely flip the switch on a circuit breaker without help.

He nodded.

"Which means . . . you're goin' to be in Greenbelt for . . ."

"However long it takes."

"And how long do you think that will be?"

Once again, the words bit into his skin. He was going to have a hell of a time soothing his hurts from this day later on. "What? You can't stand havin' me in town either?"

"It's not that, I just . . ."

"Just what?" he asked when she didn't finish her sentence.

"Nothing." She coughed. "It's fine . . . that all sounds . . . fine. I'll write your sister the check and I'll give you what you need for the house and then . . ."

"Then we have a deal. Let me know when you have the divorce papers drawn up and I'll sign them."

"Okay." She looked like she had a hard time swallowing, but he didn't read too much into it. "What happens when you're finished with the house? Are you goin' to sell it?"

"I don't know." He made his way to the front door, curling his hand around the cold brass knob. Parts of him were eager to leave while others were begging him to stay. Even if he spent the entire time fighting with her.

"Okay, well . . . Okay . . ." She cleared her throat. "I'll get in touch with my lawyer and get the papers to you as soon as I can."

He breathed in the fresh air when he opened the door. The sound of the summer crickets a relief from the incredibly thick silence between them.

"You know how wild that sounds?"

"What?" she asked.

"Hearing you say that you'll get in touch with your lawyer." He chuckled. "It's wild as fuck, actually."

Miri dropped her head and slumped her shoulders. "I know." He stood out on the porch while she waited in the doorway, her hand resting against the door. "I thought winning the lottery was supposed to feel amazing, but so far . . ."

He waited for her to finish, and when she didn't, he urged her. "So far what?"

"Nothing." She shook her head profusely. "I'll talk to you later, okay?"

"Yeah, all right, I'll be seein' you."

Before he could even make it off the third step, she'd closed the door.

5

MIRI

"**U**mm . . ." Olivia rubbed her hands over the tops of her pale arms. "Far be it from me to be the one to say this, Miri, but this is some real white-people shit you have us doing right now."

"Mm-hmm." Jade voiced her agreement.

She saw Aja grimace through the dark. "I . . . really don't want to get murdered at a place called Cunny Creek, y'all."

Jade and Olivia snorted at the same time.

"That would be hilarious, though," Jade said through a laugh.

Olivia made a noise of offense. "It sure as hell wouldn't."

"Would y'all shut the fuck up. Damn."

Miri could practically hear their jaws snap together, three heads turning toward her in tandem.

"Well excuuuuse me," Aja grumbled.

Miri flicked on the flashlight in her hand, lighting up all of their faces. The sky wasn't completely dark. The sun was only just beginning to set, but the spot they were standing in was covered in a canopy of trees, allowing very little light to peek through.

"I didn't bring y'all here to send you to your deaths." Miri grabbed the three little envelopes she had tucked in the back pocket of her shorts, handing one to each of the women in front of her. "I brought you here to change your lives."

"You are so dramatic." Olivia rolled her eyes.

None of them seemed eager to open the envelopes. She didn't blame them fully. Aside from Aja, none of them knew anything about the money she'd won. Aja hadn't even brought her win up since Miri had broken the news to her and Walker. Miri highly doubted that Aja would be expecting the gift she was about to receive.

The list of people in the know was beginning to grow faster than she could keep up. She and Patrice had finally told her auntie, with the help of a big check. Leo knew now too, and so did his sister Thea and her husband. She didn't think there was a single other person on this planet she wanted to have to break this bizarre news to. But she'd known immediately that her girls deserved something befitting her love for them—chaotic as fuck.

"Miri, I swear to God this better not be another handmade card with you and Aldis Hodge Photoshopped as a bride and groom . . ." Jade grumbled.

"Would you just open it please." Her heart was starting to thunder. She had no idea how they'd react and that made her nervous.

The sound of the envelopes ripping open was louder than the crickets. She realized immediately that the setting she'd chosen hadn't been the best after all. It had only grown darker as the sun continued setting, with the only light provided for them from her flashlight. She pointed it toward them, trying not to flash it too brightly in their eyes while allowing them to see what was inside their envelopes.

Aja was the first to react. She sucked in a sharp breath, then held the rectangular slip of paper closer to her face.

"What the fuuuuck," Olivia whispered breathlessly.

Jade didn't say anything. Silent as a church mouse, she raised her eyes up to Miri's. "This isn't real." She said the words matter-of-factly. Leaving no room for argument.

"It's real," Miri said.

Aja made a choking sound. "But Miri, this is . . . this is too much."

"Did you rob somebody?" Olivia whispered.

Miri groaned. "I really need to get better friends . . . Look, they're real. I swear. If you take them to the bank in the mornin' they're goin' to clear. Every single one of 'em."

"This is six million dollars, Miri," Jade said. "Times three. I don't . . . I don't understand."

"I won the lottery. Two hundred and twenty million fuckin' dollars. I promise you, this is very real and very much the least I could do for y'all."

Three pairs of eyes blinked at her through the darkness. So wide she almost expected them to start hooting like owls.

"You won . . . the lottery . . ." Olivia said the words slowly, feeling them out in her mouth.

Miri nodded. "The Mega Millions jackpot."

"When?" Jade asked.

"Um, about a month or so ago."

Jade reached out and sent her fist jabbing into one of Miri's upper arms. "Your ass can't hold water, you expect me to believe you kept this from us for a freakin' month?"

Miri rubbed her hurt dramatically. "Hell, give 'em back then, since you don't believe me."

"Now, we didn't say all that," Aja stammered. "We're just . . . shocked, not ungrateful."

"Definitely not ungrateful," Olivia agreed.

Aja dragged her eyes off the paper to finally look at Miri. "It's just . . . hard to wrap our heads around." She held up her check, somehow knowing better than to say that she had been keeping it a secret too. "Six million doesn't feel like a real number, much less two hundred and twenty million. Like . . . what does that look like in a bank account?"

Miri snorted. "That's not . . . really how it works. I took the lump-sum option rather than get payments over the next thirty years. That means the jackpot was reduced, and after taxes, it was reduced even further. I actually put the money in a trust that gets paid out to me every month with the option to withdraw whatever I want whenever I need to as long as I bring it up with my financial advisor first."

"Financial. Advisor." Jade whispered the words slowly.

"Yeah, it's unbelievable as hell." She let out a dry chuckle. "So, all the money isn't sitting in my little savings account at the Greenbelt Credit Union, but there's sure as hell enough in there for y'all to cash those checks."

Everyone went quiet again, the only sound the crickets and the rustling of trees. But she could practically hear the wheels turning in their heads.

"Does this . . ." Jade paused, then cleared her throat. "Does all this have anything to do with the fact that I saw Leo Vaughn picking up his nephew from the elementary school this afternoon?"

"Fuck," Miri cursed under her breath. She'd been hoping to avoid that topic altogether until she could wrap her head around it fully. But the longer she went on, the more she didn't know if that would ever happen. "Yeah."

Olivia gasped so loud it startled the rest of them. "Is he here tryin' to take your shit?"

"I thought you said y'all were split up," Aja remarked.

"They are," Olivia said. "Have been for years. Are you tellin' me he crawled his ass back here the second he heard you got some money in your pocket?"

Something in her felt defensive at the accusation. Which was ridiculous. It wasn't like at one point she hadn't thought he'd do exactly the thing they were accusing him of. But hearing them say it, people who had known him, been close to him, loved him, made something ugly twist in her belly.

"He didn't even know I'd won. I called him here to tell him, to ask him for a divorce and offer him a lump sum."

"Why in the hell would you do that?" Jade asked.

"He's entitled to something just for being my husband, and what I'm givin' him now is much less than what he might get if he wanted to sue me."

"And . . . how much is that?" Olivia physically leaned forward. "Wait . . . is that another nosy white-person question?"

"Yes." She, Jade, and Aja said it at the same time.

"But it's fine," Miri added. "I'm givin' him enough to fix up his auntie's house."

"That's not bad," Aja said. "Sure as hell better than half."

"Exactly, plus I get a divorce out of it so it's basically a win-win for me."

She could practically feel Jade's eyes boring into the side of her head, but she kept her eyes in the general direction of where Aja and Olivia were standing. It was fully dark now, the light even more scarce, but she didn't need to see Jade to know exactly what the look on her face was saying. Nor did she need to see it to feel it.

"Everything's going to be fine." She forced the words out. "He'll probably be gone by fall and I'll be rich and divorced and . . . it'll all be fine."

"Okay." Olivia said the word but sounded far from convinced.

"It has to be," Miri pushed. "I have so much shit I

want to do, y'all. I've never had this many options before. I can't even focus on one. None of it has really sunk in yet, but I know that this shit with Leo is just a speed bump on the way to my future."

"Goddamn right." Jade grinned. "You could probably buy Greenbelt if you wanted to and name yourself the mayor."

Miri grimaced. "I'd rather throw all the money into the Atlantic, to be honest. Sounds like it would be a better investment and less stressful."

All four of them laughed until, suddenly, something rustled in the grass. Loud and terrifying enough to make them jump.

"Okay, well, can we discuss your endless possibilities somewhere that isn't crawling with snakes and critters?" Aja asked. "Because these checks you cut us are only worth anything if we don't get eaten by something."

"Yeah, um, let's go. It's scary as fuck out here." Miri shivered.

"While we're at it, we really need to talk about your news-breaking skills." Olivia was the first one on the trail, not even turning her head to speak to Miri following behind her. "There is no reason we couldn't have done this in somebody's house away from the mosquitoes."

Jade snorted into the night air. "A dramatic bitch until the very end."

6

MIRI

Leo wasn't staying at his sister's place. She and her husband, Ahmir, had welcomed two young sons and a brand-new pit bull puppy. As much as he loved and missed all of them, he'd gotten too used to his own company to give it up completely overnight. So he'd chosen instead to stay at the only bed-and-breakfast in town.

Morningside B&B was owned by Mr. and Mrs. Burgos, a Puerto Rican couple who had retired to Greenbelt and opened their home to customers what seemed like forever ago. They offered impeccably clean rooms at a reasonable price that included breakfast and dinner every night.

Miri and Leo had spent their wedding night there. At the time, it had been the happiest night of her life.

Now, she tended to avoid driving by the small downtown street the hotel resided on.

She'd reluctantly agreed to meet Leo there to hand him the check she'd written for his sister, as well as discuss the start of the house project. The wannabe strategist in her wanted desperately to meet on neutral ground. But that didn't exist in Greenbelt. Not when the two of them had called this place home, filling every corner of the small town with some memory of them. She also didn't want the eyes on her.

Had they met at Minnie's, there would have been rumors about their reconciliation spreading around town within the hour. By the weekend, people would have been coming up to Miri and asking her if she'd gotten herself pregnant.

No, it was better to meet at Morningside. As much as the thought of being in a small room with him made her itch, at least she knew they'd be away from prying eyes. And knowing Mrs. Burgos's reputation for being one hell of a secret keeper, she felt confident that she could leave this meeting as unscathed as possible.

At least, she had been, until she'd found herself showing up nearly a half hour before their scheduled time. She'd spent all morning preparing for this. She'd gotten up early to try and steel herself emotionally. She'd found a morning meditation on YouTube in hopes that it would calm her mind—in the end, it hadn't worked, so she figured she didn't do it right. She'd even timed everything out perfectly, planning to strategically show up ten minutes late. Just long enough to make him sweat a little.

And yet, there she was. Eager as a fucking beaver to be in front of him again. So shameless about it that she didn't even wait around in the car until the allotted time. She just had to make her way upstairs and knock on Leo's hotel room door like she didn't have an ounce of sense in her head. It was made of a heavy wood, so she couldn't hear anything behind it, but when the knob turned, she froze. And when it swung open, her mouth went as dry as a Communion wafer.

What. The. Fuck.

Fuck him.

No, she shook her head, the cough in her throat hurt when she forced it back down.

Leo wasn't wearing . . . well, anything really. He had a white towel wrapped around his waist but the rest of him was bare. Brown skin the color of walnuts glistened with fat droplets of water. Even his beard, a bit rugged and not fully formed in some places, was wet. He was broader than she remembered, his chest more barreled, his shoulders stretching so wide they nearly took up the entire doorway. His stomach wasn't one built of hours spent in the gym, pretty with symmetrically sculpted muscles. It was slightly rounded but hard. Like he was used to digging into nachos and beer after long days of working with his hands and body.

He hadn't looked like that when he'd left. He'd been just as tall, but skinnier. With bony elbows and thighs a third the size of hers. The ones he had now were like tree trunks. And what was between them . . . well, she couldn't see that as well as she could see everything else, but she knew it was there. It wasn't fully at attention, but it was certainly presenting enough to tent the material some.

Her mouth went even drier. That, she remembered. And well. Well enough that her entire body flushed as memories played behind her eyes. The insides of her thighs tingled and she clenched her jaws tight.

Leo cleared his throat, and when her eyes snapped to meet his in response, she realized that she'd been staring at his dick. She didn't know for how long, but being caught so blatantly filled her with rage.

How goddamn dare he come to the door dressed like some kind of fucking extra in the second *Magic Mike* movie?

She'd never do that to him. If she wanted to tease him to the point of a heart attack she'd at least have the respect to come to the door in a chiffon teddy or something.

Then again, the thought of his hard body in something so pretty and delicate made her realize that she would have found herself in exactly the same position as she was now . . . which was to say . . .

Fuck. Him.

"Are you goin' to come in or just stand there and stare at my dick all day?"

"What?" Her chest seized.

Leo grinned, all teeth and smugness. "Nothin'."

"You are such an asshole."

He didn't say anything, just stepped aside, allowing her into the room. It was small, barely big enough to fit a double bed and an armoire. But the window was large and overlooked the beautiful garden behind the house. Suddenly, Miri felt like they were all over each other. Only a foot apart, she could smell the soap emanating from his damp skin. So good it made her mouth water. Like the thirst she'd felt before was about to be quenched.

Maybe meeting in his room hadn't been such a good idea after all. She'd come thinking she had the upper hand. Now, all she had was a head full of horny thoughts and nipples hard enough to break Bubble Wrap.

"Um . . ." She tried to say something to ease the burden of her own libido but she couldn't think of anything.

"This looks like the room we stayed in on our wedding night, doesn't it?" He wasn't even looking at her when he spoke.

Miri flitted her eyes around the space. In all honesty, it did look a lot like the room they'd stayed in. Which wasn't surprising. It was a freaking bed-and-breakfast, the damn place only had six rooms. But the bed had the same iron-wrought railing she'd clutched onto during their first sex as "man and wife."

That memory was a fire poker in the back of her brain and she gritted her teeth. "I wouldn't remember," she said with all the meanness she could drum up.

Leo cleared his throat, mouth turned down as he tried again to find some type of common ground. "You want to see what contractors I got in touch with about fixin' up the house?"

She nodded, her eyes glued to his tight ass flexing underneath his towel as he walked over to grab the tan folder on the single bedside table.

"So, Jackson Miller and his daddy look to be pretty good. They've got good references. I think they even worked on that place the mayor's sister-in-law opened a few years back."

A surge of annoyance ran through Miri, like it did every time Plus One Salon & Spa came up. A gaudy place run by racist rich white people who would rather serve their guests with fancy gimmicks and watered-down cocktails than provide quality service. It didn't matter how much people in town ate that shit up, it pissed Miri off to no end. Watching the business her aunt Wanda had built, the one that had helped feed two different generations of their family, dwindle more and more just because they couldn't afford Swedish massage chairs at every pedicure station.

But that wasn't true now, was it? Now, they could afford it . . . *she* could afford it, like she could afford just about anything else.

"But Demetrius Davis just started his own company. He's only done one job so far but—"

"You want to support a young Black man doin' his own shit."

"Exactly." He gave her one of his easy smiles.

"I'm all for it," she said, her horniness having been

smoothly pushed aside by her anger. "We went to school with Demetrius, I think he was a few years ahead of us but his brother Vonnie was in our class."

Leo snorted, but it was far from playful. "Yeah, I remember."

"What?" She did not appreciate his tone.

"You kissed him," he said blandly. "Sophomore year, at Blue Diamond. You had his little skinny ass pushed up against the claw machine. Probably tryin' to make me jealous."

Miri snorted, crossing her arms. "I sure as hell wasn't. It's bold as hell of you to assume that I was tryin' to make you jealous. Maybe Vonnie was just a good kisser."

Leo curled his upper lip like he'd smelled something foul. "You don't even remember that you told me your lips kept gettin' stuck in his braces, do you?"

"Doesn't mean it wasn't good."

She had no idea why she was pressing the argument so much. She didn't even remember the kiss, not really. She'd kissed a lot of people before she and Leo had made it official their junior year of high school. Football players, girls on the step team, a Ferris wheel attendant at the county fair, even Olivia a time or two. She didn't remember anything about goddamn Vonnie Davis, but she didn't want Leo thinking she cared about his ridiculous jealousy enough to give in to him. Because she didn't. Not one fucking bit.

Miri smirked. "A little pain never made anything less pleasurable for me. You of all people should know that."

It was his turn to break. His bluster faded, forcing

his fists to clench tight at the fabric around his hips. His thick lips gaped a few times and his eyes couldn't quite meet hers anymore.

Miri softened. This was the Leo she knew. All soft eyes and shy smiles. He'd been so different from her, less extroverted, quieter, more thoughtful. The calm and security he radiated had drawn her in and made her want to cling to him tight. He hadn't looked like the old Leo when he'd shown up on her doorstep. There had been more anger in his eyes, apprehension, and so many other things she didn't know him well enough to recognize anymore.

When she'd flustered him, the look on his face had reminded her of the eighteen-year-old not-quite man who had proposed to her under the weeping willow in his auntie's backyard. With a voice so gentle it would have been swallowed up by the breeze if she hadn't been so close to him.

It was gone quickly, though. The scowl was back and it wasn't nearly as unattractive as she tried to convince herself it was.

"We'll go with Demetrius, then. He told me he could start next week, but we have to get an inspector out to the property to check out the foundation and all that."

He turned his back to her, and Miri swallowed hard at the sight. Scars riddled his skin now, not too many, but most of them looked like they'd happened because of general life screwups. Some darker than the rest of his skin, one near his shoulder had actually keloided. Every single one a map across the hard muscles underneath.

She had to stop herself from reaching out to trace them. He opened a suitcase, pulling out a pair of underwear and tugging them on underneath his towel.

"Did—" She coughed to hide the breaking of her voice. "Did he give you an estimate?"

"We're still lookin' at about three hundred thousand once all is said and done." He kept his back to her as he rubbed deodorant under his arms. "I want to do it up nice. Turn it into somethin' Auntie Roberta would have liked. She was the only one in the family who was able to actually own a home here. It deserves to be done up right."

"I agree," she said, nodding, her eyes turned down to the metallic polish on her toes. There was a tear in the strap of her sandal. A fraying in the center that caused some of the fake leather fabric to dig into the top of her foot. She'd had them for years. Every spring she took a hard-bristled toothbrush to them, scrubbing them until the white soles were as bright as they could possibly be. She could afford to throw them away now. Hell, she could afford twelve pairs of the same sandals she saw her favorite Instagram baddies parading around the Maldives in. That didn't feel good, though. No Gucci flip-flops could ever be as comfortable as the twenty-dollar flea-market sandals she'd haggled over, could they?

"You should come by later this week." Leo's offer forced her out of her own head. "See what you're payin' for. Plus . . . Auntie would have wanted you to be part of it. She loved you."

"She loved me as your wife," she corrected. "But I'm not anymore."

"Yes, you are."

The words came out so fast they made her head spin.

"We haven't signed those papers yet. You haven't even gotten them to me. You're still mine and I'm still yours."

"For now." She meant the words to sound like a threat, but they were weak. "And it's only because I've been busy. I haven't been able to send for them yet, but I'm gonna get with my lawyer later this week. In fact, I'll bring them out to the house. How does that sound?"

"Sounds fine to me. Come on out, bring yourself and them papers, and we'll kill two birds with one stone."

She narrowed her eyes. Leo had turned around to face her, still naked except for a pair of burgundy boxer briefs. His face was blank and she hated it. She knew it sounded cruel but she much preferred how he'd looked when she'd originally brought up the topic of divorce. He'd looked shocked and every bit like he'd wanted to say no. She hated herself for it, but that look had made her feel . . . well, something. This one, wholly apathetic, made her feel something too. But something less satisfying and more along the lines of shattered.

"Fine." She said the word like a child, trying not to pout.

"All right, well, I've got a few errands to run, so . . ."

Her jaw dropped. "Are you kickin' me out?"

"You're welcome to stay." Leo shrugged. "Watch me get dressed. I know how much you used to like that too."

The noise she released was half shriek, half huff. Who was this man? Because he wasn't Leonard Vaughn, that was for damn sure.

"You just . . ." She struggled with her words. Eager to get the last word in, to feel like she'd won whatever this was. "Cover yourself up, you don't need to be walkin' around town lookin' like some kind of barrel-chested harlot."

His laugh was loud as it rang through the room. The kind of bark that bounced off the walls so hard it made her jump once it reached her ears.

He was laughing at her. And it didn't matter that she knew there was no malice in it, she couldn't stand it.

This did not feel like winning. In fact, it felt like she was losing.

Resisting the urge to stomp her foot, she stormed from the room. Trying to maintain enough respect for the Burgoses' home not to slam their door. But she couldn't stop her feet from stomping down the stairs when she heard his laugh deepen from the very bottom of his stomach.

She. Hated. Him.

7

LEO

Auntie Roberta's house sat on about an acre of land. It had been sharecroppers' land, sold to her in the '60s when the family that originally owned it had moved out west. The home had been built in the early 1900s. A solid two stories, three bedrooms, and one bathroom on the ground floor.

He'd watched enough late-night HGTV to know that this would probably be called "the perfect starter home" these days. But this wasn't a starter home. This was a home that had housed just about every member of his family at some point. It had provided comfort and security. For them, it was a forever home. At least, it had been at one point. Now, it was damn near dilapidated. The wood floors had been rotting for years, the foundation had cracked, multiple parts of the roof caved in. The family had spent years watching the state of the place get worse and worse. There hadn't been anything they could do about it, though. Not when they were all struggling to keep clothes on their backs and food in their bellies. They'd been approached multiple times about selling the place, largely for the land it sat on. It didn't matter how far the house fell into disrepair, though; it belonged to the Vaughn family. And it would be a cold day in hell before they handed it over to someone who didn't understand what it represented to them.

Still, Leo never thought he'd be standing in the musty living room surrounded by samples for brand-new hardwood floors and quartz countertops. It was exciting, but overwhelming too. He didn't know what the hell he was doing. It was so much more complicated than he thought it'd be. He'd figured that fixing the place up would involve more hammers and nails than talk about proper lighting.

Miri showed up right as Demetrius walked the inspector to the door. She had one of those smiles on her face that she used whenever she had to fake her way through a situation she didn't really want to be in. Bright and pretty but tight around the corners. Her cheekbones were pushed high but her eyes were guarded.

"Hey." She waved, stepping aside to let the inspector through. "It looks like y'all are busy in here."

"We are." Demetrius closed the door, pushing his thumbs through his belt loops. "Your boy here wants a full overhaul. Just about everything in this house is either gettin' changed or updated. It's a hell of a job."

Leo saw her face pinch slightly at his phrasing of "your boy," but he also couldn't help but notice how Miri smiled at the other man, all bright and unguarded. It made him want to pick up one of the sample tiles on the floor and throw it at Demetrius's head.

Miri dug the tip of her tennis shoe into a weak spot in the floor, making the wood creak. "Y'all are changin' it completely, are you? Turning it into one of those houses that looks like hell to live in? All that glass and marble floors and stuff?"

Leo snorted at the thought. "Nah, we're keepin' the soul of the house the same. We're not changin' the layout or anything, but the kitchen and bathroom need to be gutted, and just about everything needs to be replaced. We're tryin' to make sure we find things as close to the originals as possible, but some of that stuff is expensive. The wood, the baseboard skirting, it's . . . a lot."

"Well, money certainly ain't an issue," she said.

Demetrius raised an eyebrow but kept his mouth shut.

Leo snorted. "I'm not tryin' to run your pockets any more than I already am."

She cut her eyes to Demetrius like she was suddenly aware that they weren't having this conversation alone. Leo knew that she still hadn't told many people about her big win. No one that wasn't already close to her. He would have known if she had. He was positive that somebody would find a way to bring it up every time he had to stop by the Piggly Wiggly or pick his nephews up from school.

She probably would've had people knocking on her

door day and night too. But then, this was Greenbelt. A place so quintessentially southern that he couldn't imagine folks on their last even considering asking her for a dime of her money, but they'd sure as hell talk.

Silence stretched between the three of them. Demetrius's head swung back and forth between Miri and Leo, both staring off with shifty eyes, trying to explain what they'd inadvertently revealed to him.

He cleared his throat. "Imma go . . . uh . . . see what kind of gravel is on the driveway and let y'all figure out whatever the hell this is."

Neither of them said anything until they heard his feet beat against the last step on the porch.

Miri crossed her arms over her chest and Leo's eyes couldn't help but stray to the knotted button-up shirt she wore. The knot was pushed up right underneath her breasts and her cleavage spilled out between the multiple buttons she'd left open. She had never liked wearing a bra, and he found himself eternally thankful that one thing hadn't changed since he'd been gone.

The silence lingered. He had no clue what to say to her. Nothing that popped into his head felt right.

"I, um . . ." Miri cleared her throat. "I came because you basically guilted me into it, but if you're just goin' to stand here all day starin' at my titties, I have some other things I could probably be doin' instead."

"I was not!"

"Yes, you were," she laughed. "Them eyes damn near popped out of your head."

He had enough pride not to keep denying what they both knew was the absolute truth. "Hold up, you didn't only come here for that. You were supposed to bring the divorce papers too." He gestured his hand at her. "You got 'em hidin' in that tiny backpack, or . . . ?"

Miri rolled her eyes, but he could tell it was more her trying to cover up her embarrassment with bluster than actual frustration.

"My lawyer is on vacation right now so we'll have to hold off on that."

He felt like a dog the way his ears immediately perked up. She was bullshitting him. Leo didn't know if she was telling him a half-truth or an outright lie, but he knew something was off.

Any normal person would have been mad. Not him, though. He saw it for what it actually was—an in.

Hesitation poured out of her and it made hope rise in his chest. More than he had felt in years. It was damn near enough to make his spine straighter. Despite all her insistence that she was ready to be done with him, there was something there that told him different. It might have been small. But, fuck, even if it was as tiny as one of the paint splatters on his boots, he could work with it. It was like a light went on in him. Nothing too bright, still shrouded in a certain kind of hesitance he couldn't shake; it was dull, like the old lanterns his father used to bring along when they went hunting for crawfish before sunup. But it was there, right in the middle of his chest, lighting a fire under his ass. He didn't want to let the moment pass without doing something, anything to see his plan to fruition.

"Come here." He felt bolstered, and held a hand out to her. "I want to show you somethin'."

"And you need to hold my hand for that?" Miri snarked.

"It's up there." He pointed toward the ceiling. "And the stairs are a hair away from caving into the basement. Those little shoes of yours ain't goin' to help much, either."

She pursed her full lips, the dark plum color so inviting he almost wanted to sneer at the audacity. How could something look so tasty even when it was showing him disdain? It wasn't fair. A man shouldn't have to brave that tightrope of temptation and determent without some kind of safety net to fall into when his balance finally failed.

She narrowed her pretty, dark eyes at him before she took his hand. He paused for a breath. It wasn't lost on him that this was the first time he'd gotten to touch her in a long time.

He'd spent years dreaming of this moment. In those dreams they'd always been in a much nicer place with much less clothing, but he would take what he could get. Nose full of sawdust and all, his wife's skin was soft and warm but her grip was firm in his. Like she refused to let herself be in his hands without some kind of defense up.

There had been a time when she'd been as soft as Spanish moss for him. Curling around his body with a gentleness that made his skin hypersensitive. He didn't like this newness. But he deserved it. It reminded him that this was all his fault. Not that he needed the reminder all that much when it was the first thing on his mind when he woke up every morning and the lullaby that lured him to sleep each night.

They moved up the stairs slowly, him first, making a path with his feet that she followed diligently. When they got to the top, he turned left, and her breath hitched the second he did.

There were only two things that way: a storage closet that his auntie had used to hold the Christmas decorations, and his old bedroom. When Leo and his sister had first moved into this house with their aunt, Thea had slept in the room and he'd mostly spent his nights either on a pallet on the living room floor or on the couch. But by the time he'd started high school, she had moved out and he'd gotten the space to himself. It was small, barely big enough to hold his twin bed, a desk to do his homework on, and an old dresser.

The walls were a pale yellow color. The room had originally been a nursery for one of his older cousins and there had never really been the time to change it. His Jerry Rice poster was still up, though, right there above his folding closet doors. The one he'd kept above his bed was still there too. The December 2005 issue of *King* magazine with Trina on the cover. He'd spent a lot of nights as a kid with his head at the foot of the bed, staring at that picture.

Being in here made fondness settle in his chest. And it wasn't because of the Michael Jordan bobblehead, or the old study workbooks stacked in the corner, it was because he and Miri had so many memories in this space. He turned to look at her. Miri's face was relaxed and her eyes soft, and he knew instantly that she was thinking about it too.

His mind raced, working hard to think of one of the better memories circling through it. There was nothing like good old-fashioned nostalgia to soften somebody up even further.

Reluctantly, he let go of her hand, running his thumb over his palm like he could press the heat hers left behind into his skin so he'd never not feel it. He sat on the edge of the bed, thighs spread a bit and arms crossed. The old box spring creaked under him—but that was familiar too.

"This thing never could be quiet, huh?" He looked at her, breath caught while he prayed for her to answer him.

She walked a little closer to him. Not near enough for him to reach out and touch her, but it was still progress in his book.

"Wouldn't let us get away with shit." She chuckled, eyes staring out into the land behind the house through the lone window.

"Not at all," he agreed carefully. "Auntie Roberta would be right downstairs sittin' on that couch and as soon as she heard the bed creak even once she'd be up them stairs to bust in the room."

"'There's only one kind of studyin' y'all can do in that bed, and don't none of it have anything to do with algebra.'" Miri mimicked his aunt's voice well enough to make him bust a gut.

"I'd have to keep your smart ass from sayin' some slick shit about how two becoming one is technically algebra or some foolishness."

"I was offended," Miri scoffed. "We weren't even having sex. It was mighty bold of her to assume I was down for doin' anything in that raggedy twin bed of yours."

Leo raised an eyebrow. "Now . . . If I remember correctly that ain't all the way true."

She damn near rolled her eyes out her head and across the lawn. "All you remember is me lettin' you get up my shirt a few times. Maaaaybe a few French kisses, but that's it."

"Hmmmm." His skepticism was completely fake. He knew every single thing they'd gotten up to in this room, and she was right. Most of the intimacy hadn't been physical in nature. This room hadn't seen a lot of that kind of action—not with him, at least. But he'd learned so much about her here. They'd been sitting on the floor with their backs resting against the bed when she'd first told him that she was bisexual. Her body had been tensed, like she was waiting for him to say something horrible. He was all of sixteen, full of love he didn't understand and very few pretty words, but he'd thanked her for telling him and told her that he fully intended on being her person—and that he had no problem proving himself against whoever else wanted to take his place—no matter their gender.

The memory of it made his smile widen and Miri huffed, clearly taking it for smugness.

"If you remember *correctly,* we had a place for gettin' into all that."

He knew exactly what "all that" meant, and he refused to be ashamed over it. He just stared her down, smirk across his lips. Something in his gaze must have challenged her, and Miriam Butler had never been one to back down from a challenge. She walked closer to him until their shins were touching. She loomed over him, which meant that he had a perfect view of her cleavage. Dark brown like the rest of her, smooth and supple and fat, peeking up through the couple buttons she also had undone up top. He wanted to bury his face in it. Take in her scent, mark her with his tongue until they glistened from him even under the dull light bulb of the ceiling fan.

"Trust me." There was something in his throat, something that made his words come out rough and haggard. "Trust me, Miriam, I fuckin' remember . . . The real question is, do you?"

He had to bite back a smirk when she scoffed. Subtle as it was, her offense was real, and it was exactly what he wanted. Another in. One more sign that their shared history didn't have her as unaffected as she liked to play like it did.

She stepped even closer, nearly close enough for her knees to brush against his. He widened his thighs. When her eyes flicked to the space between them, his dick hardened behind his dusty jeans.

"The back room at Strike's, the one with the plaid couch and the old TV that only ever played the copy of *New Jack City* that was stuck in the VCR," she said, the edges to her words coming out a little smoother.

"I tried to make it romantic," he offered, eyes intently on hers.

Her fingers fidgeted at her sides. "The dollar-store candles and throw blankets from the church yard sale you added definitely set a very specific mood."

Her eyes were on his, her gaze was soft. The corners of her mouth were tilted up slightly, not quite into a smile, but a far cry from the scowl he'd become accustomed to from her.

Leo wanted to press freeze on this moment. To preserve it in ice, a space where they existed only like this. Them staring at one another, with the sweet pinches of nostalgia coloring the edges of everything they thought and said. A week ago he couldn't have ever imagined he'd be here with her, not even in his wildest dreams. Now, it was the best he'd felt in longer than he cared to admit. For a second, it seemed like the moment might actually go on forever. Then, there was a crash downstairs, followed by a curse. And soon Demetrius was calling up the stairs to tell him that one of the contractors was there to see about the plumbing.

His eyes flicked from her to the door, but as soon as they were back on Miri that slightly dreamy look was gone. Her arms were crossed, guarded, and her lips were a straight line.

"Anyway." She coughed. "Looks like the place is goin' to be nice." She waved an arm around at the room. "You should turn this into a home office, finally make it useful for somethin'."

And goddamn if that wasn't a punch to the gut.

8

MIRI

For the second time in as many days she was breathing in sawdust. Only this time, the tickling of her nostrils wasn't accompanied by the tangy scent of Leo's cologne. The annoyance was still there, maybe even more genuine than it had been before, but it was different.

She stood in the grandiose living room of a model home, watching with an upturned nose as her mother picked apart every detail she saw.

"I don't know who in the hell chose these decorations." Patrice pinched the tan drapes between her fingers, then sniffed. "It looks like a damn funeral home in here."

Miri wanted to tell her that the home didn't look like any funeral home she'd ever been in, but she kept that thought to herself. Granted, it *was* rather bland. Some kind of "farmhouse chic" style that had clearly been bitten from the style of that too-smiley couple on HGTV. The walls were a light tan color that was probably supposed to be inviting but read more like the lobby of a bank. The ceilings were so high it almost felt oppressive, and the hardwood floors made her lower back hurt the longer she stood on them. She didn't love it either, but it was the best their area had to offer and she wanted her mama to have the best.

"This is the model, Mama. You can customize it however you want. You can have carpet instead of all this wood. You can have that window in the kitchen you always wanted. We can even make it ranch style if you don't feel like fussin' with steps. It's whatever you want, Mama."

Patrice sniffed, then looked over at her. Miri felt tiny under her gaze. She'd never felt particularly scrutinized by her mother. Patrice tended to take her as she was. There was plenty of discipline, along with everything else that reminded Miri of the Black mothers she'd spent her life around. Very little judgment, not for her or many other people in this world. Her mama had already said that she'd been around enough rough-ass blocks enough times that she had no room to judge anybody else's shit. What Miri was feeling wasn't that, though, it was the knowledge that her mama saw something in her that even she didn't see. Some emotion buried so deep in the back of her head that the rest of her mind had shunned her into refusing to recognize. Her mama could see it, though—by the look in her eyes she could see it clear as day. There were only two people in the world who could do that. Patrice Butler and Leonard Vaughn. It was like a superpower for those two.

Only she fucking hated when it happened.

So she averted her eyes. Focused them on the ceilings, all textured and flecked with stark white paint. The house they were standing in was probably worth four of the one they'd lived in her entire life, and they still couldn't get away from those popcorn ceilings?

"Mama," she whined, when Patrice's gaze narrowed in on her even more.

"Little girl." Her mama drew in a long breath like she was gearing up to shout tongues in church. "I know what you think you're doin', bringin' me out here into this neighborhood where every single one of the damn eyesores they're callin' houses looks the same. But I don't want it, I'm just fine where I'm at."

Miri huffed. "Mama, where you're at has a leakin' roof and radiators that don't work half the time. Where you're at is barely fit for any human, let alone my mama. We . . . we have more now. We can do more. I can do more for you."

Patrice's hands went to her hips. "I raised you in that house, Miriam. Fed you, clothed you, came home after workin' two jobs to tuck you into bed. I watched the kids in the neighborhood grow up along with you. Watched when Miss Byun finally got it in her to get rid of that no-good husband of hers. I . . . I don't want to leave that, baby. Not for this." She swanned her arms around, gesturing to the house. "Surrounded by all these people who wouldn't have pissed on me if I was on fire before and probably still wouldn't now. I ain't sayin' I don't appreciate what you're tryin' to do, because Lord knows I'm honored by it, but this ain't what I want."

Miri found herself at a loss for words. It wasn't like she had any real examples to follow, but wasn't this the first thing everybody did when they suddenly got money? Buy their mama a big ole house for her to grow old in? The basketball players, the actors, hell, even Willis Pierce had gotten his parents a McMansion in this very neighborhood once he'd expanded his used car lot into Charleston. What in the hell was she supposed to do when her mama didn't want that?

"Mama, I can't . . . I can't just have all this money and not give back to you. All that stuff you did, the way you took care of me, I have to pay you back." Miri shook her head. "No, Mama, I'm not gonna not give back."

Patrice's face softened. "Bein' your mama is not somethin' I need to be rewarded for, little girl. Not by you or anybody else. I decided to have you, I decided to keep you, and that's that. The only thing you owe me is the respect of your elder, and you've always given me that."

That was crap, but Miri knew she couldn't say it. Patrice had given her so much more than a full belly and a warm bed over the years. She'd been supportive and attentive, her biggest fan. When Miri had told her that boys weren't the only ones who caught her eye, she'd put a rainbow bumper sticker on her car. When she'd stated that she didn't want to take out thousands of dollars in student loans to go to college and instead wanted to marry a boy when she was freshly eighteen and train to be a nail tech, Patrice had sighed, puffed on a cigarette she'd stolen from Auntie Wanda, and given her blessing. Miri's life hadn't been long, but she'd managed to make so many mistakes in her short time. Mistakes that she'd needed to make, but that had ostensibly changed her forever. She was grateful that her mother hadn't kept her from that. And had never, not even once, kicked her when she was down. She knew there was no real way she could ever repay her for that, but it didn't mean she wasn't going to try.

"What if I try to buy our house," she said with widened eyes. "I can talk to Mr. Simmons. We've lived in that house for dang near thirty years, maybe he's tired of bein' a landlord."

"Hmmm . . ." Miri knew then that meant her mother was listening, interest piqued, so she kept going.

"We could renovate it too." She clapped her hands together as the idea built up. "Replace the floors, get you a state-of-the-art kitchen, update the electrical system and plumbing, all that . . . plus, I'm sure that even with all that we'd spend less than we would buyin' one of these houses."

That did her in. Patrice's lips were pursed but Miri could see in her eyes that she liked the idea. She'd watched far too many home renovation shows not to have secret dreams of undertaking one herself. Miri was sure she'd be getting opinions on the uselessness of shiplap and the staying power of quartz countertops for weeks. She didn't care, though, she welcomed it.

"Okay . . ." Patrice's tone was hesitant. "But I want you to give me a budget to follow, I don't want to be out there spendin' like I ain't got no sense."

"I can do that." Miri knew full well that any budget she had in mind had a cap with more zeros than either of them knew what to do with.

"All right." Patrice nodded. "You can buy me the house and my new Cadillac, but that's it."

"Don't forget your cut of the winnings," Miri reminded her.

She grumbled. "Come on, little girl, let's get out of here before white people start showin' up with them fake smiles and nasty-ass pies."

Tink Alexander had the softest hardworking hands Miri had ever touched. Skin the color of baked clay and so smooth you'd think they'd been worked over by loving hands. She supposed they had. Tink had been her first repeat customer. The first person in Greenbelt to let her take a pair of clippers to their nails and allow her to experiment with her designs. Tink worked on an assembly line at a factory in Beaufort, building overpriced SUVs. He came to her every week and a half for a manicure before he had her aunt thread his eyebrows.

Today he'd requested that she do something inspired by Gemini season. Because he couldn't do his work with acrylics, she had to work her magic with his natural nails. It was a challenge, so she was fully in her element.

Here, nothing mattered except her art. She wasn't knee-deep in contracts for things so complicated they made her head spin. All she needed to focus on was painting a tiny bohemian-style sun on Tink's left ring finger.

"My granny told me that you and Miss Patrice were gettin' ready to buy the house." Tink's deep voice was deceptively innocent.

"I guess word got around faster than usual." She sighed. "We dang near just brought it up to the landlord."

"That's how Granny found out. Said that old white man who owns that house y'all live in was down at Minnie's talkin' about how y'all offered him a whole heap of money to buy it out from under him."

Miri rolled her eyes. For as long as they'd lived in that house, she'd never known their landlord to be anything other than retired. He owned a few houses around Greenbelt and a small apartment building in Beaufort. He did the bare minimum to maintain them too. As far as she could remember, not a single one had been updated in fifteen years. Not quite slums, but if your issue was anything less than a home-destroying fire or your roof caving in . . . good luck. There was no lost love between the Butlers and their landlord, which was why they'd made him an offer with the intent of having to go back and forth with him as few times as possible. They'd offered him $250,000 on a tiny run-down two-bedroom house that he'd probably bought for $20,000 when he'd gotten it in the '70s. It was a drop in the bucket for Miri now, but still more than the man deserved. And by a whole hell of a lot. She didn't know how she or Mama had thought he'd keep his mouth shut about it.

"Yeah," she answered Tink, trying to keep her hands steady and her eyes on her work. "We been living in it for dang near twenty years, figured it was about time to actually call it ours."

"He said y'all are offering to pay him an arm and a leg for it . . ." Tink prodded.

"Hmmm."

"And, well, you know Folake, my sister-in-law, is the loan officer over at the credit union and she said y'all didn't come see her about borrowin' any money."

She kept silent as she finished tracing the thin rim of black polish around the oval shape of his nail. "Isn't it against the rules for them to share personal information about clients anyway?"

Tink chuckled. "Not if you ain't a client."

"Boy, don't start with me! My family has been putting our money into that credit union for longer than I've been alive."

He gave her a smirk. "Oh, I know. Which is why I also know they'd never give y'all's Black asses a dime, let alone enough of them to fund somebody's retirement."

"You are so damn nosy," she groaned.

Tink blew her a kiss. "I've known you long enough to warrant it. What happened, Miri? You and Miss Patrice rob a bank or somethin'? You find out the house was sittin' on an oil well? You win the lottery?" He snorted when he said the last one.

Miri coughed and tried to hide it by clearing her throat. She didn't know what her plan was supposed to be with this . . . whole thing. Keeping her "big news" from most everyone had seemed like the right idea at first. That's what she'd always heard during those odd, nebulous conversations when people discussed what they'd do if they won the lottery and suddenly got rich. "You don't tell anybody," they'd say. "Not even family. Because all of a sudden, everybody will want somethin' from you."

Was that what she was hiding from? Being asked for money?

No.

Honestly, most people she knew were too prideful to ask outright. And the others, well, she hadn't been too proud to ask somebody to let her hold twenty dollars a time or two in her life when she was down that horrendously either.

It wasn't that. It was, well, she didn't know what it was inside her that begged to be locked down tight so far away that even she forgot about it, but she was inclined to listen. Even if that meant she had to lie to someone she'd known practically her entire life.

It wasn't the worst thing. Miri didn't know whether she was proud of it or not, but she was a pretty damn good liar when it came to most things. Little white ones about not absolutely hating Olivia's cat, Buffy, or pretending she was about to start going to church regularly again when she ran into one of the elders at the grocery. The only people she could never quite make her little stories curl over for were her mama and Leo. Which, ugh.

This lie seemed pretty harmless. At least in the vein that it kept her from having to see Tink's face change when she told him the truth.

"It's nothin' like that," she answered him finally. "We've been savin' for a while. We always knew we'd want to buy it one day and we were finally in a position to, so . . . we did."

"Hmmm." Tink looked dubious, so she glanced up and flashed him a smile.

"And it's because of loyal customers like you that we were able to." She finished the top coat on his pinkie and guided his hand underneath the curing blue-light machine. "So, thank you."

9

LEO

Leo had always been one of those kids with more cousins than he knew what to do with. Cousins on his mama's side, cousins on his daddy's side, play cousins; hell, even kids in his grandmother's neighborhood who came around a little too often. This was not something he'd always appreciated. The majority of the time, he'd felt the exact opposite. All those kids running through his house, some of them much younger and others just old enough to be bossy as hell, had been overwhelming. Instead of sharing a box of Piggly Wiggly–brand ice-cream sandwiches with Thea, he had to share them with Little Sam, Darius, Shina, and everybody else they knew too.

The older he got, though, and the more time he'd spent isolating himself from everything that had ever meant anything to him, the more he regretted not appreciating the company more. There were only so many lonely motel rooms you could stay in before you realized that the vibrating massage beds didn't make up for real company.

Miri had always been his best friend. The person he'd confided in first and foremost, but she wasn't only his best friend. She'd always been more than that to him, even when he'd been too young to realize there was such a thing as something else. Outside of her—and Thea, he supposed—the only other friend he could qualify with the word "best" was Quentin Perry.

Leo's second week of his freshman year of high school he got switched out of his first-period Algebra 1 class because of overcrowding. His schedule had gotten all switched around, completely taking him out of the one class and lunch period he shared with Miri. And even though he couldn't bring himself to complain about it to anyone but his sister, he'd been furious.

He'd sat down in his new assigned seat in Honors Biology and found himself face-to-face with a short, skinny Black boy. Light skin, with the silkiest waves he'd ever seen, and a tight yellow polo. Quentin had looked him up and down, raised an eyebrow, then immediately turned back around in his seat. It wasn't the look of somebody who was trying to size his shit up, either. It was the look of somebody who found him unimpressive as hell.

Admittedly, Leo had started off his fourteenth year a little dusty. He'd given up on getting his hair lined up, trying to grow it out enough to get straight backs like D'Angelo. He was growing taller than his aunt could afford to keep him in updated clothes. So instead of wearing high-waters, he wore his uncle's old clothes. Ugly-ass jeans, T-shirts with Black Rodeo advertisements, and button-up shirts older than he was. He had one pair of Jordan 1's he could still fit into, but when he wasn't wearing those down to the toes, he had on a pair of dusty work boots.

Quentin, on the other hand, looked like a B2K background dancer—one of Lil' Fizz's cousins. Leo had disliked him immediately, but weeks later, when they'd been paired up to work on a project together, Quentin had mentioned that *The Meteor Man* was his favorite movie, and Leo had no choice but to begrudgingly like him.

Two decades later and the boys turned men had never truly fallen out of each other's graces, not even after months of no contact. Which was why, when Leo was greeted by Quentin with a light jab to the ribs as he stood outside on the other man's porch, he had enough shame not to swing back.

"So . . . what? You was just gon' show your ass up in here without telling anybody?"

Leo sighed, mentally preparing himself for the berating he was about to get.

Quentin didn't miss a beat. "I had to hear that you were here from Chuckie's raggedy-ass mama." He jerked a thumb over his shoulder to where his husband, Charlie, was standing. Arms crossed with the most patient, pleasant smile on his face.

"Hey, Chuck," Leo greeted the other man, earning himself a wink.

Quentin's tone was biting. "I oughta whoop your Black ass, Leonard."

"Didn't you already do that?" Leo gestured to where his kidney was still trying to mold itself back into its original shape.

"Not enough."

Quentin's words were half-joking, but Leo could feel the hurt behind them.

"I'm sorry, Quen." Leo put a hand on his shoulder, squeezing. "It happened fast. One minute I was on a job site and the next thing I knew I was tucking tail and running home."

"Why? Just got a wild hair up your ass?"

Leo bit down on the inside of his cheek. Quentin was his boy, he trusted him with his life, but he couldn't tell him the real reason he was back in Greenbelt. One, because Miri's lottery secret wasn't his to tell. And two, because there was no way he was about to admit, out loud, that he was fool-headed enough to try to fix a marriage as broken as his was.

"It was time," he said instead, not quite telling a lie. "I was tired of being away from Thea and the boys . . . Greenbelt . . . you . . ."

Quentin curled his upper lip, but his eyes softened. "Got tired of being away from Greenbelt. Boy, getting out of this town might be the best thing you've ever done."

"You're still here."

"I'm only here because Chuckie might not survive more than thirty miles outside this place. He's too much of an invasive species to survive anywhere outside Greenbelt."

Charlie snorted. "Yeah, that's what it is. Not because you can't be more than fifteen minutes away from your mama without freaking out."

Leo couldn't help but bark out a laugh. Quentin Perry was a lot of things, but he was a mama's boy first and foremost.

"Both of y'all are nasty." Quentin pointed between his husband and best friend. "Nasty and messy and ain't shit."

Charlie clipped Leo on the shoulder fondly, leading him into the house behind Quentin.

Leo toed his shoes off by the door, placing them on the rack next to the others. Quentin had convinced his mama to make their household a "shoe free" one when he was younger and hadn't looked back since. Leo didn't need a reminder, it was practically instinct.

Quentin was a guidance counselor at Greenbelt Junior High, and Charlie was part owner of his family's small but incredibly successful chain of roadside BBQ shacks. Their home was gorgeous, perfectly suited to two people with no kids, disposable income, and good taste.

It was old, maybe even older than his aunt's house, but it had been remodeled beautifully. Still classic and made to highlight the older features, it was all cherry-wood floors, glass, and colorful art on white walls. Even their couch, which looked incredibly soft, was some kind of off-white color. It made Leo anxious to sit on it.

"It's fine," Charlie whispered, "it's got a cover on it."

"Like some new-age version of the plastic your granny had on the couches in her nice family room." Leo laughed.

"Exactly," Quentin remarked, returning from the kitchen with a tray of drinks. Beers for the two of them and undoubtedly something with gin for Charlie—who drank like somebody's uncle.

"Thea told me you were redoing your auntie's house," Quentin said. "You're probably not buying furniture and things yet, but when you do, remember to get the couch covers. They'll save your life."

Leo snorted. "All right, I will."

"How's it going, anyway? The remodeling? You doing a lot of it yourself?" Quentin handed him a beer.

"Yeah, I mean I can't technically help with the plumbing and electric stuff if we want it to be up to code, I only know the basics about that," Leo said. "But I can lend a hand with just about anything else."

"Is the house in good shape?" Charlie asked. "I know it's kinda just been sittin' there since she passed."

Leo took a long drink before answering. "Not as bad as it could be, I guess. But the floors had to be completely stripped. And the insulation is shot, which is probably why we used to wear coats in the house when it got cold. We were lucky to not have termites or pests, but everything is just . . . old. There's stuff in the house that needed to be fixed a decade ago, hell, two even. But the money was never there."

A wave of guilt strong enough to make his toes curl

washed over him. If he'd stayed, if he hadn't been such a coward, even if he'd just brought his behind back sooner, he would have noticed everything that needed to be done. He would have done something about it too, he would have made sure his family's only real tangible showing of success and permanence hadn't turned to shit.

"That ain't your fault." Quentin leaned toward him over the coffee table. "That's how this goes, you see this all the time, especially around here. Even when we find a way to keep property in the family, handling the up-keep becomes too much when you've barely got enough to get by. I could give you a list of ten Black families in Greenbelt right now that are this close to having to sell their family homes to developers because they can't afford to maintain them."

"I know." Leo shook his head. "We weren't too far off from that. Between the property taxes and the costs of just keeping the water running, it was gettin' to be too much. There's no way I would have been able to do what I'm doing now if it hadn't been for—" He stopped abruptly, swallowing down what he'd been about to say.

"For who?" Quentin's ears practically perked up.

"If it hadn't been for my incredibly industrious nature," Leo said with as much confidence as he could muster.

"Right." Quentin's lips pursed again. "Ol' lying ass."

"I'm not—"

The other man held a hand up and Leo had to bite back the urge to finally send a jab of his own.

"Anyway . . . I don't care if the money for fixing up the house 'fell off the back of a truck,' I'm just glad it's

getting done. I would have hated to see it bought by
some white people and turned into some soulless internet
bed-and-breakfast."

Leo shuddered. "Jesus wept."

"Exactly." Quentin raised his beer. "Just . . . you know,
if you knocked off a bank or something, I deserve a cut."

"The hell you do. I could barely get you to share a
plate of fries with me. Stingy ass."

"You know I don't share my food, not even with my
man."

"Especially not with me," Charlie said with a smile.

"What about all those free lineups I gave you? Or all
the times I was a real one and let you know when whatever you decided to put on that day looked goofy," Leo
asked.

"Was that you helping me or was that just you being
a hater?"

"A hater?" Quentin snorted so aggressively Leo had
to bite back a laugh. "Boy, you know as well as I do that
Miri wouldn't have looked at you twice if I hadn't gotten
you together. Then where would you be?"

He finished his thought in its entirety, but as the
words tapered off, it was clear that Quentin hadn't meant
to say them out loud so boldly. In an instant, the energy
in the room changed.

Charlie sat next to him on the couch, his glass sitting
on his knee, the hand wrapped around it tightened at
the knuckles. Across from him, Quentin's skin suddenly
looked sallow. Leo's best friend was a man who meant
what he said and said what he meant—always. But that

didn't mean he didn't have any sense of decorum. The beer, the excitement of seeing him, they loosened Quentin up—and made it harder for him to pretend that things were different from the way they actually were.

Low tolerance for bullshit and pretenders—it was why Leo admired him so much, even when he himself was doing his fair share of bullshitting and pretending.

"I'd be even worse off than I am now," Leo joked, trying to lighten the mood.

He could see on Quentin's face that he wanted to dig, ask all kinds of questions about his situation with Miri. Leo also knew that he didn't have answers for any of them.

Charlie, probably a better man than either of them, lightened the mood in an instant. "Worse than you are now? Is that . . . is that possible?"

Leo's mouth dropped open in shock. "Oh, fuck y'all." He stood up, faking like he was about to leave. "I don't even know why I come around, y'all are trash."

Quentin cackled. "Sit your ass back down, boy. You're here because you love us and you ain't going nowhere. Not again."

His chest swelled and he did as he was told. He figured it was as good a time as any to stay put.

10

LEO

Leo's sister, Thea, had two sons. Six and ten years old, they were active little boys with pointy elbows, innocent smiles, and enough energy to run a power plant. Only seeing the boys a couple times a year, he'd never quite been able to fully get used to being around kids on the regular. A week spent together in a little beachfront condo in Hilton Head every summer had nothing to living with them. Leo decided to leave the bed-and-breakfast after he realized he'd be staying a while and instead of spending a ridiculous amount of money he didn't really have on a room, he finally asked his sister if her spare bed was still open. Thea and her husband had taken Leo's rent-free stay in their house in stride, but it wasn't entirely free. His sister and brother-in-law had decided that having him around was the perfect opportunity to make up for the time they inevitably lost raising two young kids. Any second Leo didn't spend working on the house, he was watching the boys. Picking them up from school, playing ball with them, letting them teach him those little dances they learned on their video games. He was far from complaining, though. One, because he'd never been much for complaining in the first place. And two, because it was basically a dream come true for a man who'd never really had the chance to be much of an uncle.

They were a lot. But they were fun. Which was why he didn't think twice about saying yes when they asked him to take them to Strike's.

It had been what felt like a lifetime since he'd been, and he figured times had changed enough that there would barely be anyone there. Time passed slowly in Greenbelt, but the dollar movie theater had started playing new releases and pretty much everybody had all the entertainment they could handle on their phones. The way he saw it, the boys could rent some skates, go around the rink a few times until they got tired, then he could take them to Minnie's for some cobbler. Instead, he pulled into a packed parking lot, so overrun with cars that he had to park on a strip of grass off to the side.

He held his breath as they made their way in, paying the cover charge and going through the metal detectors. The place was practically unchanged. Lit up with flashing lights, thin dark carpet, and the sounds of worn wheels on hardwood. The scent of popcorn and bad pizza was in the air and music was bumping so loud it made his chest vibrate.

Back when he was young, Strike's had been the place to be on any night you could get your homework done on time and make the five-dollar cover charge. Especially for the young Black folks in Greenbelt. Parents could drop their kids off with reassurances that they'd be safe and out of their hair for a few hours. Safe from the good ol' boys that liked to make trouble and the sheriff's department that stoked the fires. The old heads were always in attendance too. Ones who'd spent the '70s turning roller skating into a way of life, smooth as hell while they glided around the place to Zapp & Roger.

The old heads on the floor looked a little closer to his age now than he wanted to admit and the music was something he couldn't readily recognize, but the beat was good, and he found himself nodding along to it.

He jogged to catch up with the boys as they ran toward the skate rental booth. They gave their sizes to the teenage girl behind the counter, and as she disappeared through the stacks to grab them, an older man came back through the storeroom.

Leo recognized him immediately. Willie was a short Black man with dark red hair, a big soft-looking belly, and freckles all over his wheat-colored face. He'd kept Leo's scrawny butt out of trouble plenty when he was a kid.

"Well, I'll be damned." Willie's eyes lit up, a wide-toothed grin slowly taking over his face. "If it ain't my best employee, back from the dead."

The boys turned around to look at him, eyes wide. "Uncle Lee, you worked here?"

"He sure did," Willie answered for him. "Couldn't skate a lick when he came to me. By the time he graduated high school he was one of the floor managers."

"Your mama worked here too," Leo told them. "She worked the food stand, used to sneak me free hot dogs and everything."

"Did you get to skate for free?" Jamir asked.

Leo snorted. "Yeah, little man, it was my job to skate."

"Here." Willie handed the boys their skates. "Why don't y'all go on out there while I catch up with your uncle."

Leo's stomach dropped as he watched the boys walk off, heavy tan skates in hand. There weren't many people in Greenbelt outside of his family he felt guilty about, but Willie Strike was one of them. He'd given Leo his first job—under the table—at twelve, sanitizing the skates for twenty dollars a day, and allowed him to grow as he aged. Willie was the reason he had enough money to take Miri out on their first date and to get Thea tickets to see Beyoncé for Christmas in 2006. He'd taught him the meaning of hard work and passion and Leo had never forgotten it. Not even when he had to quit his managerial position at the rink to take on a construction job once he and Miri got married. He'd thought he was making the right choice. He'd thought he'd be bringing in enough money to take care of his wife the way a husband was supposed to. But he'd been wrong. When he realized how wrong he'd been about, well, everything, he'd been too embarrassed to work up the nerve to tell Willie goodbye.

Now, here he was, nearly a decade later, staring at the same man, Willie, who'd aged physically but had a spark in his eyes that didn't look a day over twenty-one years old.

"Boy," Willie chuckled. "I never thought I'd see your skinny hide again." He looked him up and down. "Not so skinny now, I guess, but still."

Leo leaned forward, elbows on the counter. "If I'm bein' honest, sir, I didn't entirely plan on comin' back anytime soon."

Willie didn't say anything for a few long moments, just looked at Leo, shaking his head, a wry smirk on his lips. "You youngins, man. You get a taste of what real love is like and go runnin' like you can't handle it. Ain't you ever listened to Teddy Pendergrass? You can't lie to yourself, boy."

Leo fought the urge to roll his eyes. "It's not that simple, man. Teddy, Marvin, Al, they all made that shit— love—sound simple, but it ain't."

"No, it ain't simple," Willie agreed. "But it sure ain't as hard as y'all are makin' it out to be."

"Y'all?" Leo laughed. "Me and all the young dudes out there, you mean?"

Willie shook his head and pointed. "Uh-uh, you and that one over there."

Leo's gaze followed the older man's finger like he was in a movie. Right there, across the room, but on the side of the rink closest to him, Miri skated by.

It was clear that she hadn't noticed him. She was in a groove, head and hips bopping to the beat as she skated alongside Jade Dunn and another Black woman he didn't know. She had on a tiny pair of denim shorts that cupped her full ass so thoroughly he was jealous of them. She had on a cropped T-shirt that fell just below her breasts and her big afro was on full display.

Jesus Christ, that woman.

He didn't know whether he wanted to rush home and jerk his dick at an image of her that would now be living in his head rent free, or to propel his legs forward. In the end, he did neither, just stood there, watching her like a fool while Willie kept speaking. "And don't think I forgot about y'all defiling the couch in my storeroom."

Leo's mouth gaped. "We . . . we didn't . . ."

"Don't even try to lie to me, boy. I may have been born at night but I wasn't born last night."

Leo coughed.

"Anyway, nasty and lovestruck as y'all were, I would have bet everything I had on y'all makin' it to the end of the line." Willie shook his head with a sad smile.

"You would'a lost a hell of a lot of money, then."

"Because you went runnin'."

"Because she put me out." Leo was apparently in a mood to argue.

The older man snorted. "If I had a dime for every time my wife put me out, I'd have been retired twenty years ago."

"This was different," Leo said. "She meant it . . . she . . . I, I wasn't a good husband. I wasn't a good provider. I wasn't doing a thing but pulling her down into the dirt with me."

Willie shook his head. "So damned extra . . . ain't that what y'all say? Extra?"

Leo ignored the question. "I'm not bein' extra, I'm tellin' the truth!"

"Yeah, all right, but whose truth are you telling?"

"I—" Leo shook his head. "I don't understand what you mean. The truth is the truth. It doesn't belong to anybody."

"Not when it comes to things like murder it don't, but when it involves love and life and all the rest of this stuff, everybody has their own truth. You tellin' me that you're sure hers is the same as yours?" Willie jutted his chin out to where Miri was skating.

"Of course. Because that's what it is. No ifs, ands, or buts about it."

"She tell you that?" Willie's eyes were sharp on him.

Leo's throat suddenly felt thick. "She didn't have to. I knew what it was. I knew enough on my own to realize I didn't deserve her. Not back then anyway."

Truth be told, he wasn't entirely sure he deserved her now either. Shit, how different was he from how he'd been back then? He was less skinny, he'd grown a bit more into his ears, built up some muscle. But he was still shit broke with a family name that didn't mean dirt and very few prospects for his future. The only real difference between now and then was that he wasn't trying to fool himself into believing he could continue to live without her.

So here he was, trying to use whatever few tools he had to win her back when she had all the options in the world. His Miri was rich as sin on top of being fine as wine. She could take her pick. He was just hoping desperately, foolishly, that he could convince her to pick him. The same way she had when they were kids. Hell, maybe this made him worse than he'd been before. But he didn't have the strength to stay away anymore. It might kill him. And if it was his time to go, he wanted his heart to bleed out because she commanded it to, not because he was too much of a coward to allow her the chance to stitch it back together.

For what seemed like the hundredth time since they'd started talking, Willie sighed deeply, the kind of sigh that instantly transported Leo back to trying to sneak in late as a teenager only to find his auntie sitting in her rocking chair on the front porch. Just waiting for him. Ready to dig him out.

"Damn kids," Willie muttered. "A hard head makes a soft ass, boy, remember that."

"What's that got to do with anything?"

"It means, the more you try to deny your shit and her shit, the worse it's going to be in the end. I've been married four times, boy, you can quote me on that."

Miri was making her way around the rink again, only this time something compelled her to look up. And she did. Right at him. Her eyes widened for a split second, then narrowed before going back to normal. She tilted forward to slow herself down and stared for a few long moments, face as expressionless as possible. Then, she quirked a brow at him. As if struck by lightning, Leo turned to where Willie was still behind the counter. "Let me get a pair of skates, please."

The urgency in his voice meant next to nothing to the

old man. "Why should I? So you can go out there and spout that garbage you just told me in her face?"

"Come on, man, please." Leo was not above begging. "If you don't give them to me, I'll go out there in my socks."

"The hell you will. I'll have one of these young boys snatch your ass up so fast, that big head of yours will spin," Willie muttered, going over to the racks. "You still a size thirteen?"

Leo grinned. "Yes, sir."

The older man slapped the heavy skates down on the counter with more force than was necessary. "Go on then. Let history repeat itself."

The words barely registered. He couldn't remember stopping to put his skates on, but the next thing he knew, he was skating up to Miri on humiliatingly shaky knees.

"We are trying to have a peaceful girls' skate." Jade was on him before he could even fully approach. "Now your big-ass head is blocking out my view of the lights."

"Jade . . ." The pretty brown-skinned woman Jade and Miri were with looked scandalized as she admonished her softly.

Jade didn't look fazed in the slightest and Leo took it in stride. She'd called him bigheaded once when they were eleven and hadn't looked back since.

"Girl," Jade huffed. "He ain't nobody. Just some of Miri's old work."

His eyes cut to his wife. She looked halfway mortified and half like she wanted to laugh.

"I think I need to start calling you that now." Miri smirked, catching his eyes. "My old work."

Leo shook his head. "I do not agree."

He didn't care for how finite it sounded.

"Well, now that we got that out of the way, why don't you take those shaky knees and go skate with the rest of the kids . . . away from us."

"All right now, Jade . . ." Leo was only willing to let her go so far.

Jade crossed her arms with an eye roll, looking every bit like the girl who always tried to get him to pretend to be the cat when they played house as kids.

"Miri doesn't—"

Finally, Miri cut her off. "Miri is a grown woman. I'll tell him to fuck off when I want him to fuck off."

Jade didn't say anything in return, but the two shared a long look that seemed more like a full-on conversation on his end. He had no clue what they were saying, but in the end Jade released a long, dramatic sigh.

"Fine," she said, before cutting her eyes to Leo and turning her nose up. "But don't try anything cute, because I'll be here watching."

"Go, Jade," Miri laughed, pushing the other woman's arm.

With one last withering look at him—which he grinned right back at—Jade and the other woman were off to continue their round at the rink, leaving him alone with Miri.

She spoke first. "If you're stalking me, just know that

I carry a Taser and I'm not afraid to point it right at your face."

The fact that he knew she was entirely serious made his stomach dance.

He'd always had a thing for the mean girls.

"Not stalking." His tone was more serious than he'd meant it to be. "I'm out with the boys."

He pointed to where his nephews were using the provided skate helpers to move around the rink. He watched her face soften as she took them in.

"Seems like a pretty good excuse to me," she told him. "Almost too good."

"They've never been here before," he said. "Between the new park, that arcade in Beaufort, and all the stuff they've got at home, I guess something as simple as going skating is boring."

The song blasting through the speakers faded away, then the fast, banging beat of a Sean Paul song accompanied the flashing lights. The song wasn't anything close to romantic, but it was familiar. Something that didn't conjure up a specific memory but the intimate knowledge that he and Miri had probably been in this exact same spot at some point in history with this exact same song playing. She looked so different than she would have back then, but the way he felt standing next to her was exactly the same.

"Skate with me." He sent the wheels on his feet forward instead of reaching out to grab her hand. No one could ever say that he wasn't actively trying to behave himself.

He only got about a foot ahead of her before her legs started moving, so quickly that she danced right by, leaving him to stare after her like a damn fool.

All he could do was what he'd done their entire lives—chase her.

When he caught up, Miri's grin was shameless. She moved her body to the song as she rounded the rink, all hips and shoulders, effortless, like it was impossible for her to miss a beat. He was less sure on his feet—it had been over a decade since he'd had anything but Jordans or work boots on his feet. He had to put at least half his attention on not busting his ass, 30 percent on keeping an eye on the boys, and every bit of the 20 left on trying to catch peeks of Miri's ass.

He looked up the second he heard her snort. The song had changed to something he didn't know, obviously a song that the teenager in the DJ booth was into. Everyone in the rink over the age of twenty-five became noticeably less enthusiastic.

"What?" he asked.

"You're bad at this now." Her smile was softer than her words.

"It's been a long time," he grumbled. "I haven't skated since I left."

There was something in her answering expression that almost reminded him of surprise but he couldn't make heads or tails of it.

"I remember when you used to be the best skating dude in here." She spun around, skating backwards now as she faced him. "It was pretty sexy, to be honest."

Her voice was wistful. Like the reminder, that at one time she'd been attracted to him, made her long for the past.

Another sign that there was still something there. If he didn't grab the moment by the balls, he might as well leave, as alone as he'd come.

"Go out with me." There was no subtlety in his words, no finesse, which meant it was probably closer to the real him than he wanted to admit.

Miri stopped skating, forcing him to come to a standstill with her in the middle of the rink.

"For what?" she asked. "So we can go sit in a booth at Minnie's together and spend months telling people that 'no, we are not back together' and 'yes, we're definitely sure'?"

"Who gives a shit what people will say?"

"That's an easy stance for you to take," she scoffed. "In a few months you get to leave, you won't have to stay here and hear the same ridiculous shit from the same ridiculous people for years. You won't be the girl who got married too young even though people told her not to, had it all fall apart, then somehow managed to screw it up again a second time."

"Maybe we won't fuck it—"

"Stop, Leo." Her jaw was clenched. "We both know that whatever we had was good for two sixteen-year-olds. We messed ourselves up when we tried to take it beyond that."

Leo shook his head. "I don't believe that."

Her face tilted up toward the ceiling, shoulders and

mouth drawn tight. "Whatever. It doesn't matter. The point is, I'm not letting you take me out on a date. That's ridiculous. Why would I do that? What purpose would that serve?"

The mean girl was out in full effect, but it only spurred him on.

"We don't have to call it a date, then, we can call it something else."

Miri huffed, scowling at him. "What good does that do if you and I both know that you'll be calling it a date in your head the whole time?"

He had to laugh at that. "What does it matter what I call it in my head?"

Leo knew he was being annoying as hell, answering a question with a question, but he maintained that he was doing his fucking best just trying to keep up with her.

"It matters," the woman damn near growled over the Jazze Pha production playing on the loudspeakers as she pushed off. "Because a date is a date is a date. Everybody knows that. And I don't want you out here getting in the habit of thinking I'm letting you take me on dates. That is not what this is."

He was quick to follow after her. "What is it, then?"

The wheels of Miri's skates beat hard against the polished wooden floor of the rink. "This is fucked up is what it is. And ridiculous." She stopped, making a tight circle back. "We are not lovers anymore, Leo. You have to accept that."

"What about something as friends then? Before we

were anything else we were friends." He moved closer to her. Grabbing one of her hands, he stroked a thumb over the warm skin on the back. Then, he pressed it to his face. Touching it to both of his cheeks, running the tip of his nose over her skin as if he was trying to cover himself in her scent. When he finally pressed his lips to the softness there, he stayed for several breaths, until he let her go altogether. "I want to know you again, Miriam. Please . . . please."

"Jesus Christ." She tried to look unaffected but he saw everything, especially the small shiver that ran through her. "Fine. I'll . . . I'll come over to the house. I'm wearing jeans and a T-shirt, no makeup, no perfume, you'll be lucky if I don't show up in my bonnet. Hell, I'll even bring my own sack lunch. Just so that we're both clear this is very much not a date. This is . . . still a weird, fucked-up thing to be doing, but it's not a date."

"I can live with that." He grinned.

Leo didn't know how he could find a way to make home renovations romantic, but he'd be good goddamned if he didn't try.

"Fine." She nodded firmly. "Saturday afternoon. Now get on somewhere, you're messing with my vibe."

He stood in the same place, watching as she skated away from him. It didn't matter how much of her back he was seeing in the moment, progress had been made.

11

MIRI

Patrice always fried fish on Tuesdays. Most people tended to make it their Friday-night supper, but her mother insisted that fish was less expensive to buy at the top of the week.

So, every Tuesday night, no matter the season, they opened up all the windows in the house as far as they could go. Mama always put on music while she cooked, and on fried-fish nights it tended to be a lot of Teddy Pendergrass. In an effort to keep her room and clothes from smelling like their dinner, Miri always stuffed a T-shirt under the crack of her door and waited it out in her room.

That night, she sat in her room trying to figure out how to tell her mama that they weren't going to be able to buy the house.

Mr. Simmons had called her earlier that day, telling her that while he appreciated the offer she'd made on the house, he was deciding not to sell it after all. Apparently, it was more lucrative for him to keep it as a rental property. He wanted to pass it down to his kids, so they could profit off it too. They'd been given the option to carry out their lease for as long as they wanted, of course, but they'd never own the home Miri had grown up in.

She didn't know whether Patrice would be devastated at the news, but she sure as heck wouldn't be happy about it. The last thing Miri wanted was to see the look of disappointment settle back into her mother's eyes. She'd always thought that having money would mean she'd never have to see that look again.

She was learning quickly that so many of her previously held beliefs were paper thin.

When Patrice finally called out to let her know that dinner was ready, she left her room with slumped shoulders. Her mother noticed that something was wrong as soon as she sat Miri's plate down in front of her.

"Why you lookin' all sad for?" Patrice said, taking a seat across from her at the table.

Miri looked down at her plate, a nice big piece of fried whiting, homemade coleslaw, fat green beans, and a fresh piece of white bread. It made her mouth water, but she couldn't quite dig in.

"He's not giving us the house, Mama," she said, practically whining. "He turned down the offer."

Patrice paused for a second, her fork halfway to her mouth. Then, in the blink of an eye, she was taking her first bite of slaw, shaking her head. "We'll go back to the original plan, then. We'll find something else."

"You're not disappointed?"

Patrice reached across the table to grab the bottle of Crystal Miri had in front of her. "I'm not saying I'm happy to have to go back to lookin' and all that stress. But it ain't eating me up inside. Shit," she laughed. "I might even be a little happy that you ain't giving that man any more money than you have to."

Feeling slightly more settled, Miri smiled before digging into her fish, steam rising from the center as she cracked through the breading with a fork. She dipped it into the little pool of hot sauce she'd made on her plate, closing her eyes in satisfaction when the flavor finally touched her lips.

"I'll call that Realtor back then," Miri said finally.

Patrice nodded. "You gon' call her for you too?"

"I don't know what I'm going to do yet, I'm still trying to figure that out."

Something about buying a home for herself felt so permanent. Just because she had the money to do it didn't mean she was ready for it. Everything was up in the air right now, and she didn't know what thing to try to reach out and grab first. Let alone which life-changing, lifelong decision was right for her. The only thing that felt even halfway okay was staying put right where she was. She needed something familiar among all this mess.

Her mother looked at her for a long while, eyes roaming every inch of her face. No doubt reading her better than anyone else had ever been able to. When she finally pulled her eyes away, Miri expected her to say something deep and life-changing. Instead, her mama gave her a little smile.

"Eat your food, baby," she said. "You're going to need your strength."

"Why is it that every time I turn around he's got me making a fool of myself?"

It was just past seven on a Wednesday evening, and aside from Miri, Jade, Olivia, and Aja, the bar was mostly empty. With her bank account holding more zeros than she'd ever seen at one time, drinks were obviously on Miri. And while all her friends seemed to be taking things slow and steady, she'd been pounding them back for almost an hour. Leaving her words slightly slurred and her tongue much looser than normal.

"And when the fuck did he get so fine? I don't remember him bein' that fine."

Jade released a high-pitched noise from the back of her throat. "You literally always thought he was fine. Ain't that why you married him?"

Miri whined, "When I married him he was fine, fine because I loved him, and because he was the only person aside from me to ever make me orgasm until I cried. He didn't look like *this*. With all them damn muscles and the ears he grew into and those lips . . . he definitely didn't have those lips."

She was incredibly grateful when none of them voiced any opposing facts.

"I thought you were over him," Aja stated delicately, her pretty pink nails lightly tapping against a can of beer.

"I am," Miri asserted. "I mean . . . no! I am absolutely over him. But him being back brings up all these memories and confused feelings and I keep trying to remind myself why it didn't work out the first time, but then his annoying ass smiles at me or kisses my hand and I start acting like a fool."

"He kissed your hand?" Jade's eyes went almost comically wide. "Like on some *Pride and Prejudice* shit?"

"Girl, yes," Miri groaned, leaning down to rest her forehead on the table. She'd have to triple-cleanse her face when she got home but she was too distressed to care that she was definitely being grimy as hell in the moment. "He was on skates too. Like some Black *Roll Bounce* version of Mr. Darcy. I was so horny I could have died."

"I'll say this, he definitely got some game while he was gone," Olivia laughed. "Because that boy used to be all ears and awkwardness."

"Well . . ." Jade spoke, then paused like she was contemplating whether or not she actually wanted to say what she was thinking. But they'd known each other so long Miri knew she'd come out with it eventually. "Why don't you just fuck him and get it out of your system? Then you can focus on the important shit. Like how you're Big Daddy Warbucks now."

Aja cleared her throat delicately. "I can say firsthand that the whole trying to sex someone out of your system thing never, ever works. Unless you want to end up like me and Walker. I think we're pretty great, but we are definitely not out of each other's systems.

Aja and her long-term boyfriend, Walker, had met at bingo. One supposedly no-feelings-involved sex pact, a major heartbreak, and hella groveling later and they were living happily in a little rented house in Beaufort. Every time Miri saw them together she could feel it in the air. See it in their eyes every time they so much as mentioned each other. But they weren't her and Leo. Neither Aja nor Walker had a history full of roses or sunshine but they didn't have the history she and Leo had. More than twenty years of history. Entire lives weaved around each other. Nor did they have the shame that came with the failing of a marriage everyone told them they were too young for in the first place.

Miri nodded her head, pointing a finger at Aja. "Exactly. And that is not an outcome that's even possible for me and Leo, so why would I risk screwing everything up even more? It can't possibly be worth it, not when there are plenty of people in Greenbelt I can use to scratch that itch. People that are not my husband."

She told herself that her words sounded sincere, but she knew, not even deep down if she was being honest, that she was bullshitting everyone—even herself.

"If you say so," Olivia offered. "I just—"

Miri held up a hand to stop her. She knew what Olivia was going to say. She'd do that thing she always did where she tilted her head to the side and somehow managed to turn all the features on her face downward to lighten the blow of whatever crappy but true thing she was about to say. Miri could practically hear it in her head already. Liv would give her that face, maybe reach across the table to take her hand and let her know that what she was doing right now was shoving her real feelings down for pretend things that felt more comfortable to her.

She wasn't wrong. Of course she wasn't. Miri might have wanted to avoid her feelings publicly but she wasn't so fool-headed that she'd deny their existence to her own self. She couldn't always name those feelings or identify what they meant exactly, but they were there. Swirling around in her brain and her heart, turning everything upside down, making her all confused and emotional.

It was hard to spend years trying to desperately convince yourself that the only thing you felt for someone was hatred. Then to suddenly be forced to confront all the things you'd been repressing in favor of trying not to fall apart was hell on earth. Miri had spent every night cycling through those thoughts since she'd had to make that call to Leo, asking him to return to Greenbelt. She didn't want to do that now.

Now, all she wanted to do was bitch about the man. And if she couldn't do that, she didn't want to talk about him at all. No matter how much of a brat that made her.

"Can we talk about something else?" Miri asked. "Literally anything else?"

Her friends looked at each other, eyes wary, but abided by her request.

"We can talk about how I threw up when that check you gave me cleared with my bank," Olivia said with a shrug.

Aja sucked in a breath. "Me too, Walker keeps asking me what I'm going to do with it and I have no idea? It's weird knowing that I could, like, buy us a house or go on vacation or even, I don't know . . . not budget when we go grocery shopping. I know it's supposed to be freeing, and it is." She reached across the table to squeeze Miri's hands, a small, warm smile on her round face. "You have no idea how grateful I am. How grateful we all are. You changed our lives and there's just . . . no way to even articulate how much that means."

"Seriously, girl," Jade cut in. "I can teach just because I want to now instead of working three jobs just to make ends meet. I can make sure the boys on the football team have new cleats and equipment. Get plenty of school supplies to donate at the beginning of the year." She laughed. "I just don't know what to do for myself."

Aja nodded. "All that time you spend thinking about what you'd do if you suddenly woke up rich, how happy you'd be. Then it actually happens and instead you find yourself stuck."

Olivia sighed. "And since you told us not to tell anybody, we're basically all fresh off the turnip truck with this stuff." She laughed.

"You're tellin' me." Miri sighed. "I feel like I have even less of a clue what to do with my life than I did two months ago when I was broke. I don't feel happy every time I look at what's in my bank now. It's like I feel stifled. I started workin' on getting my mama a new house and a new car all within a week, yet I've barely been able to stop feeling guilty about replacing my five-year-old phone. And I . . . I hate sounding like I'm ungrateful. I understand that this is all luck and I have all this privilege, resources to help the people I love, to help Greenbelt, but I don't even know where to start. I've been poor my entire life. Some days I wake up and before I remember that I have money now my first instinct is to start stressing out about how much money I don't have. It's like I don't even know how to live when I'm not constantly panicking about money."

The eyes of all three of her friends turned sympathetic and Miri had to avert hers to swallow down the shame she felt at her own thoughts.

"I think it's going to take time," Jade said. "Even if your circumstances changed overnight, you can't expect your mind to. You need to start slow. What's somthing that you always wanted but could never get? Something that you dreamed about but never let yourself actually believe you could have?"

Days ago, her mother had asked her a similar question after Miri had told her that she planned to stay in the dingy little home they'd been renting forever instead of buying herself a home. She hadn't had much of an answer then. Not because she didn't know what it was, but because it embarrassed her to admit that. So she'd shrugged her shoulders and forcibly changed the subject.

These were her girls, though. Even if they didn't, Miri felt like they knew every single excruciating detail of her life. Every fear, every futile hope, every desperately made wish. She didn't have to worry about worrying them like she did her mama. She didn't have to fear adding yet another burden onto their plates.

"This is going to sound so ridiculous," she warned them. "Like for real."

Olivia released a good-natured snort. "We already knew it was going to be."

"I want a puppy." Miri spoke it like a shameful confession. "And look, I know that there are plenty of dogs out there taken care of by people even poorer than me, but I never felt like I had it together enough to get one. Didn't have enough money for the adoption fee and for the extra our landlord tacks onto the rent every month if you have a pet. Didn't have money for all the supplies and cute things I wanted them to have. Or the vet fees, the unexpected costs. Plus, between all the jobs me and Mama had to work, we barely would've been able to give a pet the time and attention they need and deserve. But damn if I didn't want one so bad I could cry over it."

"That's it." Aja grinned. "You're getting a puppy. That's where we're starting. Give you something to love and take care of. Show yourself that you're allowed to have nice good things in your life."

Miri's heart soared and thundered at the same time. Instinct kicked in, trying to force her brain to immediately begin calculating in her head the costs that came with being a dog owner, the way she'd done a thousand times before. Then, she immediately started to convince herself that it was a bad idea. That she shouldn't do it—or even worse, couldn't. Tears brimmed the corners of her eyes and she had to stop her top lip from quivering. Why was this so hard? Letting yourself have something nice shouldn't be hard.

She glanced up from the table, looking at the kind faces of her best friends, each of them with gazes that made her chest fill with warmth.

None of them said anything, but their faces were a reminder of something important.

She could do anything with their support. All that was left was for her to believe in herself. It was a thing that she'd had to fight for a lot over the years, something that she was having to fight for now. But she'd be damned if she didn't.

"Fuck it," she said, voice shaky. "I'm getting a dog. A cute one with a fluffy tail and sweet little ears. And I'm goin' to love the shit out of it."

Jade grinned back at her. "Hell yeah you are."

12

LEO

There wasn't a single thing that was romantic about an old house in the middle of a full-on gut job. When Miri had agreed to come to his auntie's house to see him, she'd made some comment about helping him pull up old baseboards. He'd gone along with it at the time, but he had no intention of making her work. The house was his project, his way of showing her that he was different, stronger, more capable, but just as willing. It was bad enough that she had to be the one paying. He didn't want her breaking a sweat.

He'd spent the morning running around trying to straighten up the living space as much as possible. Moving what materials he could out of the area, sweeping up, and carting things he'd prepared for the day from his sister's house in his little car.

She was due in half an hour, and instead of feeling anxious like he thought he would, he felt cool, confident. There was no way this was going to work if he couldn't prove to her that he was a real man now. Not the boy she'd married. The one that couldn't provide for her, couldn't give her everything a husband should. Not even a big, beautiful ring.

He still had no money but he had something that he didn't have back then. The sheer force of will to make shit shake for his woman.

That was why he stood with pride over the small nest he'd made for them. Two beanbags he'd borrowed from his nephews' rooms. Some string lights picked up from the dollar store, along with some of her favorite snacks. And a meal made by his own hand.

He was ready for her. Ready to show how much he'd changed—all for her.

When her knock sounded on the door it was all he could do not to run toward it. He needed to keep his cool. Not be running around like a chicken with its head cut off.

Her face when he opened the door was surprised, like she'd forgotten for a second where she was and why she'd come. Then he grinned at her, saw a flicker of softness in her gaze before it was immediately replaced with stoicism.

She was wearing loose-fitting pants, black and white with some kind of abstract design all over them. Her shirt was simple, a burnt-orange T-shirt with a V-neck that hugged tight to her ample chest. Her afro was braided down into two twists on the sides of her head. She was casual and relaxed and so gorgeous he about swallowed his tongue.

"You going to invite me in?" she asked, all sass.

He said nothing, just stepped aside, allowing her to come off the half-finished front porch and into the house. Leo found himself suddenly nervous, waiting for her reaction to the setup he'd put together.

She didn't say anything at first. But the old wood subflooring creaked under her footsteps as she walked toward the cluster of items.

"You got me Cow Tales." It wasn't a question, but there was something in there that still kind of sounded like one.

"I know you said you were going to bring a sack lunch, but I had to get you something. And they're your favorite," he said. "Always have been . . . Unless . . . you don't like them anymore."

Most of the time Leo was almost painfully aware of the long history between them. Other times, he felt stumped by the fact that he knew so little about her. For all he knew, she hated the little caramel candies now. Or had grown out of her sweet tooth altogether.

"No, I do." She turned to look at him. "I haven't had any in a while, though. A long time actually."

"Why not?"

Miri shook her head. "They remind me too much of the past. Of you. You used to bring me a bag after work on Fridays, remember?"

He turned his face to the floor. "Because I couldn't afford to take you out on a real date."

"So what? You used to bring me Cow Tales and we'd eat Hamburger Helper for dinner and watch the DVDs the bootleg man used to bring into the shop. We had fun. It was nice, romantic."

Leo shook his head. His memory of that time was different. He remembered dragging himself home after doing whatever shit-pay odd job he could find, bone-tired, only to find his woman at their little kitchen table crying while she tried to figure out how they'd make their bills for the month. The self-loathing that would rise in his chest, damn near choking him as they scraped together random items from their cabinets to get a half-way decent meal. Listening to her belly growl in their bed at night when it wasn't ever enough to fully satiate her. He remembered being a failure of a husband. One who could only offer his wife dollar-store candies instead of diamonds and steaks like she deserved.

The memories made him rage. He wanted to take the bag of candies out of her hand and stomp on them, go at them with the saw sitting in the kitchen, and throw them out like the trash they were then.

"Fun would have been me being able to take you to that nice steak house in Beaufort every Friday," he told her.

Miri turned her nose up. "For what? So we could break bread with all those rich people looking at us like we were crazy the entire time? No thank you."

Leo didn't agree, but he wasn't interested in starting an argument. Instead, he pushed his anger deep down into his gut, gently taking the bag of candies from her, opening it, and unwrapping one. He held it up to her mouth, breath bated as she stared at him before gently closing her eyes and opening her mouth. He thumbed the candy inside, his dick immediately hardening when her lips closed around his fingers. The sensation of her mouth around him only lasted for a second, maybe not even that, but he had to close his own eyes to regain his composure.

"Have a seat." He bit down on the inside of his cheek, voice gruff as he urged her to sit on one of the beanbags.

She did, legs crossed, arms hanging loosely at her sides. "Um, so what are we supposed to be doing? I came dressed to work."

She absolutely hadn't, not with those thin pants and short sleeves and tennis shoes instead of work boots, but he wasn't about to say that.

"I figured we'd do something a little more relaxing." He pulled the iPad he'd borrowed from his brother-in-law out from its case under the blanket. "Like watch a movie or somethin'."

Miri's lips pursed, her eyes narrowed a bit, completely dubious.

"This is not a date," she reminded him.

"Of course not."

What he didn't tell her was that he had plans for their actual second first date. Ones that included a setting much nicer than the floor of a run-down house.

"Fine," she huffed, but he could tell her heart wasn't in it. "What do you have on there?"

He scrolled through the selection with rough fingertips. "We could watch *Love Jones*."

She shook her head. "No. Too romantic."

"*B.A.P.S.*? You used to love *B.A.P.S.*"

"I still do. It's an iconic piece of classic Black cinema, and Natalie Desselle is like chubby Black girl royalty."

"Let's watch it then." Leo placed the iPad on the little dock that helped it stand up, then stood, plugging in the fairy lights and switching off the main ones.

Miri looked up, eyes wide as she took in the display.

"I can't believe you did all this for us to watch a movie on the floor," she joked.

Leo, however, was completely serious when he spoke. "I'd do anything for you, girl. You know that. This is . . . this is nothing."

And there it was again. That flicker in her eyes that kept him going. The one that reminded him that she still felt something too. It didn't matter how hesitant she was to admit it, it was there and it was all he needed, for now.

She didn't reply to his statement directly. Instead, she swallowed deeply and turned her head. "Put the movie on, Leo . . . and stop staring at me."

He grinned as he took his seat in his own beanbag.

His grin was a constant throughout the movie. He snuck coy peeks at her as they watched, and every once in a while he caught her looking at him too. Sometimes with her eyebrows turned down and other times with something soft in her eyes. Neither of them spoke,

though. Him, out of trying to fulfill her desire to watch
the movie unbothered, and her out of . . . Well, he didn't
actually know. But when the movie was over and the Al-
fredo he'd made had been eaten, she turned to look at
him expectantly. He wasn't interested in putting on another movie, though.

"What next?" she asked.

He sucked a breath as he stood, back and knees aching a bit from the lack of support the beanbag chair provided. "Come outside with me, will you?"

"What for?"

"I want to show you something."

She stood too, heaving in that way everyone over
the age of thirty seemed to. "If you're talking about your
dick, I'm going to stab you."

"Miriam, when have I ever—"

She cut him off. "I'm just sayin'. No funny shit."

He took her hand. "Come on, you'll see."

Instead of taking her out the front door, he walked
them toward the back of the house. It looked like a war
zone. Scraps of materials, dust, and power tools that
looked more intimidating than any weapon he'd ever
seen. "Follow my steps," he told her, tucking her hand
into his back to pull her a little closer. "I don't want you
to get hurt."

"You're going to get sick of holdin' my hand like
some kind of schoolchild, boy."

"Sure won't." He led them out through the kitchen
and opened the back door, smiling up into the sky.

Right there, beyond the back porch and deep into

the large yard, was a little shed. It didn't look like much. Relatively small, made out of a light cherrywood, with a vaulted roof; Leo was prouder of it than almost anything he'd ever done.

"I started on it while the guys were doing the floors inside." He led her off the porch and into the grass.

"A shed?" she asked, not unkindly. "For like, tools and stuff?"

There was a door in front made out of the same wood as the rest. What she couldn't see were the windows on either side and at the back.

"No, Miriam. Not for tools." He opened the door.

Much like the outside, the interior wasn't much to see yet. All it had was four walls and a sturdy floor, but he had plans for it. The sun was beginning to set and the large, clear windows provided a perfect view of the colorful sky.

"I plan on fixing it up real nice. Making sure there's heat and air and all that stuff."

She looked thoroughly confused. "Why do you need heat and air for a shed?"

God, did he not want to lie to her. Even at his worst as a husband he'd never sunk that low. But he couldn't tell her the truth. Not all of it, at least. Not yet. He wasn't trying to run her off before he'd even really gotten a chance to get her back.

"I, uh . . ." Leo rubbed his palm along the back of his neck. "I built it with you in mind."

"Leo . . ."

"Not for you," he lied quickly. "But I remembered

when we were living together how much you talked about never really having a space of your own. Not then and not when you were living with your mama. And it made me think, I guess. I figure my sister will have the house when it's done, and with her husband and the kids, I bet she feels the same way. So I built this for . . . for her. So she could have a place that was just hers."

Miri walked around the one-room shed, her fingertips tracing the windowpanes and small divots in the wood.

"That's really kind of you." Her voice was small, quiet. "I'm sure she's going to appreciate it. I know she will. I sure as hell would if anybody ever did anything like this for me."

He wanted to tell her that they had. He had. He'd put together each piece of the little building with his own two hands with only Miri and her happiness in mind. He was doing the same with the house, too. He didn't want to leave it to his sister. Not just because she was more than happy in her own home, but because with every change of tile, with every new bit of insulation placed into the wall, it felt like new life was being breathed into him and his relationship with Miri. Every decision he made, he did it with her in mind. In the ridiculous, foolish, desperate hope that she would love him again. That she'd want to make up for the time they'd missed by spending the rest of her life with him.

He bit his tongue to the point of damn near bleeding. Clamped his lips tight and walked over to her. His feet were heavy with the weirdness of his omissions.

As soon as he was in front of her he put his palm to her cheek. It was painful not to touch her and pure torture to feel her skin when she wasn't really his.

"You deserve it," he told her. "You deserve everything. You know you do."

Miri's eyes fluttered closed and she leaned into his touch. "I have everything now. More money than I know what to do with. Endless opportunities and . . ." She shook her head. "None of it feels right."

He brought his other hand up to her face, thumbs stroking the apples of her cheeks. "What do you need, sugar?"

Her lips quivered at the old endearment. "I don't know. That's the problem, I don't fucking know."

He brought her to him then, hand resting at the small of her back as she leaned into him. Her arms went around his waist and a shiver ran up his spine.

"You've got to stop worrying about other people, Miri. What they need, what they want, what they think or expect. Fuck that. You deserve to focus on yourself. Just you."

He meant it too. Even if it meant that ultimately, she had to leave him behind for good. It would kill him, but he'd accept whatever she needed if it meant her happiness.

"I don't know how to do that." She mumbled the words into his chest. "Where do I even start?"

"Think about what you want right now, right here in this moment."

She looked up at him, those brown eyes wide and

misty. She tried a few times to speak, her lips moving but nothing coming out.

"I want to kiss you."

The wind was knocked out of his body in an instant. For a second he was positive he hadn't heard her words right. Like somehow, someway, his hopes had materialized themselves into real-world delusions. Allowing him to hear words come out of her mouth that she hadn't really said.

He pulled back a little, forcing himself to look at her face. He only let himself realize that her words had been real when he found her eyes closed tight, like she was bracing for the consequences of her admission. Leo found himself aching to soothe her.

His hands went to her face again, the apples of her cheeks warmer than before as his fingertips lightly touched them.

"Open your eyes, Miriam," he said. "Look at me."

Her actions were slow but when she finally opened her eyes, they were more guarded than he'd ever seen them.

"Do you want to kiss me, really? Think about it. Think about if you really want that."

"I know I do." Her tone made him ache. "I don't even need to think about it. I fuckin' know it. I just don't know why. You're the asshole that left me. You fuckin' left me, Leo. Just like that." She snapped her fingers. "It took me years to get over that shit. I must be the most fool-headed woman alive to want to kiss you right now, but I do."

Even though Leo firmly believed that leaving her had

been his own way of keeping the woman he loved from being held back by him, that didn't mean he didn't feel the guilt of it every day. Especially when her pain was presented to him so honestly.

Hands still framing her face, he walked forward, prompting her backward, until her shoulders met the glass of the large window.

One of his thumbs stroked over the soft skin of her juicy bottom lip. Her mouth opened the slightest bit. His face was so close to hers that the warm little puffs of her sweet breath hit his face. The hard thumping of her heart was easy to decipher with the pressing together of their chests. Leo's was calm, steady. He didn't feel nervous or anxious or even halfway scared. The relaxation that swept over him was hard to explain but he understood it keenly.

This wasn't his first kiss with her—not even close. There had probably been millions of kisses between them throughout the years. And even though it had been a long time since the last one, his body knew the feel of her. Having Miri in his arms, trembling in anticipation of his kisses, felt like coming home after a long time away. Like fresh linens on the bed and a long, hot shower. It made him almost slack, sluggish but not sleepy, just placid.

When his mouth touched hers, it was a soft press of skin. A teaser. His tongue ran over the edge of the deep bow of her upper lip and they both shivered.

As much as he wanted to draw it out, tease her until she was all wrung out and writhing, he couldn't wait.

His dick was hard as a rock beneath his jeans and he couldn't find it in himself to hold back any longer. So he took her lips, tasting the soft caramel-and-creme candies she'd eaten for dessert. Her mouth was sweet and warm and she kissed him like she was drowning in him. He pressed against her even more, her back firmly against the window, letting her feel how hard she was making him.

His teeth nipped at her bottom lip and she shuddered, then pulled away from him with a gasp. She put both of her hands to his chest and pushed, not hard, but with enough force to let him know that he needed to move away from her.

"We shouldn't have done that." Her lips were swollen and her voice was hoarse. "That was a bad idea."

"No." He shook his head. "That felt right. Damn near perfect. You know it too."

Miri clamped her eyes shut, shaking her head more profusely. "No. No, no, no, no. I'm such a fuckin—" She stopped speaking abruptly. "Do you remember the day you left me?"

"Like it was yesterday. It runs through my mind on repeat."

"Yeah." She chuckled darkly. "Mine too. It was a Tuesday and I remember getting off from work at the shop early. I went home and I took a nap. It was my night to make dinner. And I—" She drew in a sob, making her shudder.

Leo reached out to comfort her but she moved back immediately.

"I just threw together some food. Baked chicken and mashed potatoes, broccoli that was close to going bad." Her eyes were a million miles away. "When you came in, I was sitting on the couch waiting for the chicken to come out of the oven, and the second I saw your face, I knew something bad was about to happen. I thought you were going to tell me you'd cheated on me or something."

"I spent all day going over the decision in my head," he said softly. "I'd been thinking about it for a few weeks. But that morning when I was opening the mail, I saw that we had a red notice for the power bill. Miri, we were about to be living in the dark and barely had any groceries in the fridge. And I . . . I couldn't figure out what the hell I was good for if I couldn't make sure my wife had the most basic things necessary for her to just live. Not even thrive, but live."

"You think I didn't feel stressed out about that too? You act like I expected you to be some kind of superhero and swoop in and take care of everything. I never asked you to take care of me, Leo. That wasn't our deal."

She was right, she hadn't. But she hadn't needed to, either. He'd grown up with what felt like a very clear understanding of what a husband's job was—to take care of his family by any means necessary. And when it became clear that he wasn't capable of that, he'd been forced to question what worth he brought to the role at all.

Miri kept going, tears pooling at the bottoms of her pretty brown eyes. He'd been the one to put them there, yet again, and he felt lower than low about it. "You didn't even say hi to me, didn't give me a kiss or a hug. Your eyes looked so . . . I don't even know, gone. I almost thought you were high or something at first. You just looked at me and said, 'Miri, I need to go.'"

She made a choking sound and let out a sob. His fists clenched at his side. He didn't deserve to comfort her.

"You didn't even let me get a word in. My brain was all over the place. I couldn't figure out if you meant, like, you needed to run out. I couldn't wrap my head around how you were actually fucking leaving me. My silly ass just stood there while you disappeared into the room and came out with a duffel bag full of stuff, and that's when I knew."

"That's when you yelled at me." He'd been thankful for her reaction then. He had been hurt by it, but it had solidified his belief that he didn't deserve her. How could he, if this was what he turned her into? All that pain and anger and frustration, it had taken every little bit of stubbornness he had in his body not to fall at her feet and immediately take back what he'd said.

"I called you all kinds of bastards." She chuckled darkly. "I was trying to get you to fight with me so you'd stay . . . but you didn't. You left. You just left me, Leo. Standing in the living room, chicken burning in the oven, with my heart broken all over the floor."

"There's nothing I regret more than that, Miri. I swear to you."

She snorted, and he knew that his swears and promises meant fuck all to her, just like it should be. "You regret how you left or the fact that you did?"

"Both, if that makes sense."

She didn't believe him. But fuck, he needed her to. He wasn't the most religious man, but he felt the need to repent for his wrongs against her. He stepped toward her again and this time she let him. He was gentle as he took her hands in his.

"Miri, I am so sorry. You have no idea how sorry I am."

She shook her head back and forth.

"I am, I am," he stressed. "I lov—"

"No." She stopped him abruptly, forcing him to drop her hands. "How dare you say that to me? After all this time?"

"I—I'm sorry." His words were pathetic, useless.

Her face transformed, her expression suddenly meaner than any snake he'd ever seen. "I hope you don't think that just because you came back and I'm not that poor little girl you married anymore, that we're going to get back to it like shit's sweet."

His brows furrowed for a second, not fully understanding what she meant. "Miri, I don't . . . I don't care about the money . . . that's not—"

She interrupted him again. "Since when? Because when you left, the money was all you could think about."

"Because we didn't have any," Leo stressed.

"And me having some now doesn't change anything. Just because we don't have to skimp and scrape to get by doesn't discount how you were a shitty husband to me."

In an instant, something gave way in his chest. She'd cursed him, sneered at him, but she'd never called him that. Miri had never admitted, out loud, what he'd known all along.

"I know I was a shitty husband," he admitted. "Money or no money."

Miri shook her head, wiping away angry tears. "Leo, what you can't seem to get through that thick skull of yours is that money had nothing to do with you being a bad husband. It was the fact that you left. You abandoned me. Without any say or input or thought on what I might want, you ran away and left me here to deal with everything. And I don't give a shit what you think you were doing, I'm definitely not about to sit back and let you do it again."

She fled the space then, her long legs making sure strides away from him as fast as they could manage.

He wanted to run after her. Do some goofy movie stunt where he stopped her and took her by the hand, confessed all kinds of romantic shit, pulling her into his arms and kissing her with so much passion that she realized how much she still loved and wanted him. But this wasn't a movie. If he did that, Miri would beat his ass. And she'd be well within her rights to do so.

Instead, he just stood there, watching her run away from him for what felt like the hundredth time. His chest aching so much that he wanted to rip his heart out for a bit of relief.

The worst part of it all, though, was that he knew she was right and he had no idea how to make things better.

13

MIRI

Mama went to church three days a week, every week. Monday for choir practice, Wednesday for Bible study, and Sunday for regular weekly service. Miri, however, was lucky if she found it in her to show up for a Sunday service once a month. But she'd written Greenbelt First Baptist a check for five million dollars for the "building fund," and even though she'd donated it anonymously, her mama insisted that she show her face and put her butt in a pew.

It had been a week since she'd let Leo kiss her in his little she-shed and she still couldn't figure out how she felt about it.

On one hand, it had been fucking fantastic. She left panting, her pussy as wet as the tears in her eyes on the drive home. On the other, she'd practically offered herself up on a silver platter to be hurt again.

She'd always been hardheaded, but this was on a completely different level.

When she'd gotten home, she'd made herself come while simultaneously crying in the shower. It had been a long time since she'd felt so pathetic. She was Miri. She was a bad bitch. And being around Leo didn't make her feel like any less than the bad bitch she knew she was, but it did make her feel raw and vulnerable, like she'd been flayed down to the softest layer of her flesh. That was much less pleasant. In fact, she hated it.

As she sat next to her mother in the older woman's favorite pew, she hoped that Reverend Mosley would have a word strong enough to take her mind off it all. The money, the confusion, Leo. All she wanted to do was sit there and listen to the men's choir stomp their way through "Trouble in My Way."

But whatever peace she may have found in the few minutes she'd been sitting there, making out the patterns in the stained-glass window, was completely shot when she saw him.

Leo was dressed in an old, too-tight black suit, talking to his brother-in-law. His sister was holding someone's baby and conversing with one of the elders while her two sons played around their father's legs. It was rude to stare, Miri knew that, it had been drilled into her head a million times. But there was no stopping it. She'd tried not to think about what she would do when she saw him next. So much so that she'd repressed the desire to practice any type of speech about her feelings or expectations.

So there she sat, staring Leo down like somebody raised by a gang of chickens in a barn somewhere.

Her mama looked over, saw her so intently focused, then followed her line of sight. When she laid eyes on Leo, she harrumphed.

"Little girl . . ." It was all warning.

"I'm not, Mama!" Miri answered with indignation.

"Last thing you need is to be gone off on that boy again. You remember last time, don't you? I darn near had to peel you off the concrete."

"I know, Mama." Miri didn't know what else to say.

Patrice put her hand on Miri's knee, squeezing through the thin, cheap material of her only real church-appropriate dress. "You got everything you could possibly have right now. You can have anybody you want. Boy, girl, or otherwise. You always could. I don't want you sittin' around waitin' for that boy when you have so much more in front of you."

She was exactly right. Fuck Leo. Fuck him. And fuck the dusty Toyota he'd rode into town in. Thinking he was coming back like some kind of dusty white knight.

Lord forgive her.

It wasn't right to try so hard to whip up anger in church. But it was necessary when the other thing she was feeling was longing. Longing that was absolutely useless.

Miri turned her head toward the pulpit. Reverend Mosley was quiet as he flipped through his Bible, his dark bald head already shiny with sweat.

Even with her eyes forward, her peripheral vision was vigilant. Watching as Leo led his family to a pew that was on the other side of the small church and a few ahead of the one she was sitting in. She couldn't quite see all of him when he sat down on the end, but his face and profile were clear. The broadness of his nose, his big lips, the way the jaw on the left side of his face was a little sharper than the one on the right.

He had no right to be so fine. Not when he made her want to strangle the hell out of him. Here she was, thinking of sin after sin in church while he sat there cool as you please, tapping his feet along to the music the organist had started playing.

She barely heard the words when the preacher started talking. All she did was stare at Leo, her lips drawn and her jaw tight, like she was trying to will him to look at her out of sheer spite.

He never did. Not through three different sermons, five hymns, and the taking of Communion.

And with every second that passed, every second that he kept his eyes forward instead of on her, her anger became more and more oppressive.

Greenbelt didn't have its own Humane Society, so she'd had to go to Beaufort. She'd spent hours on the shelter's website, looking at the listings of animals, falling in love with each and every pair of sweet puppy eyes she looked into.

The front office was hectic, the energy happy but chaotic. It matched the way she was feeling perfectly.

She'd thought about asking her mama to come along with her, then the girls. Her mind had been filled with thoughts about needing some kind of moral support. Ultimately, she'd come alone. This was, in some kind of way, a pivotal moment for Miri, something she'd hoped for practically her entire life. This was hers to experience, only hers. And if that meant crying on the floor of the kennel while some teenaged attendant stood by in horror, it was whatever.

The kennel supervisor was a short, college-aged Latina named Juana with an incredibly endearing smile and extensive knowledge on every dog they housed. Miri followed behind her, half listening, half trying desperately to see if she could lay eyes on "the one."

They were close to the end of the line, Juana still smiling as she told Miri that people usually had to walk through a couple times before they were able to make a choice.

Miri turned, preparing to head back to the front, when she saw a flash of brown and white.

Apparently she'd missed the little thing before, but it was making itself known, zooming its little body back and forth in its cage with breakneck speed. Miri could have sworn it was grinning.

"That's Ginger," Juana told her. "We think she's somewhere about seven months old. She's a Jack Russell terrier and only been with us a few weeks. Someone found her wandering along the side of a busy road with no tags or chips or anything and brought her over. Since no one claimed her, we figured she'd been abandoned."

Miri squatted down in front of the cage, fingers through the links. Ginger ran up to her, panting, licking at her fingertips for a second before going right back to her zooming. "She's so little," Miri said. "It's a miracle she survived."

The longer Miri stared at her, the more she saw. Her left ear had been clipped on the tip, she ran with a small limp in one of her hind legs, and there was some sort of scar on her back. Miri wanted to grab her up and tuck her into her chest immediately.

"She's a strong girl," Juana said. "You want me to take her out?"

"Please."

Ginger ran to her as soon as the door was opened, practically forcing Miri to pick her up. She could feel the excitement radiating through the animal's whole body.

"Oh my God." Miri spoke into her fur. "You are the sweetest, cutest little thing." She took Ginger in two hands and held her away from her. "You want to come home with me, baby girl? Huh? You want to come live at my house?"

Ginger, of course, couldn't answer. But her tail wagged and Miri could have sworn Ginger grinned.

"I want her." She looked over at Juana with a smile.

"That's great," Juana said, all enthusiasm. "So, we like to make sure that we have as small of a come-back rate as possible for the animals we get adopted. Essentially, this means that we do a home inspection and have a relatively extensive application process. I don't think it'll be an issue but we have to make sure we're sending the animals into a safe environment with people who are dedicated to caring for them and giving them good lives."

"I absolutely understand. I'll do whatever you need," Miri said, her eyes back on Ginger's panting face.

"Fantastic, we'll have you fill out some intent-to-adopt paperwork out front and officially take Ginger off the adoption list. We'll need to keep her until you're approved, but it shouldn't take longer than a couple weeks. You can do the application here, and all that's left will be for us to find a time to perform the home inspection."

Juana motioned for her to help put Ginger back in her cage. With great reluctance, Miri placed a kiss on her little head, sat her down, and watched as she went to lie in her bed.

"What does the house inspection look like?" Miri was already planning her thorough cleaning strategy in her head.

"Nothing too intense. We don't have income requirements or anything like that. We just need to make sure that, whether it's the home itself or the yard, the animal will be able to play and roam freely without falling into too much danger."

Miri let out a puff of air. "Right, okay, good. We don't have much of a yard but my mom and I have lived in our house for twenty years and we've made sure to keep it up best we can."

Juana stopped Miri when they reached the desk of

an older white man—presumably the one who would help with her applications. Juana's smile grew more understanding. "Trust me, anybody can love and take care of an animal if they're able to. It's rare that we get high-income people coming in here anyway. They tend to go to the breeders." Her nose turned up like she'd smelled something funky. "We get the everyday people. Folks who just want an animal to love on. So we are in no way looking for perfection. Only safety."

Miri was still nervous, terrified that the small things in the house that needed to be fixed would disqualify her. But she supposed that was normal. Still, that they weren't looking for perfection was a relief. The last thing she wanted was to come all this way, just to be told she was unfit because the carpets in her house were wearing thin. Especially when she couldn't bear to move out of it now.

She took a deep breath, squaring her shoulders and managing to greet the man behind the desk politely. The only thing left to figure out was what she was supposed to put on the "income" section of the forms.

14

LEO

Quentin had convinced Leo to wake up at the ass crack of dawn on a Saturday morning to go to some sort of combo farmers' market / flea market. Leo had been to plenty of rubbish sales and church donation bin pickups, but Quentin had explained that this was different. He'd used words like "local honey" and "antiques" to describe it, words that meant next to nothing to Leo, if he was being honest. But he'd agreed because he wanted to spend time with his boy. So much so that it didn't matter what the hell they were doing. It also didn't matter when the market got rained out by a summer shower.

Leo hadn't spent his time away from Greenbelt making friends. Honestly, he'd done the exact opposite. He'd avoided almost all meaningful connections. Partly because he knew that no one could compare to the people he'd left behind, and partly because he didn't feel like he deserved it after what he'd done. Almost a decade spent in some kind of self-imposed isolation and Quentin could have asked him to help unclog his toilet and he probably would have been fully on board to help.

So much of his brain space had been rightfully filled with guilt over leaving Miri, but he was starting to see that he'd been shortsighted. Thea, Ahmir, and the kids, Quentin, all his cousins, hell, even all the church aunties. He'd cared about them, which probably meant that they had cared for him too.

Was it ridiculous that he'd never really considered that? The possibility that the people he loved would love him back and—in return—miss him when he was gone?

Thea had been telling him for years that she missed him. That she wanted him back in Greenbelt with her and the family. And to be honest, he'd dismissed it as the kind of stuff everyone said when their family moved away. When he thought about her and everyone else back home, he'd imagined them as almost unchanged. Going about their lives completely normal as if he'd never been there in the first place.

Now, sitting across from his best friend in a booth at Minnie's Diner, he wasn't so sure.

"You know we still come here every Tuesday night," Quentin told him, eyes on the laminated menu as if it hadn't remained unchanged for longer than both of them had even been alive.

"You and Chuck?"

"Yep, and my mama and daddy too. Every Tuesday, rain or shine. Who does shit like that anymore?"

Leo didn't know if there was a single Greenbelt citizen who could consider themselves as anything other than a regular at Minnie's. Even his aunties, who hated anything that wasn't made by hand in one of their kitchens, made their way down to Minnie's for a meal on the regular. It was a Greenbelt institution. The one thing that brought everyone in town together to some extent. They might not have liked each other, but they sure liked Minnie's peach cobbler or meat loaf and cabbage.

"You know Greenbelt." Leo laughed. "I left for eight years, came back, and I swear not a thing has changed. Life still feels the same."

"Does it?" Quentin's face drew in, not in anger, but in thought. "I don't know . . . Sometimes it seems like this place changes more and more every day. Maybe the people more than the town itself." He took a long sip of his sweet tea. "Greenbelt High is as run-down and ramshackle as it was when we went there, but Jade Dunn is one of the assistant football coaches now."

"Wait, what?"

Leo had never had the desire to play competitive sports, but you didn't have to be on the team to know how important high school football was in the south. Greenbelt may not have been West Texas but there was nothing more important than watching the Greenbelt Bull Sharks play. Some type of hype for his home team was ingrained in him, but he knew the good ol' boys club that ran Greenbelt's sports—and most other things—liked to keep things real traditionally racist and misogynistic and every other kind of messed-up, backwards thing there was to be.

Jade was Miri's best friend, her oldest friend, and he'd known her well at some point. Which meant that he knew how hard she went for football—especially Greenbelt football. This would be a dream come true for her.

"Yeah, man. She's been the O-line coach for about five years now. Greenbelt's back, baby, feels like it did when we were in school. All that energy in the town, everybody's happy when we're winning!"

Their waitress returned with dismissed apologies for taking a little long with the food. A fried bologna sandwich and chips for Leo and meat loaf for Quentin. It wasn't until she left and they'd already dug into their meals that Leo continued.

"Since when do you care about football?"

Q had been like him, in the spirit just enough to enjoy the fun of it.

The other man rolled his eyes. "Chuckie's ass . . . which is ridiculous as hell because he ain't even from here."

Leo had to laugh. Chuck was from Beaufort and the two towns had always had a bitter sports rivalry.

"He has a personal vendetta against the Bulldogs because they wouldn't let him on the team. So we cheer for the Bull Sharks half out of spite and half because he's gotten soft. And of course, being the supportive husband I am, I need to turn up with him."

Quentin's words were backed by a quiet, amused

smile. His "I do it to appease him" act was paper thin. The man was clearly in love.

"I'm happy for you, Q." The words came out of nowhere, but they were honest. "I really am, it's good to see that there's still real love out there."

Quentin tilted his head to the side. "You in your feelings about Miri again, huh?"

The words weren't unkind but they made Leo's abs clench.

"I'm always in my feelings about that woman." He shoved a couple chips in his mouth. "The last time I saw her we kissed. It was . . . unbelievable. It's been so long since I've been that close to her, and for a second I thought we were back, Miri and Leo. I felt that shit." He shook his head. "But I said something ridiculous and she ran off. Hasn't talked to me since."

"What did you think was going to happen, Leo? Eight years of nothing down the toilet just because you put your tongue down her throat."

Truth was, he didn't know what exactly he'd expected to happen. Or maybe he was just lying to himself. Maybe he had expected shit to work out like a fairy tale. She'd called him back—no matter whether it was for a divorce or not, he was still waiting on those papers, after all—and he'd work his ass off to show her that what they really needed was to stay together. When she'd leaned into him, her eyes full of longing and want, the first thing in his mind had been *This is it. It's finally happening.*

It had only taken seconds for him to find himself thrown back into the real world. The one where his wife

could barely be in the same room as him for longer than
five minutes without having to flee.

"Maybe," he admitted. "But we both know I'm not
that bright when it comes to that woman."

There was no hesitation in Quentin's agreement.
"True. She had your nose wide open from the start and it
hasn't closed since." He shook his head. "I told you then
and I'm telling you now. I feel like all this mess could have
been avoided if y'all would actually just learn how to talk
to each other. Especially you—you and that damn martyr
complex are going to get you fucked up every time."

"Boy, I do not have a martyr complex."

Quentin scoffed. "Ohhhh, look at me, I managed to
get the finest woman in town to fall in love with my little
broke ass and it was pure torture for me."

Leo's mouth dropped open. "You're so grimy . . ."

Q kept going. "Everybody feel bad for me because
my beautiful wife was so supportive that I had run away
about it."

"Okay, now you're doing too much."

Quentin chuckled. "I'm fucking with you, but you
know I'm a little bit right. You were young and didn't
know shit about shit but you made the wrong decision.
And I'm not even talking about you leaving Miri, either.
I'm talking about you leaving all of us."

Leo's eyes settled on the helping of untouched cabbage on Quentin's plate. He always ordered it, even
though he hated it, even when it was no big thing to sub-
stitute mashed potatoes or more corn bread. Every time
he got meat loaf, he got a side of cabbage, and only after

he'd finished everything else on his plate and in his cup did he manage to choke it down. He knew that Quentin did it because his mama had always insisted on it when he was young. He couldn't help but note that the man had more dedication to choosing that cabbage than Leo had to choosing to be a good husband and brother and friend. It made his stomach roil in disgust.

"I'm a coward," he said.

"You're not a coward, Leo. You're just a man." Quentin rolled his slim shoulders. "Which is the same reason you're having such a hard time figuring all this out. I don't know how much of a chance you have with Miri, I mean, judging by the way she's acting, I'd say it's probably more than you might think. But I do know that you're sitting here across from me with the chance to be the kind of friend you used to be. I love you, man, and I know you love me too. The same goes for your family and everybody else that's been here waiting for you: All you need to do is show the fuck up, Leonard. Just show up for us."

Leo's stomach jumped into his throat, pulsing and clenching. He tried to swallow it down, all the emotion. Guilt and shame collided with hope and relief so fast and violently that it almost knocked him out of his seat.

He hated to admit it, but he hadn't come back for this. For anybody else but Miri. She'd called him and he'd come running with only her on his mind, and even that wasn't at all selfless. So what kind of person did that make him? He didn't know the answer, but it wasn't looking good.

"Fuck, man . . ."

Quentin simply nodded.

"I'm trash."

"As hell."

"I'm a fuckin' bad friend."

Quentin's mouth turned down a bit. "Not always, you just lost your sense."

Leo rubbed a hand over his face, his head suddenly hurting. "I'll get it together, man. All of it. I swear I will."

"You're lucky I believe that too."

The basement of Greenbelt First Baptist Church smelled like mothballs. It was spotless—shiny linoleum floors and walls that were scrubbed weekly—but it was simply too old and dank not to have that particular smell.

Saturday night, after his day with Quentin, he'd agreed to stop by the church and bring some tables and chairs upstairs for Sunday's potluck. He'd already taken three trips from the storage room in the basement to the little activity room and had at least three more to go. Briefly, he considered calling Ahmir and the boys to come help, but he figured he could use the workout to help relieve some of the tension between his shoulders.

It was creepy as hell down there. Eerily quiet except for the sound of the boiler. The fluorescent bulb above him blinked a few times and he stared up as if daring it to go out on him. With his attention taken, he didn't notice the sound of another person entering the space until he felt a presence behind him.

Nearly scared shitless, he jumped, face morphing into one of terror at the thought that he was suddenly joined by someone else. The expression deepened quickly when he saw that the other person was none other than Patrice Butler.

An ax murderer could have been standing there and he'd have been less scared.

"Sister Pearlie told me you were down here," she said, looking at him with so much scrutiny it made him feel naked.

Leo crossed his arms over his chest, already defensive. "Um . . . yes, ma'am, I'm helping bring some things upstairs for tomorrow."

The woman went silent for a few long moments, her eyes squinting as she narrowed in on his face.

"I didn't come down here to be mean to you, Leonard." She'd always refused to call him anything but that. "My daughter is doing a fine job of that herself."

The way she grinned made him shiver, letting him know that she was intensely proud of the amount of shit Miri was giving him.

"But I did want to talk," she continued.

He cleared his throat, praying for his voice not to break like he was upstairs kneeling in one of the pews. "About what?"

His question was ridiculous. There wasn't a single thing in the world this woman would want to talk to him about aside from the fact that he'd broken her daughter's heart.

"About what you're doing."

"I . . . don't think I know what you mean."

Ms. Patrice huffed, a scowl appearing on her face that reminded him so much of his wife's that he couldn't help but soften some at the sight of it. "You're back and that's all well and good. Did what you were supposed to do and accepted the very generous offer Miri made you. But, Leonard, you're still sniffin' around."

Leo took a second to gather his thoughts, figuring the best way to respond to her. This was a woman he'd known all his life, a woman he respected and loved. A woman he was technically related to by marriage. It made him feel good that Miri had people in her corner willing to throw down to protect her, even if it was from him.

He wanted to give her the respect she deserved, but he also wanted to make it clear that she wasn't the one who was going to make him back off. The only one with that power was Miri.

"Ms. Patrice . . ."

The woman must have heard something in his tone that gave her pause. She huffed, then squared her shoulders, no doubt bracing for the impact of his bullshit.

"You know I love her," he said simply.

"Oh, I'd never deny that," she answered, mouth pursed.

"And you know that I messed up. *I* know I messed up."

The woman seemed intent on interrupting him. "You did more than 'mess up,' that's the first thing you need to realize."

Leo didn't want to curse in front of her, but what choice did he have but to express himself in the most intense way possible. "You're right," he told her, shaking his head. "I got everything all messed up. I'm not trying to pull anything over on anybody, Ms. Patrice. I'm just trying to get my wife back."

"And what makes you think I'll allow you to even try?"

It was his turn to stare at her. The straightness of her narrow shoulders, the glint in her eyes. He didn't remember much about his own mother, but even he could recognize the look of a mama ready to kill to protect hers.

"With all due respect, ma'am"—Leo swallowed—"I don't think that's for you to decide."

Ms. Patrice approached him until she was all up in his shit. Her eyes were hard and he found himself unable to look away from them. "I've known you since you were knee-high to a grasshopper. Chasing behind my girl with those big eyes and ears. I remember thinkin' then that she was going to be the one to break your heart, leave you cryin' in your auntie's lap." She gritted her teeth. "Even when I gave her my blessing to marry you, I figured it'd last a few years, maybe. That I'd have to talk her off the ledge of cheating or something and be there for her while she figured herself out. Maybe I'm the fool, but I saw the way you looked at her, like nothing else in your life mattered, and I just knew you were going to be the one hurt in the end. Not her."

This was a sentiment Leo wasn't unfamiliar with. He'd spent their entire first year as a couple waiting for the other shoe to drop. He wasn't completely worthless, he knew that at least. But Miri . . . Miri was something else.

Every room she entered immediately brightened. Every smile she flashed made days better. There was something undeniable about her. Something that drew people in and made them want to stay. And all of this was only made more intense by the fact that she was a choosy thing who wasn't interested in letting any old body close to her.

Everyone, including him, had expected her to be the one to break his heart. This was what everyone had prepared for. This was also why everyone had been sent scrambling when he'd done what he did.

It was wild. He knew it. And it definitely didn't make him feel good to be aware of it. But it was the truth, nonetheless.

Patrice reached out and grabbed his arm. Her grip didn't hurt but it was urgent. "You don't know what it was like for her when you left. It was like she left with you, trying to follow after you with her spirit even when her body was at home with me. There were days when I had to brush her teeth and comb her hair. I can't let her go through that again, Leonard. And I don't care how much of a meddling old bat I have to be to make sure it doesn't happen."

Leo caught her eyes, trying to convey every ounce of honesty he had in his body. "I'm not going to let that happen. If she lets me in again, she'll be the only one who gets me to leave her side."

"I might believe you," she said. "I can at least see that *you* believe you."

"Now I just have to get her to believe it," he finished for her.

"I'm not sayin' I support you. But I'm not sayin' I'm going to dump your body in with the hogs either, not unless you muck it all up again."

"I appreciate that." He flashed her a relieved smile. "But you don't have to worry, because I'm not going back to that. Not ever."

Ms. Patrice didn't say anything to acknowledge his promise. Instead, she tightened her grip on his arm for a moment, then nodded her head at something behind him. "Pastor Franklin wants you to bring the bingo stuff up too, the elders want to enjoy a few games of Bible Bingo at the potluck tomorrow."

"Yes, ma'am," he said, nodding, relieved that their conversation seemed to be ending.

"I hope she gives you all the hell in the world" were her parting words as she left him alone under the blinking fluorescent lights with his top lip sweating.

"Wonder where she gets that from," he mumbled to himself, housing two stacks of folding chairs onto his back with all the strength of a man paying his rightful penance.

15

MIRI

The Piggly Wiggly was sparsely populated. Miri knew it would be. It was a Wednesday afternoon, right after twelve o'clock. The only people out were the retired folks and teenagers skipping school. And for both of those groups, there were far more exciting places to be than the grocery store, whether it was the bingo hall or Greenbelt's version of a "Lovers' Lane."

It was exactly the reason Miri chose to wander the aisles of the Piggly Wiggly. She had a small list of things she needed to pick up for her mama but there was something incredibly relaxing about staring at countless different versions of the exact same item. She was standing in front of the Cheez-Its, wondering about the mindset of the person who came up with the cheeseburger flavor, when someone cleared their throat behind her.

She moved out of the way immediately, embarrassed she'd been blocking someone's way. She almost threw her handheld basket across the aisle and booked it when she saw who it was.

Thea stood across from her with a cart full of items. Tall like her brother, with the same wide nose and gorgeous dark eyes. The look on her face, however, was all Thea. Mouth drawn in a line so tight there was no mistaking her displeasure.

Miri instantly felt admonishment. Thea was almost ten years older than her and Miri had spent such a large portion of her life considering the other woman a big sister of sorts, so she couldn't help her reaction. They'd been close once. Miri didn't have any siblings of her own and she'd been nothing but grateful when Thea Vaughn had adopted her as such. She'd been even happier when she and Leo married, knowing that she wasn't only getting a husband she loved, but a sister too.

It hadn't taken long for it all to fall apart, though. The second Leo left Greenbelt—and her—she and Thea became something tantamount to strangers. It wasn't Thea's fault, either. Back then, Miri couldn't bear the sight of her, not for a long time. She looked so much like him that the mere vision of her gorgeous face had made her want to cry. Miri's fragile state lasted a long time, years even. She still sometimes felt like she was so damn close to shattering.

In those early years, she wouldn't have been able to help herself from getting down on her knees to beg Thea for any information she had on Leo. Where he was, who he was with, if he was ever coming back, why he'd left her. Her need for answers would have overshadowed any normal conversation they could have had. So she'd stayed away, and so had Thea, their relationship turning from familiar to strained smiles at church and head nods if they saw each other out in public. Miri hadn't actively sought her out in eight years, and nor had Thea. The shock of her doing it now was almost enough to make Miri crumble.

"Hi," she said awkwardly.

"Hey." The straight line of Thea's mouth gave way to a small smile.

"How have you been?" Miri asked, even though she knew the answer—well, some of it at least.

Thea made a face. "Don't act like you don't know." She called Miri out with blatant exasperation. "You bought my house. You made sure my kids have a shot at an actual future. You put money in mine and my husband's bank accounts. *You* did all that." She twirled her pointer finger in the circle. "And you didn't even bother to come and let me thank you properly."

Miri hung her head in embarrassment. "I didn't know how," she said honestly. "I didn't think you'd want to see me."

Thea sighed and Miri looked up to see her hands tighten on the handle of her cart. "You know, you and him are so damn perfect for each other."

Miri didn't need a lick of help figuring out which "him" Thea was referring to.

"Both of you are just as stubborn as you want to be,

bullheaded to a fault. And you let it cloud everything else in your view."

Something hot started burning in Miri's chest. Apparently, indignation felt a hell of a lot like heartburn. "I wouldn't call it being stubborn. I have valid reasons for not approaching you. I mean, damn, Thea, it's not like you've tried to approach me either."

"That's true. But if I'd gone out of my way to completely change your life, I like to think I'd get over it pretty quick. At least for long enough to let you express your gratitude."

"I didn't do it for your gratitude." Miri hung her head.

"I know you didn't," Thea said, giving her a small smile. "Leo told me everything. But I also know he didn't stipulate a specific amount. That was all you. Because even though we're too chickenshit to talk to each other and you barely know my kids or even me anymore, I know you love me. Because I love you."

Miri's eyes brimmed with tears, sticking to her eyelashes, making them heavy and hard to see through. "Thea . . ."

The other woman held a hand up, immediately stopping whatever mush-mouthed apology Miri was trying to string together. Thea reached into her purse, pulling out a little card and handing it to her.

"Jacobi's turning seven on Sunday. Why don't you come and see the party you helped make possible."

Miri's chest seized again. A child's birthday party meant family. And not only Thea, her little family, and Leo, either. Aunties and uncles and cousins. All of them with their own views of her and opinions on what had happened between her and her husband. They probably hated her. Or worse, pitied her. She knew that her own family—extended or not—were always open about their thoughts on her situation. She'd heard enough of them over the years to send a shudder down her spine at the thought of having to field them from the Vaughns.

She hated feeling this unsure. It reminded her of the state of mind she'd had in her early twenties. Married with no husband, and so fragile she could cry at the drop of a hat. It had taken a long time to grow out of that, to build a shell around herself that made her feel confident in its unbreakability. Leo hadn't even been back for an entire summer yet and she'd cried more than she had in years.

She'd also felt more butterflies and belly flips and warm cheeks, but that was different. Confusing, for sure, but different.

"Bring your mama," Thea told her. "That way you'll have somebody to have your back if one of the aunties starts wildin'."

Miri snorted out a laugh. "God bless all the hip replacements in the room."

Thea laughed too, before giving Miri's arm a pat. "Please come, Miri. I'm serious. Whatever happened between you and Leo, I want you there. You have nephews, girl, and they'd like to meet you instead of just hearing stories about how you used to put their uncle in a headlock when y'all were kids."

"Okay. I will."

"Promise me."

Miri held out her pinkie, waiting until Thea wrapped her own around it.

Thea grinned. "Don't disappoint me. Because I will roll up on your ass."

"I know you will," Miri laughed. "And I'd deserve it."

16

LEO

A few days after his visit to Minnie's with Quentin, Leo snuck in under the cover of night. His disgust with himself had all but killed his appetite that day. Now that his self-loathing was somewhat back to normal, everyday levels, he was craving a piece of strawberry pound cake.

Leo had a sweet tooth like no other. If given the choice, he'd always choose a little something sweet over anything else. He couldn't even go to sleep at night without indulging in at least a small piece of chocolate.

Minnie's desserts were so good, though, that the diner was no stranger to clandestine cake orders at ungodly hours—which, in Greenbelt, meant any time past nine.

He showed up thirty minutes before eleven, closing time on weeknights, armed with cash and a hankering strong enough to remove him from his bed after he'd already been settled in it.

A waitress, an older white woman whose name he couldn't remember, was standing at the counter, helping some other poor soul. She flipped her red hair over one of her shoulders as she talked, and the way the fake pearl bracelet on her wrist jangled reminded him of something out of *Fried Green Tomatoes*.

After the other customer had left, Leo stepped up to the counter with the same polite but not-too-warm smile his mother had passed down to him before she'd passed.

"What can I do for you, honey?" she asked. "Kitchen's closed, so no hot meals, but we can still do sweets and cold sandwiches."

"I'll have a piece of the strawberry pound cake, please. With a scoop of vanilla on the side."

She leaned back with her arms clutching the edges of the counter, checking the little glass sweets holder. "I think we're sold out of that, sugar."

His spirits fell immediately. Had he come all this way only to settle for a piece of mulberry pie?

"Tell you what, though, I'll cut you a piece of the one we prepped for tomorrow morning just because you're handsome."

Leo grinned. "That's mighty kind of you."

"Sit tight, I'll be back in two shakes." She winked at him.

He was there alone in the diner for all of four seconds before the little bell rang over the door signaling that another customer had come in. Leo turned his head, eager to see someone else who'd had the same idea as him.

Instead of seeing one of his old grade-school teachers or a deacon from church, he laid eyes on Jade Dunn. She wore a pair of black running shorts and a sports bra, her hair tied back in the low ponytail she kept it in often.

The second their eyes connected, she froze in place. Her eyes darted back to the door like she was considering running back out the way she'd come.

He couldn't blame her, honestly. The air in Minnie's was suddenly rife with awkwardness of a very specific kind. They were in two very opposing places.

Him, the man that was trying to get his woman back after fucking up. Her, the best friend who hated the very ground he walked upon.

He held no ill feelings toward Jade; how could he? All she'd ever done was hold her friend down. And because he loved that friend more than anything in the world, he was damn near happy to be on the receiving end of the cold stare she threw at him.

"Hey." Leo was willing to break the ice, as uncomfortable as it was.

Jade cleared her throat, squared her shoulders, and joined him next to the counter.

He tried again. "It felt like a good night for a slice of cake."

Still she didn't respond, but this time she pursed her lips and narrowed her eyes at him. Not once did she glance at the dessert display. He didn't know what else to do but open his big mouth again.

"What are you thinking of getting? I hear the, uhmm, peach cobbler is better than your granny's."

"I cannot believe you are still talking." She crossed her arms over her chest.

"Me either."

Behind the counter, he could hear the waitress moving around in the kitchen. He stood there begging silently for her to come back with all the desperation of someone begging their lover to return safely from war.

"I don't like you."

Leo rubbed at the back of his neck. "I can tell."

"Good." Her face turned sour. "And you need to leave Miri alone—stop jerking her around."

Leo felt the skin on his face grow hot. "The only person that can get me to leave Miri alone is Miri. And I'm not jerking her around, I'd never do that. Shit, I'm trying to get her back."

"Miri doesn't—"

He held a hand up to stop her mid-sentence. "With all due respect, Jade, what's happening between my wife and I is a little more complicated than all this petty shit. I appreciate you protecting her, but I have no intentions of hurting her."

"Not any more than you already have, you mean." Jade refused to take her eyes off his; there was a thunderstorm happening behind them.

He was ashamed at how his hackles raised. He

wanted to deny what she was saying, defend himself as a first reaction to his guilt. But what the hell would that do but make him look even worse and make her hate him even more.

Leo took a deep breath. This was starting to look like one of those chances to show up and prove that he wasn't that fool-headed kid anymore. He was a grown man and it was time he started acting like it.

"Not any more than I already have," he said, repeating Jade's words back to her. "Not a lick more."

Her brown eyes narrowed again, this time less in anger and more in thought.

"You got a big-ass head, you know that?" She uncrossed her arms. "You might be the only person in the world more hardheaded than her."

Leo smiled. "That's why we fit so well together."

Her eyes rolled so fast Leo nearly started running off to catch them. "Or why y'all are in the position you're in now."

She wasn't wrong. To some extent he and Miri had always been this way. When they'd been young, before puberty, before the romantic love, their disagreements had been intense. Once, he'd promised Miri that he'd go to the premiere showing of some movie he couldn't even remember the name of now. Then, a group of boys from his class had invited him over for a birthday party. Both the same night, same time. He'd bailed on Miri without even giving a reason.

When he'd shown up on her doorstep that Sunday, expecting her anger at him to have worn off, he'd found himself sorely mistaken. She'd doled out a lecture almost as earth-shattering as one of his elders and then proceeded not to speak to him for two whole weeks. It had taken him two bags of Hot Fries, some Sour Patch Kids, a nut-free Drumstick, and a lot of groveling to make it up to her.

He already knew that he'd have to bring more than that for the mess he'd gotten himself into this time.

"Yeah . . ." He cleared his throat, drawing his eyes to the display of black-and-white photos on the wall behind the register.

Jade sighed so loud she had to have been trying to get his attention. When he didn't give it to her, she did it again, then one more time, until his head turned.

"Far be it from me to give you relationship advice." She grimaced. "Look, Miri is . . . she's just scared. She's scared of you. That's what all this is—she's afraid."

Leo ground his teeth together, guts churning. All of a sudden he had to fight off a strong wave of nausea. Those words made him sick. His Miri . . . scared of him . . . He could hardly wrap his mind around it.

"I—" There wasn't anything he could say to combat the way he was feeling.

Jade was relentless, though, unfazed by his little breakdown. "You did something awful. You were selfish and you hurt her and she's been trying to heal from it ever since. Now you're here again, rubbing all kinds of salt in her wounds, and she's all turned around because of it."

His guilt settled over him like a steel wool blanket. He couldn't help but consider the thought that he'd been right all along about Miri being better off without him. What good was his plan to try to get her back if all it was doing was causing her pain?

The coward's heart that still beat inside him immediately thought to run. That wasn't a solution, though. It also wasn't an option. As much as he wanted to deny it, he was home. He felt better, more filled with purpose, than he had in years, and he wasn't willing to give that up. He also wasn't willing to cause even more pain to the people he claimed to love.

Maybe he could leave her alone . . .

Maybe he could let her go . . .

Let her find someone else to love her the way she deserved . . .

Even if it killed him.

Jade let out another one of her sighs, but this time, there was something else in it. Leo didn't know if it was pity or what, but it made him pause.

"She still loves you, though." Jade's voice was low, like she couldn't believe she was saying it. "And she's never let you go. I honestly don't think she ever will."

"Jade . . ." He wanted to beg her not to fill his head with a false sense of hope, it was torture.

"I'm not saying I understand it," she snorted. "I would have knocked that big-ass head off your shoulders. But there's something about you that Miri can't let go of. So maybe . . . maybe if you can get it together and show her that she doesn't have to be scared of you anymore . . . maybe she'll finally stop running."

His mouth went dry in an instant. He wouldn't have

called what she'd told him advice, that didn't feel like it
had been her intent. Maybe more of a kick in the ass. Or
a kick in his big-ass head.

Before he could say anything, the waitress returned
with a little plastic container filled with cake and ice
cream; there was a bow around it. She handed it over to
him and he slid her a ten-dollar bill, gesturing for her to
keep the change when she tried to return it.

"Oh, hi there." Her smile widened when she saw
Jade. "You in for a late-night dessert too?"

"Mulberry pie, please," Jade said, as close to mono-
tone as she could get. "No ice cream."

Her back was turned to him as he accepted his dessert from the waitress, and even when the woman went
about cutting Jade's slice, he hung around awkwardly.
He felt overcome with the need to say something. A
thanks. An acknowledgment of her genius.

"Jade . . ." The word was mumbled, but it got her attention.

She turned her head to look at him, rolling her eyes
yet again with something that looked suspiciously close
to playful exasperation. "Just go, bighead. And get rid of
all that saltiness."

17

MIRI

Her auntie was convinced that the second she opened her salon, someone had put a root out on her. When Miri was young and silly enough to roll her eyes at things like that, she thought it was goofy as hell. Yes, there'd never been a single Tuesday in the shop's history that had ever seen a single goddamn customer walk through the front doors, but that was definitely explainable, right?

She wasn't young and silly anymore, not nearly. She believed that shit now. Every single Tuesday for as long as she could remember, she would sit in the shop, alone, with the mounted TV in the corner playing daytime's finest.

When she'd been in school, she had opened the shop at 2:40 P.M., exactly twenty minutes after she got out of class. But even now, she never opened before 10:00 A.M. on Tuesday mornings. Normally, she took the time to practice something new, either on her own nails or her little practice hand. Today, however, she was looking over her divorce papers, with Ginger going hard as hell on a lick mat on the floor next to her.

She'd been awakened out of her Tuesday-morning sleep-in by a phone call from Corey Whittaker. After he'd made a warm joke about the "good life getting to her already," he'd asked how the signing of the papers was coming along. She wasn't surprised that the lawyer he'd hooked her up with had let that little tidbit slip. Miri had been dodging emails for weeks at this point.

She didn't know which was the more excruciating thought to have to admit; that she hadn't managed to get something so incredibly important done, or that she couldn't even blame Leo for it. She'd held up her end of the deal with him, and he'd been right there ready to hold up his. And when the time had come, she'd been so full of bullshit she could still taste it. Knowing damn well she kept the papers in her glove box. Right next to her car manual and her Taser.

She wanted a divorce. She did. She wanted to be free of Leo and all the shit he made her feel. She was convinced that if she divorced him, everything else would fall into place. But then she'd read through those papers, saw things like "they agree to live separate and apart from each other" and "irretrievable breakdown of the marriage" in the text, and her stomach had turned. Something about it, them, this thing that was theirs, as mangled as it was, reading it broken down in such clinical terms made her feel so heartachingly sad that she could only ever handle acknowledging it at certain times.

Each time she opened the manila folder that contained the documents, she tried to find it in herself to muster up the sheer nerve to have Leo sign them. And every time, faster than she could blink, she got further from her goal than she'd been before.

Which was exactly why she found herself audibly relieved when Jade called her out of the blue that afternoon.

"Where are you right now?"

Miri held the phone to her ear, using her shoulder as an anchor. "Sitting in the shop, why?"

Jade sighed on the other end, her frustration palpable. "Gladys broke down."

"Again? I literally gave you millions of dollars. Why are you still refusing to get rid of that damn thing?"

She could have sworn she heard Jade growl. "I don't care how much money I have, I will not get rid of this truck. My dad—"

"Your daddy gave you that truck, I know, I know," Miri interrupted. "But he gave you that truck like a decade ago and even then it already had almost two hundred thousand miles on it. I honestly can't believe it's still going."

What Miri didn't say was that she couldn't understand the sentimental connection her best friend had to a green pickup the color of baby poop. Especially when the father that had given it to her was perfectly fine and alive in his home not even five minutes away from where Miri lived.

She'd spent a long time trying to fully understand

Jade's special reasonings behind things. The other woman was more superstitious than anyone she'd ever met, and stubborn to boot.

"Can you come get me or am I going to have to get down on my knees and beg Liv to leave work?"

As much as Miri would pay to see that happen—and to film it for posterity's sake—she couldn't not put Jade out of her misery.

"Give me ten minutes, I've got my child with me."

Greenbelt had three K–12 schools. One elementary school, one middle school, and one high school. All three of them were midsize but placed on the exact same huge plot of land downtown. The parking lots were vaguely separated but ultimately it wasn't enough to make traffic at school start and end times any lighter.

Normally, Miri had no reason to visit any of the schools. Jade was a math teacher and one of the assistant coaches of Greenbelt High's football team—the only woman in the school's history, actually. So while her friend arguably spent most of her time at the place, Miri tended to steer pretty clear. Unless, of course, she was saving Jade's hide.

She drove around the staff parking lot until she spotted her friend, legs and arms crossed, leaning against her truck with the nastiest scowl on her pretty face.

"Hey there, pork chop." Miri, to her credit, didn't even wince as Jade slammed the door.

"Please get me out of here."

"Say hi to Ginger first." She gestured to the back seat of her car, where she'd installed one of those giant doggy holders. Ginger's little self looked too adorable for words, all swallowed up and safe. "Say hiiiii, Auntie Jade."

Jade groaned, fingers on her temples. "Miriam, please do not do this."

"Say hi to her one time. It'll make you feel better. Look, just one time. I won't pull off until you do."

The other woman grumbled under her breath but twisted her body around. Like Miri had predicted, her entire body softened in an instant.

Ginger's energy, Miri was finding, was good enough to completely change the mood in even the tensest room.

The car ambled forward maybe ten feet before they were forced to stop in the line of cars trying to exit the lot.

"What's wrong with Gladys this time?"

"I don't know." Jade's grumpy pretense dropped, leaving behind her bone-tired interior. "It won't turn over. So it might just be the spark plugs or she might actually be dying."

As much as she joked, Miri knew how much the truck meant to her friend. It had meant independence, freedom, on top of being a physical monument to her father's love and care.

"I'm sure she's all right, Jadey Wadey. That old lady is too stubborn to die," Miri said. She caught a glimpse of it in her rearview mirror, as ugly and unassuming as ever.

Jade crossed one of her legs over the other. "She better be. I really, really don't want to have to go shopping for a new car. People who sell cars give me the ick."

"The ick?"

"The kids are saying it." Jade shrugged. "It's cute, right?"

"I can't tell if I think it's weird or if I'm getting old." Miri squinted as she eyed a couple of kids messing around near the edges of the parking lot. Had they been that small when they'd gone here? Surely they hadn't been.

"Well, one of those is definitely true," Jade snorted. "I'm surprised you didn't show up to the school in a housedress."

"Well, I didn't want to embarrass you in front of all your cool teacher friends . . ." Miri's voice trailed off as her eyes scanned the parking lot. They were practically at a standstill and she was tired of staring at the busted taillight in front of her.

He was literally two parking lots away, in the midst of a sea of cars and people, but she homed in on him immediately. Leo was there, a wide smile on his face and his nephews running around his legs. He was speaking to a man she remembered going to high school with.

The sun was high in the sky and beating down hard. And Leo . . . well, unfortunately Leo looked good as hell.

Wearing a white ribbed tank top, a pair of jeans that hugged his ass, and some work boots, he looked every single bit of the sexiest man in town. His brown skin had darkened even more since coming home and it was literally glistening with sweat.

Her mouth went dry and her thighs ran slick. Her heart thudded as she watched him turn his attention away from the other man toward his nephews. She couldn't see his eyes from this far away but she could see the look on his face and it was reverent.

The boys looked up at him with so much awe that it made her chest ache. Bizarrely, she felt a wave of guilt wash over her.

Leo hadn't been close to many people aside from his family, and seeing how happy he was to be around them—in the school pickup line of all places—made her hurt for him. She knew it wasn't her fault that he'd stayed away for so long, but it wasn't like she didn't play a big part in the reason for his absence.

All those feelings did was make her even more confused. If she divorced Leo, would he leave again? Would he hurt Thea and the boys by coming around even less? Was that even supposed to matter to her?

Her gaze was narrowed in on Leo as he spoke to the boys about something or other, obviously giving them good news from the way they reacted—all giggles and excited energy.

Then, whatever spell she was under was broken by the clearing of a throat.

Miri jumped, startled, and looked over at Jade. The smirk on her friend's face was so damned wicked that Miri had to push down the urge to flick her on the ear.

"Shut up," she growled.

"I didn't say anything," Jade snickered. "Just wanted to let you know that traffic's moving. If you could tear your eyes away from your husband who you 'hate so fucking much' that would be great."

She gritted her teeth. "Jade. Shut. Up."

"I'm just saying. That look on your face definitely didn't seem like hatred to me."

"See if I ever come get you again."

Jade's cackling was louder than the engine revving when they finally left the parking lot, but Miri couldn't help but sneak one last peek at Leo in her side mirror.

18

LEO

"Swear 'fore God I didn't know this much Miles Morales stuff existed," Xavier Lewis grunted from his place across from Leo. They were trying to hang a personalized banner for Jacobi over the fireplace. "I mean, where in the hell did your sister even find a neon sign that big?"

Xavier had been a couple years ahead of Leo in school, but he was close friends with Leo's brother-in-law, Ahmir. The man was a single father with four kids, and Leo's scheming sister had told him that the party was set to start two hours earlier just to rope him into helping with setup. Leo had been listening to him complain nearly the entirety of those two hours and still couldn't find it in himself to be annoyed.

First, because the other man was practically voicing all the same grievances Leo had but was too scared to voice. And two, because Thea had guaranteed him that Miri was coming.

He hadn't been able to get their kiss out of his head since it had happened. If he closed his eyes, he could still feel her soft body against his, the heavy thump of her heart on his chest. She'd tasted like candy and caramel, all lush and decadent. He had jerked off to the memory of it enough times since, he was surprised his penis was still in working order. There was shame there too, and sadness at the way she had run from him. He had no idea what he was going to say to her today, but he knew it had to be something good. He figured the best place to start would be an apology. Even if he was still trying to drum up even an ounce of regret about what had happened.

Moments after he and Xavier finally got the banner up, Thea came back into the living room. Her anxious energy clogged up the air enough to make both men twitch. She put her hands on her hips, eyes scrutinous as she took in the banner and streamers, hell, even the giant Miles Morales cardboard cutout she'd managed to get her hands on. It looked incredible. More intricate than any party Leo had ever been to. And yet, his sister's eyebrows were drawn like she wasn't quite sure.

"Do you think it's enough?" She let the question hang, as if she didn't really expect anyone to answer it. "I saw this Spider-Man removable wallpaper online but I thought it would be too much. Now, I'm not so sure."

Leo walked over to his sister, throwing an arm around her shoulder and pulling her in close until she rested her head on his shoulder. "It looks amazing, Thea," he told her, kissing the crown of her head.

Xavier nodded from his place across the room. "I'm tellin' you, my kids are going to see this and get real disappointed with their little swimming parties."

Thea didn't say anything but Leo felt her silent chuckle. He held her, watching her eyes flick back and forth across every item and decoration in the room.

When his brother-in-law, Ahmir, appeared in the doorway, the look on his face was comical.

"Finished getting the bounce house set up," he told them all before narrowing in on his wife. "What's wrong, sweetness?"

"She thinks she didn't do enough," Leo snitched.

Thea pinched his shoulder hard enough to make Leo drop his arm from around her.

"Didn't do enough?" Ahmir's tone was incredulous. "Baby, these kids are about to pass out from how fire this shit looks. You did a beautiful job, Thea."

His sister's voice was nearly shy as she looked up at her husband through her eyelashes. "Yeah?"

The look Ahmir gave her was so loving and indulgent Leo had to look away to where Xavier was standing awkwardly in the corner.

The couple stared at one another for what felt like forever. Communicating so silently, so intimately, that it made Leo envious. He and his wife could barely communicate with words, let alone looks.

When the screen door at the back of the house slammed, and childlike giggles and little stomping feet filled the space, both Thea and Ahmir immediately snapped out of it and into parent mode.

"I know I didn't just hear you slamming my door, Jacobi Aaron." Thea's voice was calm but dangerous. "I thought I told y'all's little behinds to stay outside until we were done. Ain't no reason for you to be comin' in and out the house like that."

Jacobi whined and Leo had to choke his laugh back down his throat. "We just wanted to see, Mama."

"Uh-uh." Thea was already making her way into the kitchen, arms crossed and a storm brewing behind her eyes. "You can see it when we're done. Now git. Before I call everybody and tell them the party is canceled."

Leo turned to Xavier to see him laughing silently.

It was nice to be reminded that some things never changed. Relationships did. Feelings did. Even love did. But Black mamas were timeless.

The house was packed wall-to-wall with people. Family members, folks from church, kids from the boys' school; hell, there was even a group of Thea's friends sitting around the kitchen table holding mimosa glasses that never seemed to find themselves empty. Everyone had shown up at practically the same time. One second, the house had been barren and the next it had been filled with enough people that it was hard to move.

Leo was refilling the Styrofoam coolers with ice and sodas when he heard a voice that made his ears perk up almost like a puppy's.

Patrice Butler had one of the most distinct voices he'd ever heard. It was deep and raspy, unique in its tenor. Leo had always felt a voice like hers belonged in a jazz club in Harlem instead of Greenbelt. When she laughed, it was so boisterous you could damn near hear it from a mile away. Thea had mentioned that she'd told Miri to bring her mother, in the hope she'd actually show up if she had a support system there.

He'd immediately felt a sting at the news, remembering a time when he was an integral part of her support system. What was he to her now but a memory? The pain of the past made flesh and whole? It made him hate himself even more than he already did. He'd wasted so much. Time and effort and opportunity. These days, all he was was some unwanted ex trying to get back a woman he hadn't deserved in the first place.

He made his way through the crowd, to the doorway of the living room, eyes floating around until he spotted Patrice speaking with one of his great-aunties. He walked toward her slowly, out of apprehension, and because he didn't want to be scolded for interrupting their conversation. The entire time, his eyes swept every inch of the room, looking for Miri's face in the crowd. When he didn't see her, he immediately feared that she'd decided not to come after all.

Standing to the side of Patrice, his arms at his side, he waited. She didn't even acknowledge him until after she ended her conversation. And when she did, her expression was unreadable. The woman had always held a fondness for him, but she'd been against him and Miri getting married so young. She'd never been nasty about it, or even controlling, but she hadn't made a secret of her belief that they were making a mistake. And she hadn't made it a secret at the church that she didn't want him ruining things for Miri now.

Leo didn't know how she'd reacted when Miri had told her that he'd left, but he imagined it involved some form of an "I knew this would happen." And he was not looking forward to confronting that. Her face transformed slowly, into something that was just as difficult to decipher but didn't make him feel nearly as uncomfortable. It certainly wasn't soft, but it was far from the hardness Miri often greeted him with.

"I knew you'd still be here" was the first thing she said.

Leo wanted to smile, or cry, or both. There was something flattering in her words. Like she believed in his integrity, even if it was skewed.

"After our talk in the church I told her that even if you stuck around, she shouldn't take you back," Patrice finished.

Any hope he'd had about her being on his side crashed and burst into flames. He didn't know what to say to her, his mouth held in a state of part openness as he tried to gather himself. He and Patrice hadn't had so much of a talk as they'd had a confrontation. One where, if he were being honest, she'd walked away the victor.

It hadn't deterred him from his plan of winning his wife back, but it had forced him to sit in his own mess, and that was never pleasant.

The woman kept going. "But she's never listened to me when it comes to you." She sighed. "She's in the back with your sister, watching the kids in that bouncy thing."

He swallowed, stunned almost to silence. It was his sister's house and he half expected Ms. Patrice to try to kick him out of it.

"Thank you" were the only words he'd managed to get out in the short exchange. And they felt as pathetic as they sounded. When he turned to walk away, Patrice grabbed his forearm, her weathered hand tightening on his flesh.

"I told you before, and I'll tell you again. You hurt my daughter once, boy." She moved closer to him and spoke the words low and slow. Making sure they were tender enough for him to tear into. "And that's all the chance you get. I don't know if you're after money or ass or something else, but I will hurt you myself before I see you do what you did to her before. I don't care how tough she acts, she loves your behind, maybe she always will. But she's strong enough to keep from losing herself in it now, and so am I. So think twice before you try any shit."

"No shit," Leo said. "I swear. I meant what I said at the church. I'm not here to pull one over on anybody. I just want to show her that I'm different now. That I'm willing to work to deserve her."

"And what makes you so worthy?"

"Nothing. Just the fact that I know I'm not, but I'll die trying to be."

She let him go at that, and he held his breath as he walked away, toward his wife. He stopped dead in his tracks when he entered the kitchen on his way to the back door only to see Miri standing in front of the fridge, a half-frozen water bottle pressed against the back of her neck.

He was sure she could feel it the second he walked in. And while she didn't so much as look up to acknowledge his presence, her shoulders shifted, making her back straighter. Like she was preparing herself. Like she was a predator who'd just sensed some poor prey animal wandering into her territory. Strange thing was, he didn't much mind being prey if Miri was the one taking him between her jaws.

Leo stood with his back to the door, trying to force some semblance of privacy for them. Noise came from in and outside of the house. Kids playing, grown folks laughing, and Bell Biv DeVoe on the speakers. He was squared in on Miri, though, just like he was every time they were in the same room.

"Can we talk?" he asked.

Her shoulders drew backward slowly before she turned to him with a sigh. "Why do I feel like I've had more conversations in the past few weeks than I've had in years? And why has literally every one filled me with more dread than the last?"

Miri was well known for her ability to turn anything into her own brand of clever snarkiness. But this wasn't her fucking around with him. She was expressing real frustration in her own way. Any thought he had of trying to use his nephew's birthday party to hash out some of their issues disappeared in an instant. Her face and shoulders were drawn tight, she was tense. Her eyes were vulnerable, though.

"Hey," he said, keeping his voice low and soft. "Come somewhere with me."

He held his hand out to her, breath stalled in his lungs as he waited to see the results of the chance he'd taken.

"Where?" she asked, hesitant.

"I don't know. Somewhere that's not here, in the middle of all this."

Miri looked back at the open refrigerator. "I'm supposed to be taking more water outside, though."

"Someone else will handle it."

She stared at his outstretched hand for a few more beats and he had to push down the urge to tuck it back at his side. When she reached out and entwined their fingers together, he wasted no time leading her out of the kitchen and through the crowd in the living room. Eyes straight ahead, he ignored every stare or shocked look they garnered. Downstairs was a basement that the owners of the house had half-finished before his sister had moved in. The walls were all drywalled but the floor was still paint-stained concrete. Not the most comforting place Leo could have taken her, but it was better than his nephews' Spider-Man-themed room.

Their laundry room was off to the side of the space, with its own door; it was only big enough to fit the front-loader, dryer, and some kind of wooden folding table. There was even a load of clothes tumbling in the dryer. Probably Ahmir's doing. The man never missed a chance to get some chores done. The room was a little noisy, from the dryer and those general weird-as-hell basement noises. It wasn't bad, though; it kept them from standing in awkward silence.

"What's wrong, Miri?" He felt like a fool, asking her such an obvious, simple question, but he had to start somewhere.

Miri leaned against the front-loader, crossing her ankles, and stared at a spot on the ground. He could see her moving her tongue around in her mouth like she was physically trying to find the right vowels and consonants to create whatever words were in her head.

"I'm an ungrateful asshole," she finally said, blowing out a harsh breath. "I'm sitting here pretty as can be with more money than I can wrap my head around, but instead of being happy about it, I just feel . . . stuck."

Her words came out fast, like she could hardly believe she was saying them—especially to him. Before he could say anything, do anything to even attempt to comfort her, she kept going.

"I've had this same conversation with, like, five people over the past few weeks, and every single time, I wind up just as lost as I was before."

"Maybe you need to stop having the same conversation then." He made sure his tone was firm enough to drown out the sounds of the room.

The small sink faucet dripped into the basin, filling Miri's lack of immediate response with something other than thick silence.

"What?" Finally, she looked up at him.

"Look." Leo crossed his arms over his chest, the sleeves of the thin white T-shirt he wore stretching over his shoulders. "It seems to me like you're doing that thing you always do. Where you pretend to be all tough while still giving way too much of a damn about how people feel about you."

Miri scoffed. "I don't give a fuck about what people think, you know that."

"I didn't say 'think,' Miriam. I said feel. And I ain't talking about random townies or your mama's church friends. You might not care about what they think, but the people you care about? The ones you love and admire? Hell, you care about their feelings more than your own."

"I don't . . . it can't be that." Miri frowned. "All the people I care about, I've provided for. I've made sure they're taken care of. There's no bad blood there. No animosity. Everything's good."

She looked genuinely confused. Like she genuinely didn't understand what he was trying to rap to her.

Leo let out a sigh. "Yeah, but those are the same people who know you better than anyone else. Not just the you who's perfect at your job and funny and too damn beautiful to look at straight on. But the you who's had more shit slung at you than anyone should have to wade through. They know you get real, knock-down, drag-out

sad in the winter. They know you've never allowed yourself to dream as big as your mind will let you. Them
people know you almost as well as I do, and you know,
like we know, that you're not happy. So then you feel guilty
about not being happy, which makes you even more un-
happy. And you resent us for loving you so much that we
can't pretend to feel any different."

He'd pulled her card. And it didn't matter that no one
else was there to see it, Miri was as prideful as any pea-
cock he'd seen. They both were. It was why they fit so
well. And why they'd crashed so hard, too.

Leo was trying to get away from that, though. He'd
thrown every bit of pride he had out the window once
she'd come calling for him. His pride had sent him away
and kept him away. All he wanted to be now was right
here. On top of her, underneath her, at her side. Where
the hell ever, as long as he could reach out his arm and feel
her when he got to feeling anything close to lonely or sad.

She clenched her jaw and puckered her lips and for
a second, Leo thought she was going to cry. Instead, she
grimaced. Mouth wide, teeth gnashed. Like she wanted
to sink her teeth into something and gnaw at it. He'd
always preferred her pissed off than sad. He was ren-
dered useless at her tears. But her red-hot anger? He
had plenty of things she could take that out on.

"I'm not supposed to feel like this," she said, teeth
still gritted. "You remember how happy those people
looked in the Publishers Clearing House commercials?
Like, Ed McMahon would show up at their door with
one of those big checks and tell them they were getting

five thousand dollars for the rest of their lives. All you'd see was them grinning and falling out on the floor in happiness. They'd be thankful. Not thankful and terrified or thankful and full of dread."

Leo shook his head. "That wasn't Ed McMahon," he said.

"What?"

"That wasn't Ed McMahon," he repeated. "That's a . . . a myth or whatever. It wasn't him."

Miri looked confused. "Who was it then?"

He shrugged. "I don't know, some dude. That ain't the point, though. The point is, all that was fake."

"First you're telling me that Ed McMahon wasn't changing the lives of 'everyday Americans,' and now you're telling me none of the money was real?"

"That's not at all what I'm saying, Miri, and you know it. You're just being ornery."

She curled her lip up in response but didn't comment.

"I'm saying, they showed us the fat check, but they didn't show us all the other things that came with it. Hell, that's what this country does." He spread his arms. "Everybody here knows that the more money you have, the better life is for you. You can see doctors when you need to and have your heater on as high as you like, not work yourself to death, you know, the good shit. But that don't mean it erases all the other stuff you've been through. You might have woken up rich one day, but you still went to bed broke and depressed."

"I'm not depressed," she insisted.

"Maybe not. But you are fucked up from growing up

in poverty your entire life. Just like me and damn near eighty percent of the people in this town." Leo shook his head. "You ain't one of the mayor's kids, Miri. You grew up as a little poor Black girl in Greenbelt, South Carolina."

"That ain't how we grew up, though," Miri shot back. "Our folks weren't sitting around lettin' us feel sorry for ourselves all day. They found a way to make sure we lived as well as we could, just like their folks did with them. It's what we've always done."

"I'm not discounting that," Leo said, making his tone softer. "Even after my folks died, my family made sure me and Thea were as good as we could possibly be. But you don't grow up like we did without having a whole lot of baggage too. And that load don't lighten overnight."

She went quiet, and when she tilted her head up, she gave him a look he'd never seen from her before. It was like he'd taught her something, shown her something she'd never even considered before. And wasn't that just the damndest thing.

Miri had been his first kiss, his first lover. There had been a time when, even though he was three months older, he'd felt like he'd only known a fraction of the stuff she did.

And that was part of his problem, wasn't it. That he'd been a fool-headed, shithead boy who hadn't really known how to handle that. He'd had years to accept that about himself, coming to the realization that it wasn't shameful, didn't make him "less than" just because his

204 ⌃ Jodie Slaughter

girl shined so fucking bright. He shouldn't have felt any shame in that. He should have felt lucky.

Still, he found himself glad to have shown her this thing, at the very least. Happy as he was, the last thing he expected was for her to reach out, pull him closer by the back of his neck, and bite down into his bottom lip.

19

MIRI

In a decade, if someone asked Miri to look back on this moment, she'd swear up and down that she'd just been so overcome with emotion that attacking her husband with her teeth had been the only reasonable option.

It would be a lie though, flat out.

The truth was, since he'd come back, she'd spent every second in his presence resisting the urge to rub her pussy against his lips. She was feeling emotional, her defenses were all the way down. And there he was. Standing in front of her with his mouth full of logical conclusions and his thick lips even more inviting as the words passed through them.

She decided then that denying herself the urge to fuck him was ridiculous. What was it doing, really? Her being horny and sad didn't keep his presence from being confusing. It didn't stop her heart from squeezing so tight she thought it might explode through her rib cage. And it sure as hell didn't keep her from wanting to kiss him and kill him at the same time.

Leo was still a pain in her fat ass, forever on her last damn nerve, but when she pulled him in, he came to her like he'd never forgotten how to.

When she bit down into the fat of his bottom lip, she pushed her hips against his. Wide hips guiding her as she grinded, the feeling of his dick fattening under his jeans making her press harder. Her hands gripped his strong biceps. She didn't know what the hell he'd been thinking, stepping out like that in a white tank top that was definitely a size too little. Every time he moved his arms, it lifted a little, showing a sliver of brown skin and hair just above his pants.

She'd been in the middle of having a fucking breakdown a few minutes ago and she'd still managed to notice and lock it away in the back of her brain.

"What are you doing?" Leo asked, as her fingers dug into his warm, heated skin.

She pulled back and smirked as he sucked in a sharp breath. "What does it look like I'm doing?"

"Shit." His voice was ragged. "Knowing you, probably trying to torture me."

Miri had no choice but to laugh. "That's not untrue, but I've got other things on my mind too. Like me on top of this dryer and you on top of me."

Leo pulled his head back some. "Since . . . when?"

"Since now. I'm tired of dancing around this. Let's just . . . do it."

Her eyes were half-closed and her body felt desperate. Heart thumping, pussy throbbing, she waited with slow breaths for him to respond.

When he finally did, there were no words to be heard. Leo reached down and put the backs of her knees over his arms, lifting like she was nothing more than a paper bag of groceries. Her arms went around his neck instinctively, holding on tight even after he sat her on top of the dryer.

She had on a maxi dress made of soft yellow cotton. Perfect for summer breezes and, apparently, feeling the vibrations of a laundry machine massage the bottom of her ass.

She let her hands flow down the skin of his neck, the softness of his shirt, and over his biceps until she got to his hands, resting on her calves.

"It's been so long since I've touched you like this," he said as she guided his hands up her legs. Slowly, so slowly that every inch they covered raised in goosebumps as they passed. "I forgot what you felt like."

Leo's thumbs worked in circles along the backs of her knees, the sweet touch making her ankles roll. "I tried not to," he continued. "Feels like I spent every night for years replaying the last time I touched you. I thought I remembered, but that was nothing compared to this. You feel softer, warmer, more . . . more everything than before."

"I bet it feels like being with someone entirely new." The words were spoken against his cheek. His skin was slightly rough from stubble and his aftershave only succeeded in making her feel even more heady. She felt drunk on him. Had it been like this before? She'd spent so long trying to forget that she found herself struggling to believe she'd ever felt this crazy over him. She must have, though, or she wouldn't have been so thoroughly destroyed when he'd left.

She didn't want to think about that. Him leaving, her hurting. All she wanted to focus on was how calloused his big fingers were and what they'd feel like rubbing her clit to high heaven.

"Nah." He moved his face so that their lips were almost touching. "It don't feel new at all. Feels like coming home to your bed after a long day. All you wanna do is sink into it."

He'd climbed his fingers up further all on his own and Miri had been so caught up that she hadn't noticed until he dug them into the soft fatty tissue of her inner thighs.

The last time they'd had sex, they'd been kids. Of age, yes, but they'd known next to nothing. She'd been with two other people by the time they'd officially gotten together and he'd been with none. She had taken a certain amount of pride in being able to teach him how she liked to be touched, licked, fucked. But even those preferences had been those of someone who, ultimately, hadn't known much.

Now, things were different. She'd been around a few

blocks. Exploring her attraction to all types of people with all different types of sex. She'd had women strap her down within an inch of her life. It was impossible not to be changed after that.

Miri didn't know how many people Leo had been with in his absence or how much he'd explored his sexuality. There was something a little clumsy in his touch. He didn't look nervous, but his hands trembled a little on her thighs. She couldn't shake the feeling that it wasn't just because of her.

It was time for her to take over, take the lead. Provide a firm hand and some guidance.

She took his face between her hands, bringing his attention back to her face. His pupils were blown so wide she figured he must have been looking at her through blurry eyes. Past the lust, past the desire, was a thought about how she had always thought she'd look best with a '70s Donna Summer lens over her life anyway.

But it wasn't the time for that particularly weird ideation.

"Here." She spoke softly, trying not to break the spell they were both under. "I want you to touch me here." She cupped her own pussy in her palm. Spreading her thighs a little more, showing him exactly what she meant.

"Yeah?" Leo's eyes met hers before he focused on her hand.

She pulled the gusset of her panties to the side with two fingers. "See how wet I am for you?"

"I can smell you." His nostrils flared. "I can damn near taste you too."

There was longing in his eyes, want and desperation that was reserved for her. Only her. It made her even hotter.

"Don't worry, baby. You'll have plenty of time to taste. But I want you to touch first. It's been so long since I felt you touch me." Taking a second to toe off her shoes, she lifted the heels of her feet until they were firmly on the edge of the dryer. In this position, she could look down between her thighs and see everything. Her glistening wet flesh, her soft skin, and soon, his talented body.

Leo took initiative, yanking her panties down until they were away from her cunt but still around her thighs. It made her feel bound in some sense. The same way she felt—knew—that she maintained a certain level of control over both of them. Being bound yet in charge; it was too sexy for words.

She clenched when his fingers finally brushed against her lips. He wet himself in her cream, taking his sweet goddamn time as he explored her skin.

Miri whined, trying to move her hips enough that he'd take pity and fill her up with his fingers.

"I need to take my time," he said, eyes firmly on the space between her legs. "Just in case . . . just in case . . . I need to make sure I remember exactly how you felt. How you responded when I touched you. I won't survive it if I start forgetting again."

Her chest hurt from the ache in her heart. Her desperation was palpable, but every word he said resonated with her. She wasn't sure if she'd ever admit it out loud, she could barely admit it to herself. More nights than she could count, spent in the darkness of her bed, fingers deep inside herself, trying to re-create his touch. The frustration when she'd fail, followed by tears.

It was all so damn much. Miri didn't know what they were supposed to do with all this history. It was always there between them, taking up space, reminding them of its presence every time they tried to get close to each other.

She clenched her eyes closed, tight, willing herself to forget about it all. She had wanted to feel him touching her tender spots for years, and here he was, doing it like he'd stepped right out of her fantasies.

When he finally entered her, it was with his thumb. Fat and a little rough, her slick pussy took it with no resistance. He fucked it in and out of her slowly, the sound of her wet clench drowning out the dryer. When he took it out a few thrusts later, Miri whined. But even that was cut off with a sharp gasp when that same thumb met her clit.

"Fuuuuuck." They were echoes of each other.

Achingly wet, his digit slipped and slid over her button in torturous circles. She figured she'd have to tell him how to touch her here, but he hadn't forgotten. As much as had changed about her and her body over the years, this had remained a constant. She liked head-on touches. Pads of fingers rubbing directly on her sensitive clit until she cried and gasped and shouted. It was always slightly painful but never anything less than pure ecstasy.

"I want you to make me come like this," she said. "The first time. Make me come just like this. All on those thick fucking fingers."

"You want them in you?"

"Yes. Two of them. Fuck me fast. I need it. Jesus Christ, I need it."

She didn't have to tell him twice. Keeping his thumb in rhythm on her clit, he slid two fingers into her slowly. His thrusts were maintained with steady wrist movements. Skilled and pleasurable, but far from what she needed.

Miri planted her feet even more firmly. "Leo, look at me."

His head snapped toward her like she'd slapped him. In his gaze, all she saw was openness. It didn't matter how much weight he'd put on or how heavy his work boots were, Leonard Vaughn was a man who craved being commanded by her. Just the same way she enjoyed leading him.

"You want to make me happy, right?"

"More than anything." He sounded downright feral. "You know that."

"Then make me come," she commanded. "Now."

He crooked his fingers up, no doubt searching for her G-spot. He grazed it before he pressed down and Miri felt all the air get sucked out of her windpipe. A flash of pure, deep pleasure. There then gone so quickly she might have imagined it. A harsh, high-pitched noise left her mouth before she could stop it—or beg him to keep going.

Her man was smart, though, for all his faults. When he touched her G-spot again, he did it with intent. Fingers pressing against the spongy insides of her with just enough force to bring tears to her eyes.

She gulped. "I'm . . . I'm . . ." She couldn't manage to get the words out. A warning of what was about to happen if he kept doing exactly what he was doing.

Leo hadn't forgotten, though. "I know, baby. I know." His thumb went round and round and round on her clit as he pressed inside her. Her vision went black. "I can feel it coming. Get me wet, Miri. I want it all over me."

Sirens fired in her brain, sending her heart racing even faster. Even her gasp was suspended as she threw her head back in bliss.

She came with a gush. Her toes curling as she felt it leave her and soak Leo up to his elbows. Her thighs quivered as she fought against the temptation to close them. She didn't want to hide from this pleasure, she wanted to experience every single excruciating bit of it.

"Oh. My. God . . ." Teeth chattering as she came down, she finally opened her eyes to look at him. "I'd forgotten how good you are at that."

Miri would never discount the sheer impact of a good fingering ever again.

Leo didn't seem to care much for the praise. His eyes were glued to her pussy. Dark and flushed and glistening, he stared at it like a starving man.

She wanted to let him eat. Desperately. As wrung out as she felt, she'd normally never turn down a pair of thick lips on her clit. But they didn't have time. There were no windows in the laundry room, which made it impossible to gauge how much time had passed. It felt like they'd been locked away forever and for ten minutes all at once. They weren't alone—not truly. And she had no interest in trying to explain why both of them missed cake and ice cream.

The choice between getting her pussy eaten or getting fucked was an impossible one. But the ache deep, deep inside her needed to be soothed. And that could only be done by his hard dick touching the back of her.

"Next time," she told him. Hands going to work on his belt. "Next time, I'll lay out and spread myself open and let you lick me out until your tongue hurts."

"Even after that," he said.

"But right now, I need you to fuck me. Will you?"

Leo wasted no time pulling himself out of his boxers. His dick was hard and beautiful, wet at the tip and so fucking swollen it looked painful. She licked her lips. Promising herself that she'd get her turn with it sometime soon.

He moved closer, body fully pressed against hers. Both of them groaned at the first brush of his dick against her lips.

"Do you have a condom?" Leo asked.

"No." The admission made her want to cry. "Do you?"

"No."

They stared at each other and Miri was sure he was doing the same thing in his head that she was doing in hers. Trying desperately to justify making a risky decision.

"I haven't been with anyone." Leo didn't offer any qualifiers that signified the passing of time.

"I have," she said. "I get tested regularly and I'm on birth control but . . ."

"But it's still not smart . . ."

"Exactly . . ."

When the tip of him brushed her clit she suddenly remembered that she'd never been particularly risk averse.

"This is so not smart." Blood rushed to her ears.

He gulped. "Not at all. It could . . . we could . . ."

"All kinds of things could happen."

"Right." All on its own, his dick bobbed, making her feel every inch on her most sensitive flesh.

When it settled, it was against her entrance. Not quite pressing into her, she could feel her cream wetting his skin. One push, one movement of her hips and he would be inside her, giving them exactly what they both wanted.

She reached down and took his base in her palm. "I understand if you don't want to," she said.

"I want to." His voice was rough like sandpaper. "I need to."

"So do I."

Her wrist moved, pressing him in. She barely got the very tip of him inside when a loud noise boomed on the basement stairs.

"Shit." She jumped.

They stood still and silent for a moment, trying to decipher what was happening. But when the loud sounds continued it became clear that they were footsteps.

Jumping apart, they rushed to right their clothes. Leo moved quickly to the industrial sink to wash his hands and it was all Miri could do to hop off the dryer and grab a Tide stick, shoving it into his shoulder before the door opened.

Ahmir stood on the other side, his eyes widened, then his brows raised. It was impossible to miss the little smirk that hid behind his beard.

"What are y'all doing?"

"He had a stain," Miri lied, rubbing the Tide stick around on Leo's perfectly white shirt.

"Riiiight," Ahmir chuckled. "And I'm guessing you had to take your drawers off to do that?"

Right there on the floor, in front of the dryer, were Miri's hunter-green lace panties.

"Ugh," she shrieked, snatching them up and crushing them into a ball in her palm. "Mind your business."

She practically ran out of the room, no shame in leaving both men behind.

"I want a new dryer," Ahmir called. "One that won't have my clothes smelling like eau du freak."

20

LEO

Thea had bought a trampoline for the boys, one of those big ones with the nets high up the sides to keep them from falling over the edge when jumping. Leo and Thea had spent the afternoon waiting like children for it to be delivered, then tested the bonds of their already strained relationship trying to put it together.

Three hours and two individual storm-offs later, they were enjoying the fruits of their labor with a celebratory jump. Well, Thea was jumping, Leo was letting her movements rock him as he lay on his back, looking up at that clear sky above him.

"What are your plans for Christmas?" Thea asked him, obvious joy in her slightly out-of-breath voice.

"I don't know yet."

"You don't know yet..." He could feel her mood

sour instantly, so he put a hand over his eyes, shielding them from the sun to look at her directly.

She'd stopped her jumping and was standing there, swaying and bobbing a bit to stay upright. The sun was bright and right above them. He couldn't see her face or any of her features, just the blazing silhouette of her. The sight almost scared him.

"No," he said. "I guess it all depends."

"On what? Miri?" She scoffed.

Leo shrugged.

He could hear her hands slap down against the sides of her legs. That one loud sound the perfect representation of her annoyance. "And if she decides she doesn't want you after all, does that mean we lose you again too?"

"Woah." He sat up, crossing his legs. "Hold on now."

Thea kept going without losing so much as a breath. "And even if she does want you, if she changes her mind again in the future, is that it? Just poof and you're out of my life, my kids' lives?"

"Thea, c'mere." He gestured for her to sit down across from him and, as reluctant as her movements were, she complied. "Where's this coming from?"

She slapped a hand against her thigh again. "Where do you think, Leo? Having you back has been . . . amazing. I feel like we're finally maybe getting back to the place we were in before you left. But I can't stop thinking about how your interest in us feels so dependent on her interest in you."

"How could you say that?"

"How could I not? She's the reason you're back here, she's the reason you're staying, and she's the reason you left."

He sighed, his mind immediately taking him back to the conversation he'd had with Quentin in the diner. The one that had led him to the realization of how he'd been selfish as hell. Neglecting all the people he loved and expecting them to act like he hadn't hurt them.

He was supposed to be doing better by them.

"I'm the reason I left," he told Thea, "that's not on Miri, that was my choice."

"Don't do that." She scowled. "I love that girl, you know that. I just mean . . . whatever your reasons, they were all tied up in her. It felt like you didn't give the rest of us a second thought."

If he was being honest with himself, he hadn't. His mind had been so singularly focused on his relationship with Miri that everything else had been something even farther than an afterthought. He spent so much of his time thinking about the headspace he'd been in at that time, trying to rationalize his thoughts and decisions. Every time he thought he might have an answer for something, he was knocked back on his ass by his own foolishness.

He didn't know how to tell Thea that. How were you supposed to tell your sister that you'd made such a big, life-changing decision and hadn't taken her into account at all.

From the way tears pooled in her eyes, he didn't need to. She already knew.

"I'm not saying you didn't have the right to do what you did, Leo." She sighed. "It's your life, you're the one in charge of it, but damn . . . I was raising a toddler. I didn't have Mama or Daddy or Aunt Roberta. I wanted my brother there but you weren't. It was like you didn't even care about us anymore."

It was tough to find any real stability on the trampoline, but he managed enough to take his older sister in his arms. Her little sobs melted into his shoulder and his heart twisted in his chest.

"I know." He spoke the words softly into the crown of her head. "I'm sorry, I'm so sorry, Thea."

She sniffed and lifted her head, wiping at the tear tracks running down her cheeks. "I'm just saying, I know you left to get away from whatever was going on with Miri, but I never understood why you needed to leave us behind too. You lost her but . . . I lost you both. I grew up right there with y'all, chasing after you, watching y'all act like fools. Leo, I was the second person Miri came to after she got her first period. She was my sister too." Her tears continued, but her tone colored with anger. "At least, with you, I could miss you because you were gone. I got to see Miri at the store all the time, at church, shit, I haven't gotten a full set in years, Leonard. Years. You don't know what kind of torture that is, and none of it was fair on me. All I know is that I cannot handle going through this anymore. It cannot happen again. It just can't."

"It won't." There was pure steel in his voice. "It doesn't matter what happens with Miri, I'm never doing that again. Being here again with you and the kids, it's only reminded me of how much I missed out on. I'm sorry about that."

She didn't comfort him or let him off the hook, but she did nod once. "You've got a long way to come back from, you know."

"I know."

"That means you have to help with birthday parties for like the next ten years and you have to help any time we need anything done around the house."

"And Christmas," he said. "I'll be here, no matter what."

"Promise me." She sniffed, that very specific big-sister bossiness back in her voice.

"I promise," he said.

"No, like when we were little."

"Thea . . ." Leo damn near whined like a kid.

"Eh." She held a finger up. "This is part of your road to recovery."

"Fine," he sighed.

Leo held a hand to his heart, chin high. "I, Leonard Lee Vaughn, do swear to Althea Lee Vaughn that I will be at her house on Christmas morning . . . eating her dry-ass ham."

"Boy!" She flicked him on the ear.

He barked out a laugh as he flinched away from her. "Or else she has permission to give me one big, strong kick in the ass."

She nodded. "Good. I'm holding you to that too, and if you screw me over I'm wearing boots to do it."

"I'd expect nothing less," Leo said.

He held out his hand. Thea took it, squeezing to show dominance, then released it with a firm nod. They settled into a comfortable silence. Then, as if to finalize their little deal, she suggested a bonding activity. "Come jump with me before the boys get home and hog it all."

He stood up, his eyes on his sister, joyous once more even with tears dried on her brown cheeks.

"I love you," he said.

"Shut up," she replied. "I love you more."

21

MIRI

Aja and Walker's house was ridiculously comfortable. It was like every single item in the place had been specifically chosen and placed to make everyone inside feel good. It was all softness and color. They'd purposely chosen a smaller place, and nothing inside made it feel bigger than it was. Miri got the feeling that was the point. Bigger wasn't always better and smaller didn't have to be stifling.

She'd come over with the flimsy excuse of letting them see Ginger. Walker had been trying to convince Aja to let him adopt a puppy for months. Aja was playing hesitant but both Miri and Walker knew that she wanted one just as badly. So Miri had taken to bringing Ginger over every time she visited.

She and Aja sat on the emerald-green couch, backs pressed against plush pillows and a blanket over their lap. Ginger was cuddled up in a little ball on Aja's lap, completely relaxed as the woman ran her fingers through the short fur on her head. It was close to ninety degrees outside but their AC was going strong. Another perk of a sudden windfall of money—not having to depend on a box fan and open windows to keep from melting under the Carolina heat.

Walker was in the kitchen making them lunch. She didn't know what but it smelled good. She could hear some old Patsy Cline song through the door that separated the kitchen from the living room. And damn, she'd never met someone with bigger "my granny raised me" vibes than that man.

Next to her, Aja flipped through options on a streaming service, trying to find something that both of them could be interested in. Miri had come over to chill with her girl, but she'd also come to broach a subject she'd never really considered before. She didn't know how to bring it up, or even how to talk about it. She considered herself a very progressive person, or at least, it was something she was working on every day. Of course she supported therapy, but she'd never seriously considered it for herself. Not even because she was against it. It was more that, well, she'd never thought of her problems as "bad enough" that she needed help.

She'd spent her entire life trying to mimic what her mama did, including finding a way to grin and bear it when shit got tough. Patrice rarely complained, and Miri had come up thinking that was the way to get through things. But between the stuff going on with her money and Leo, and her confusing feelings about it all, she was finding it more and more impossible to just keep moving along like everything was normal.

"Your therapist is a Black woman, right?" The words left her with no finesse and even less subtlety.

"Um . . ." The surprise was written all over Aja's face. "Yes, she's based out of DC."

"And she's, uh . . . helpful?"

Miri knew how to ask for recommendations for braiders and nail techs and T-shirt makers. She knew what to look for there. How to gauge the quality of someone's work and decide if she wanted to give them a try. Therapists . . . she didn't know the first thing about that. Could the help they provided even be quantified in the same way? There was no IG page she could visit to see before-and-after pictures of people in crisis now living perfect lives. That wasn't how mental health worked. But life would be so much easier if it was.

Aja put the remote down and turned to face her, carefully shifting Ginger in her lap. Her friend's sweet face instantly made Miri feel less tense. Aja had eyes like a child, endlessly kind and forever welcoming. This was exactly why Miri had chosen to come to her with this instead of the internet. And yet, here she was, beating around the bush like a fool.

"Dr. Sharp is amazing." Aja's tone was emphatic. "I've had five different therapists and she's the only one who's helped me make actual headway in healing and learning to live with my mental illness instead of trying to 'logic' it away. She's even done a few sessions with both me and Walker."

Miri perked up even more. "You and Walker?"

"Yep. She's a certified couples counselor too. It's not uncommon for both or either of us to shut down sometimes, and she's helped us cut through all the noise in our heads to come back together."

Couples counseling. She hadn't even thought of that. Maybe . . . no, never mind. Miri wasn't part of a couple. Hadn't been in a long time. Just because she and Leo had screwed didn't mean they were back together. Hell, she hadn't even talked to him since the party. She needed to focus on herself.

She brushed right past her own question and Aja's subsequent answer.

"I'm thinking of going to see somebody about . . ." She waved one of her hands around. "Just, everything, I guess."

"That's a great idea. I encourage everybody to seek out therapy if they have the means to. It can be really helpful. Even if you're not in crisis at the moment. Having somebody to go to for help who you don't have to worry about hurting or treading lightly with is life-changing."

"Would you . . . um . . . is it overstepping to ask if I can talk to the lady you see?"

"Not at all," Aja said. "It's not like she'll talk about us with each other. Only thing is, I don't know if she's taking new clients. I'll send her an email, though, and see."

Miri blew out a breath of pure relief. "Thank you.

I've been in here stressing out about what I'd do if you had said no. The only therapist I know in Greenbelt is the lady that works down at the high school. She's been there for about a thousand years and I think she's busy enough as it is."

Aja reached out, giving her shoulder a gentle, comforting rub. "Don't worry. If Dr. Sharp can't take you, I'll help you find someone else who's just as good."

Her words made Miri deflate. But not in a bad way. It was like all the hot air and anxiety that had been filling her body head to toe dissipated so fast she had to lie down, putting her head in her friend's lap. Ginger licked her face, before resettling.

"I love you, Aja," she said. "Like, seriously. I'm so fucking glad I met you."

"Me too." Aja rubbed a warm hand over Miri's forehead and into her hair. "And I'm glad you reached out to me about this. You . . . haven't seemed much like yourself these past few weeks."

Miri closed her eyes. "I know. Probably because I feel like I have no fucking clue who I am anymore."

"Mmmm . . . it's not just the money, is it?"

Miri didn't answer, but she screwed her face up.

"Is it about your husband?"

"Ex."

"Right, ex-husband. Even though you're not divorced."

"I don't need a slip of paper to tell me I'm divorced," Miri said, half serious, half mimicking the tone of countless straight men who'd told women the same thing about marriage so many times over.

They shared a chuckle and Miri hoped Aja would let the discussion fall away with a little grace, but she didn't.

"Leo," Aja said, in that soft voice of hers. "Is this about Leo?"

"Of course it is. It's about Leo and my mama and me and you, Jade and Olivia too. It's about everybody in this town. But, I mean, yeah . . . it's about Leo."

Aja was quiet for what felt like a long time. So long that Miri almost opened her eyes to see if she was still there.

"I don't know if you remember this, but that summer Walker and I met, before we got back together, I was just heartbroken. Like, completely out of it."

"I remember." It had been incredibly difficult watching her new friend fall apart like that. So much so, that even after Aja and Walker had made up, Miri was the last one in Greenbelt to forgive him for hurting Aja. Except, maybe, for the man himself.

"Well, at some point, we were in my old place, and I was crying on your shoulder, and you told me a little bit about your situation." Aja's eyes went even softer somehow. "Not the specifics, just that love hadn't always been kind to you either. You told me that you'd never really been able to let Leo go. You said you loved him. And you told me that the only thing that would help me heal was time."

"I remember." Miri tensed, anticipating the point her friend was trying to make.

"I spent a lot of time thinking about what you said. And it was true . . . for me, in some ways, at least. But

I think . . . I think there's a reason you loved him for so long even after he left. I think there's a reason you still love him now."

Miri opened her mouth to object, but Aja kept going like she was completely blind to the bullshit.

"I don't think you ever really got a chance." Aja pursed her lips, her hands never stopping the calm stroking of her hair. "And now he's back and everything's all confusing and maybe you realize that you could have a chance with him now. I'm not saying it's going to work and that everything will be perfect. Maybe it'll crash and burn. But if you don't figure out what it really is you want out of that relationship, you're going to be right back here in my lap in ten years, telling me how tragic it is that you love him just the same. Either let it succeed or let it fail, girl. But you've got to pick."

Miri finally opened her eyes but they were blurry. She didn't even bother blinking away her tears. She let them fall, and let her friend wipe them away the same way she'd done for her.

"You're the worst," she said, throat watery.

"I love you too." Ginger let out a bark. Aja laughed. "And you."

22

LEO

"What do you think?"

Demetrius stood next to Leo in a pair of old Dickies, Timbs, and a T-shirt, both of them covered in dust and damn near dripping in sweat.

It was almost a hundred degrees outside. That morning, he'd called Demetrius to let him know that it was all right if he and his crew took the day off because of the heat. The brand-new central air had just been installed but a lot of time would still need to be spent outside or with all the windows and doors open.

He'd told him that he wasn't in such a rush to get the floors done that he was willing to risk people's lives. He hadn't been lying, not even a little bit. But he also wasn't in a rush to be done with his project. Not when he could feel his relationship with Miri rebuilding every minute. He was good to languish a little bit for now.

"They look good." Leo crossed his arms. "Reminds me of how they looked when Auntie Roberta was alive. Just . . . shinier or something."

"We tried to keep it as close as possible to the originals. My guys worked hard to salvage all the wood so we could repurpose it. This wood in here." Demetrius squatted down and tapped. "It was taken from some old lumber that they used to help build the church."

Leo squatted down too, running his hands along the smooth, glossy floors. "Aunt Roberta would have loved that."

"Saved you a bit of money and put a little more history into the house."

"I appreciate it, man, for real."

Demetrius brushed a hand over his waves, and if Leo didn't know better he'd almost think the man looked shy.

"We should have the baseboards done by the end of next week and the guys will be coming in to work on the bathrooms too. Have you looked over those fixture guides I gave you?"

He had. Leo had sat at Thea's kitchen table for hours looking at every single brass drawer handle and copper faucet in the thick book, trying to figure out which ones would be best. It had ended up being a monumental waste of time because he knew he wouldn't be satisfied if he didn't get a second opinion on his choices. Miri's opinion specifically.

He'd spent all this time trying to avoid the reason he was fixing up the house. Not just because somewhere, the woman who raised him would be happy about it. But something else too. There was no way in hell the family would put all this work and money into it just to sell it off. Especially not to some old Antebellum-money racists who'd buy it for pennies on the dollar and turn it into some kind of tourist trap for the same kinds of people that had weddings at plantations.

This was theirs. It was the only thing most of the Vaughn family had any real claim to. Even if they hadn't gotten the chance to fix it up, it could fall to rubble, and find its way back into the earth before any of them let it go.

So many thoughts on how he could never let it go and so few on what to do now that he knew he never had to. Thea had her own space, and the rest of the family had either spread out over the years or settled into where they already were. Greenbelt wasn't a place where many people without a lot of money were able to own homes, but it was a place where you could rent the same apartment until you died. That left him.

But this wasn't a house built for one man. All that space, all those rooms, all that yard. It was made for a family. Not necessarily kids, but them too. Aunt Roberta's home was a place of love and it didn't feel right to think of just him occupying it—like some kind of half-living ghost haunting the halls every day and night.

If he was meant to live here, he was meant to live

here with her—with Miri. He'd always been the quiet type, content to hang in the back and enjoy company from afar. She, on the other hand, was always at the center. Shining bright, all personality. And he never got tired of watching her.

The same way she could fill up a room with brightness, she could make a home come alive. And there was nothing more Leo wanted than for her to breathe life into this one.

It didn't matter whether or not his doorknobs were silver or what color the walls in the kitchen were if she wasn't there to make it all fit together.

He couldn't make heads or tails how close he was to making that happen, though. One minute he was inside her, covered in her scent, surrounded by what felt like her love. The next, she wouldn't respond to simple text messages.

Leo wasn't interested in "just" sleeping with her. He never had been. It was part of the reason he hadn't been with anyone else before her or since. Whatever the thing was that existed inside people and allowed them to fuck people without being totally, completely, frustratingly in love with them, he didn't have it. This wasn't something he'd ever shared with Miri. He'd known it for a long time, though; when other boys his age had practically made chasing tail a game, he hadn't even been able to feign interest. It was something that he was relatively comfortable with as a child. But when he was young—even grown but young—it had been one more feature of his personality that he considered a bug. One more thing that reminded him of how different he was, how . . . nontraditional.

He needed to talk to Miri. To put all his shit out on the table and figure out where they could go from there.

He loved her.

More than steaks and Mobb Deep and Greenbelt High School basketball.

He loved her so much that he was trying to build the perfect home for her. One he hoped she would agree to live in with him. He recognized that it was fucking crazy, trying to make his wife love him again with the help of a house older than both of them combined. Especially when she had enough money to buy her own house. One that was bigger and newer and . . . didn't have him in it.

But fuck if he wasn't gonna try. If he had to die hopeless and alone, at least he'd do it with the full knowledge that he hadn't given up without a fight.

"I'll get my answers to you soon," he told Demetrius. "I've got to make sure my choices are the right ones first."

About ten miles outside of Beaufort, Puck's Hardware was one of the oldest Black-owned businesses in the county. They'd managed to outlive Jim Crow, multiple recessions, and the big corporate stores moving into the area.

When he was a boy, before his parents had passed, he'd come here with his father often. Both he and Thea. They'd ride on the bench of Daddy's old pickup, windows down, Otis Redding on the radio. Passing the weeping willows and houses covered in Spanish moss, high on the innocence of a good childhood.

Puck's had a medium-sized copper statue of a Black man out front and sometimes he and Thea would stay outside, trying to climb on the man's head instead of going in with their daddy. Other times they'd join him. Popping the lid on the off-brand pop he bought them to share, trailing behind him while he looked at things they didn't know the purpose of.

As a grown man, any hardware store reminded him a little of his pops. The smell of wood and the high ceilings, it always brought him comfort. But none like Puck's. Whenever he'd snuck into Greenbelt over the years, he'd always make the time to go by there, even if he didn't need to buy so much as a nail.

He had a lot hanging on this trip, though. And the woman walking the aisles with him was at the center of it all.

"I know I'm paying for all this stuff, but I can't understand why I couldn't just give you some cash. I know even less than normal about—" She stopped in her tracks and picked up a tool from a bin, reading the label. "Never mind, I know what pliers are, but still. There's no way I can be of any help here."

"Not true," Leo argued. "I need to pick out all this stuff for the house and I don't trust anybody's opinion but yours."

Miri raised a brow. "Not even Thea's?"

"She's busy. Plus, she has her own place to worry about."

She huffed. "You are so full of shit."

Leo stopped walking right in the middle of the aisle and she followed his lead, both of them turning to face each other. "How am I full of shit?"

"You know what?" She shook her head and rolled her eyes, like he was just the most annoying person on earth. "Never mind. I don't even want to get into it with you right now. What was it you wanted my opinion on?"

"There are a few things, like I said, but we can start with the faucets since we're over this way."

He led them further down the aisle to the two small rows of display sinks they had. "Puck's doesn't have as big a selection of hardware as some of the bigger stores, but what they do have is better all around."

Miri put her hand out, her long, pretty fingers stroking over the bronze brush of a dark-colored faucet. "That's bronze," he told her. "It's beautiful, good on wear, but it'll build up calcium deposits over time if you don't look after it well."

"What about this one?" She moved across the aisle, on to the next.

"Good old stainless steel," he said without even looking at the little sign. "Everybody uses it for a reason. But I think you deserve something a little more sophisticated than that."

"Sophisticated sinks." Miri's bark of laughter made him smile. "What are you thinking, then? A faucet made out of diamond clusters."

"Not quite." He took her by the hand and stepped across the aisle to the last faucet in the line. "These are for a compression faucet," he told her. "Fancy way of saying that you have to tighten down to turn the water off. It's probably the cheapest type of faucet in here but it's reliable, and it feels satisfying to use." He took her hand and put it on the faucet, making their fingers glide over the little round handles.

Her skin was warm and she was standing so close to him that he could smell the oils she used on the soft skin at the base of her neck.

"Quentin would call this vintage." He said the words softly, saying anything in hopes that she would speak so he could hear her voice. "Vintage is, uh . . . hot right now . . . I think."

"That's because it's gorgeous." Miri looked down at their hands with an odd look on her face, but she didn't separate them. "It looks like something Dorothy Dandridge used in *Carmen Jones* or something. Imagine me, like, elegantly turning on my sink and washing my face without getting water all over my pristine nightdress somehow. Real glamorous like."

He didn't have a lick of trouble picturing that in his head. Only, in his view of it, he was right there with her. Watching her while she did her night routine, more content than he'd ever been.

"I think they're classic." He swallowed down the words he wanted to say. "I wouldn't be surprised if the house's original bathrooms had faucets like these."

"Like paying homage to what was there before." Her voice went soft.

"That's exactly why I thought you'd like it."

She nodded her head. "I do. I like it a lot."

"We'll do these then," he said. "In all the bathrooms."

Miri moved away from him, naturally instead of with the shock she tended to get when she realized she'd gotten so physically close to him. "This is more fun than I thought it'd be. What's next?"

Leo couldn't fight off his elated smile. She looked happy, without any reservations. Maybe this was it. Maybe they were finally, finally on the same page.

"Lighting, I think. We're keeping all the ceiling fans, but we need to replace the light shades."

Miri laughed as she fell into step beside him. "I can tell you've been watching hella HGTV."

He grinned. "Ahmir turned me on to *Property Brothers* and I haven't been the same since."

The lighting displays were higher up on the shelves, causing them to crane their necks. "I like that one." He pointed to a set of traditional frosted bell-shaped covers. "They remind me of my granny's house."

Miri turned her nose up. "Which is exactly why I like the one—"

They were cut off by a light laugh, both of them turning their necks almost comically fast to see an older Black woman looking through bulbs.

"Picking out stuff for the house?" she asked when she saw them looking at her.

Leo answered her almost immediately. "Yes."

"Um . . ." Miri's response was more uncertain.

The woman placed a pack of light bulbs into her little basket and smiled over at them. "Reminds me of me and my husband. We couldn't ever agree on anything until I did my magic and made him see my side."

Leo chuckled but he could feel Miri stiffen up next to him. The lady walked off without making more conversation and almost immediately Miri took a large step away from him.

"I cannot believe I'm doing this again." She spoke more to herself than to him. "This is so weird. Why do I keep fucking doing this?"

"Doing what, Miri? We weren't doing anything."

"We were right there in that spot, playing that game that you like to play so much. Perfect little husband. Perfect little wife."

His head spun. "All we were doing was picking out light fixtures. It was innocent."

"Leo, you haven't made an innocent choice concerning me since you got here. And I'm not mad, because it's not like I've done any different, but at least I've tried to be real with you."

"Oh, I've been real with you, you just don't want to accept it."

She took a step back, an affronted look on her face. "What the hell is that supposed to mean?"

"You knew what it was from the second I told you I didn't want to get divorced. Shit, you had to bribe me," Leo scoffed.

"Yeah, and somehow I still haven't gotten said divorce."

"And whose fault is that? I'm sure as hell not the reason the paperwork keeps getting 'turned around.' If you wanted it as much as you say you did, I would have been made to sign those papers before you ever even considered giving me money. You're just as stuck as I am."

He took three steps, meeting her where she stood, taking her hands in his. "That's why I'm just . . . trying to get us to realize it so we can move past it."

Miri swallowed, her jaw flexing dramatically. "What does moving past it even mean at this point?"

"I don't know," he said quietly. "I just know that I need to put it all out there, and I need you to consider it. I'd planned on trying to do this in any place but the fucking lighting displays. Maybe by the paint samples or something instead, but, fuck it. Miri, I love you. I've loved you since before I even knew what that meant and I've never stopped. No matter how many times I've tried. You . . . you're everything. You're funny and smart and fine as all hell. And I don't know if I deserve you or not. I don't know if anybody does. But I do know that I didn't come all the way back here just to let you slip through my fingers."

Leo felt like he was proposing all over again. When he'd done it the first time, his proposal had been filled with promises that he hadn't been able to keep and the kind of declarations that came from a kid who didn't know shit about shit. Truth be told, the only thing he knew now, for certain, was that he didn't know shit—not really—except for the fact that he was hers.

"There ain't a decision I've made about this house that I haven't made without you and me in mind. It's my home, and I realize that. But"—he squeezed her hands— "it can't be mine if it ain't yours too. I don't know how to not be what everybody thinks I should be, but I can try. I swear I can try."

"You brought me here to . . . to what? Pick out light fixtures and wallpaper. Not even because you're hopeless at decorating but because you want me to . . . live with you?" Miri's voice went high-pitched.

"Not just live with me," he said. "Not like roommates."

"Like a couple?" she asked, her voice small. "Like real married people?"

"Yes. Because we are real married people, baby. And I want us to start acting like it."

The balloon inside his chest popped when she dropped his hands. Her expression was clear, all humiliation and anger, and it sent the air flowing out of him. He stood there, deflated, as tears filled her eyes.

"I'm sorry." He tried to apologize, walk it all back. To tell her that he was just fucking around. He was willing to say anything if it meant the look on her face would disappear.

"No." She held a hand up. "It's . . . it's . . . I just. Jesus, Leo. I can't do this. I can't. There's so much happening. Just, it's too much. It's too much . . ."

She turned on her heels and ran, not looking back when he called after her. His stomach lodged itself in his throat and he had to choke it down to keep from throwing up in one of the display toilets. He walked toward the entrance in a daze. He searched for her when he exited, figuring that maybe she just needed some air and space.

Then he sat down on a bench, unhidden by the bright

sun, and waited. He'd wait for her here. The drive back to Greenbelt would be the second-most painful one of his life. But he wouldn't leave her here.

He'd wait for her.

He'd wait.

23

MIRI

It took her forty-five minutes to get a rideshare so far out in the sticks. She sat in the freezing-cold dining room of a Krystal, picking at chili-cheese fries until they practically disintegrated into their cardboard container.

She cried the entire way back. Her head halfway out the window, constantly failing to blink back fat, salty tears.

What the fuck? What had he been thinking?

He might as well have proposed to her all over again. The part that fucked her up the most, terrified her to the core, was that she wanted to say yes. So bad. So fucking bad.

She'd spent weeks living in her run-down childhood home when she didn't technically need to because she couldn't imagine resting her head anywhere else. Not for any length of time, at least. The only other place that didn't feel completely cold and unfamiliar was Aunt Roberta's house. Whether it was covered in old shag carpet like it had been during her childhood or the pristine hardwood that had just been installed, every time she walked through the door she felt calm.

But her feelings didn't mean anything. Her feelings were what led her to this moment. Married but alone, rich but broke in so many ways, completely and totally foolish. Leo's words had moved her and she'd wanted, so damn desperately, to tell him yes.

At first, she'd thought it would be easy to just fall into it. The visions in her head were crystal clear. She could see them brushing their teeth in tandem, right in front of the new bathroom vanity mirrors she'd picked out for them. She could see them having grits and eggs in the kitchen with the back door open, spring breeze filling the room. She could see herself in a house that was hers. And his. Old and comforting. Filled with all kinds of ghosts but still home. It was the only place in the world she thought she might have a chance of loving more than the house she lived in with her mama.

That was a dream, though. Something sweet to fantasize about. A full minute couldn't even go by before she startled herself awake. This was a man who had left her. A man she'd loved and who had claimed to love her but had given up on their relationship without so much as a weigh-in from her. That hurt was still there. Ever-present in her chest, refusing to let her trust Leo completely—or at all, really. Every time she looked at him, she saw the boy she'd loved her entire life turned into the man who'd thoroughly broken her heart with his abandonment.

She didn't know how to overcome that. To her, it seemed like one of those traumas that stuck around forever.

So, she'd done the only thing she could think of. She let all of that anger and spite and sadness well up along with her eyes, until she was nearly choked by the desire to do the same thing he'd done to her.

Run.

She'd left him standing there in the middle of a hardware store with no clue where she'd gone and no clue when or whether she'd be back.

After over an hour in the back seat of a strange car with a man making wary glances at her in the rearview mirror every five seconds, she almost collapsed on the floor when she finally made it home.

Immediately, she closed all the blinds and drew the curtains, throwing herself in her bed, outside clothes and all.

She lay there for hours in the dark, switching back and forth between angst and anger. Crying was the only thing she could do to release the emotions for both. By the time she finally fell asleep, the salty water tracks down her cheeks were making her skin feel tight. She expected to spend a night in bed, soak her pillow in tears, sweat the feelings out of her body with a long night's sleep.

Only, one night turned into two, and before she knew it, she'd gone nearly a week; only leaving her room to use the bathroom.

Another bout of dreamless sleep was snatched away from her with the sudden presence of harsh sun in her eyes. Instinctively, she tried to roll over, facedown into her pillows. A sharp slap to her behind stopped her.

"Uh-uh," her mother's voice said, hard as Miri had ever heard it. "Get up."

"I can't." Miri pouted, her eyes still clenched shut.

"Little girl, I don't care whether you take the son of a gun back or not, but you have got to get up out this bed."

"Don't call him that," Miri mumbled, completely outside of herself. "He's not a son of a gun, he's a bastard."

Patrice swatted her ass again. "Don't cuss."

"I don't want to get up, Mama. I deserve a few more days to sulk."

"You have been in this bed for four days, Miriam. And I'm a single grandmother with no help taking care of her grandbaby now."

Miri stopped, looked over at her mama, and saw Ginger in her arms. Her baby girl, all big eyes and floppy little ears, so damn sweet it made her eyes water. She sat up so her back was to the headboard, reaching her arms out for her mother to hand her the dog. The second Ginger was in her arms, she instantly felt a little better. Thanks to little kisses on her face, and that wagging tail, Miri melted completely.

Her dog had been her only consistent form of comfort and affection. Not for lack of trying when it came to her mama and the girls, but because, sometimes, it felt easier to accept Ginger's love. Her sweet puppy didn't know anything about Leo or her stupid lottery money—all she knew was that her collar was luxurious and Mama always got her the good treats.

There was nothing Ginger loved more than being in somebody's lap. So it was no surprise when she plopped down, let out a little sigh the second a hand sunk into her fur, and finally relinquished attention back to the two women in the room.

Miri reached out a hand to search for her phone, only to look at it and see days of missed notifications and, indeed, a date on her home screen that was far from what she expected to see.

Every joint in her body felt tense from not being used. Her mouth tasted disgusting and she felt even worse. She couldn't remember the last time she'd eaten something or gone to the bathroom.

Her mother sat down on the bed beside her, the same hand she'd used to swat her, stroking her face. "I hate seeing you like this again."

"I know, Mama." Miri clenched her eyes tight until she saw white behind them.

"This is exactly what happened when he left before." Patrice stroked a thumb over her left cheek. "You wouldn't talk to anybody, wouldn't eat, for months. For a minute it felt like you were just going to . . . poof, disappear."

Miri leaned back against the headboard, her face tilted up to the ceiling. "Mama, I really cannot hear an 'I told you so' right now. I just can't."

Patrice stroked a hand down her shin. "It's not an 'I

told you so,' it's an 'I'm worried about you.' You're keeping all this locked up so tight, too tight, like you always do. Hell, just like I always do. And I need you to know . . . that's not going to work. Not if you want to be happy."

She was feeling grumpy. Probably a combination of the lack of food and the situation at large, but she couldn't help but get a little smart.

"Well, I guess it's a good thing I don't know what I want then, huh?" Miri turned her face up like a child, her nails scratching at the warm, soft space behind Ginger's ears, smiling when she heard a little contented rumble.

Patrice chuckled. "Of course you know what you want, girl. You're just being dramatic."

"How?" Miri threw her arms out. "How does everybody else in the world seem to know what I want more than me but can't actually explain to me what that is."

"These damn kids, always need to have everything spelled out for them." Patrice mumbled the words, more into the ether than to Miri. "You want what every other human wants. To feel seen, to feel loved, to feel at home. That's all we want. The only difference is how we manage to catch it when it hits us and what we do when we find it."

"You make it sound so simple."

"I ain't say all that, now. I just said that you're the same as the rest of us."

"That sounds nice and all, but it doesn't change how my husband told me he wanted to be with me the other day and the only thing I could think to do in response was just . . .run off." Miri shook her head back and forth like she couldn't believe her own actions. "Every single thing about this situation, everything about Leo and me, feels like the worst, most humiliating, painful thing on earth. I know I'm being dramatic, but every time I look at him or think about him, all the bad moments start flooding my brain. And it feels like nobody else could possibly understand this pain because nobody else has ever been through it. This pain has to be unique. I have to believe that or else I won't survive it."

Miri's eyes welled up again, and she didn't try to keep the tears from falling. Patrice cupped the crown of her head in her warm mother's hand and brought her face to the space between her neck and shoulder. "You know, sometimes I forget that we're not dealing with any old kind of love when it comes to you and him. We're dealing with first love, and that's a whole different ball game."

"It is?" Miri sniffled.

"Oh yeah. Have I ever told you about mine?"

Miri shook her head and her mother chuckled. It was a low, smoky sound and Miri couldn't tell whether it was full of mirth or sadness. Maybe both.

"Well, her name was Candice—"

That made Miri gasp. "Mama! What? You mean you're . . ."

Patrice rolled her eyes. "Your generation did not invent girls liking girls, you know. Anyway, this was before you were even a suggestion, back when I lived in Orangeburg for a while. We worked at the bank together. She was the security guard, I was a teller. It was all cute at first, we'd do a little bit of flirting, eat our lunch together, stuff like that. But the more time we spent together, the more it became clear to me that I loved her. And not like a friend. I'd never loved anybody like that before, let alone a woman, and I didn't know what the hell to do about it."

Miri looked up to see Patrice's eyes covered in a misty, faraway haze. "What happened?" she asked softly.

"Well, one day, she and I were back at my apartment. I'd made us dinner and we were going to go see a movie, and I remember seeing her sitting at my kitchen table and all I could think was 'Damn, if she don't look like she belongs right there.' So I kissed her. Then and there, that was the start of it."

Her mother had never talked much about her past loves. All Miri really knew of her father was that Patrice only knew his first name. A one-night stand with a wandering man, a broken condom, and a daughter that looked like someone whose face she could hardly remember. Miri was on the edge of her proverbial seat. "How long were y'all together?"

"Not long." A small, tender smile played across Patrice's lips. "A little over a year. We even moved in together a few weeks after I kissed her. It was the best time of my life until I had you. In the end, it fell apart because we wanted different things. She wanted to settle down and move up north and start a family. I just wanted to . . . Well I don't know, I wanted to do the same thing we'd been doing. So she ended up leaving. She moved to New Jersey and met somebody and got what she wanted."

"But you still love her." It wasn't a question.

"I think about her every day. What could have been,

what was. But then I remember how my choices got me you, and I wouldn't give you up for anything. Like I said, she was my first love. That's special. And even when it ends, it stays with you."

"I get it," Miri said. "I do. But I don't see you completely unable to function because of it."

Patrice sighed. "I've had thirty-some years to come to terms with what happened between me and Retta. You haven't. And while I still love her, probably always will, I ain't *in* love with her. Not anymore."

"I'm not in love with Leo." Miri's eyes were on her comforter. She never could lie to her mother straight-faced.

"He sure wouldn't have the power to make you feel all this if you weren't."

Miri huffed and threw herself down to lie on her side. Ginger gave a startled bark. "Shhh, baby girl, I'm sorry." She scratched her behind the ears, and finally, she looked at Patrice. "Mama, I don't know how to turn it off. When he was gone I could just . . . push it down, pretend like it wasn't there. But ever since he came back, it won't go away. I wish it would. I wish I'd never brought him back here. I wish I'd never won the stupid lottery. I wish everything would go back to the way it was a couple months ago."

"Is that what you really want?"

Miri didn't say anything. Because, well, she didn't know. Every day that passed, the antsy energy under her skin seemed to get more and more uncomfortable. She had the number of Aja's therapist on her phone with the assurance that the woman would be accepting her call. She hadn't managed to make the call yet, though. She told herself it was because she was busy with work and Leo and . . .

The truth was, she was scared. Not only would going to therapy force her to confront all the things she'd been actively repressing. But she'd have to do the work to fix her own shit too. And that was terrifying all on its own.

If she didn't, though, it wouldn't be long until she was right back to where she was now. Wallowing over her own life, actively making herself miserable.

All this time she'd spent praising herself for being a Fully Grown Bad Bitch when what she really was, was a coward.

She couldn't keep this up, didn't want to. So, if that meant looking at a stranger through her computer screen and telling her all the dirty details of her life, she'd just have to get the fuck over it. Because she was sick and tired of the other option—the easy one.

"No," she told her mother. "It's not."

24

MIRI

There was water damage on the ceiling in the kitchen. It wasn't directly surrounding the lighting fixture in the center, but it was right next to it. The drywall in the ceiling was stained a rusted brown and it bulged some in the middle where it was clearly filled with water. The second she saw it, her first thought was to call the landlord. Something she absolutely hated her and her mama having to do.

Every time something went wrong in the house, Miri and Patrice tried to take it upon themselves to see if they could fix it first. Not because they wanted to, but because their landlord, Mr. Simmons, was a crotchety old bastard who acted like they were asking for the world by requesting that he do the things he'd signed up for by becoming a landlord.

Sometimes, though, the issues were too big to handle with their small but well-equipped toolbox.

Miri imagined calling Mr. Simmons. How it would take no less than three separate calls to finally get through to him. She could imagine him on the other line, his pale face, completely unused to working in the sun, turned up in annoyance as he sighed and told her that he'd get around to it. It'd probably be a month before a contractor stopped by and by then, the damage would, no doubt, have gotten worse.

She needed to leave.

Pay Mr. Simmons the change it would take to break their lease and take her ass somewhere else. This shit was getting old. She'd spent the past couple months—hell, maybe even the past few years—completely moving in fear. Every decision she'd made seemed like it was in reaction to something else.

How many times had she heard Leo call himself a coward since he'd been back? Almost too many to count, but she was beginning to think she had just as much right to call herself the same.

She'd had all the time in the world to think about her place in life over the past week. To reassess her beliefs and decisions, racking her brain, trying to sift through all the muck to get to what she really wanted.

Ultimately, all she knew was that she was sick and tired of being sick and tired. Whether it was self-induced or not, she was so over it. This house, the forced indecision about Leo, she deserved better than what she'd been allowing herself to have.

It felt like everything she'd ever wanted was within her reach now—she just had to figure out how to have the strength to reach out and grab it all.

A loud, hurried knock on her door drew her attention away from the stained watermark on the ceiling, startling her instantly. Her lips turned down and she flung the door open without looking out of the peephole.

"Why are you knocking on my door like the cops?" she asked the second she laid eyes on Thea.

"I'm heavy-handed." The other woman shoved past her into the house, toeing her shoes off and plopping down on the couch without so much as a hello.

"Um . . ." Miri stood next to her awkwardly. "Why are you here?"

Thea hadn't been to this house since before Leo had left.

"I bought something for Ginger," she said, pulling a little toy out of her purse, squeezing and making it squeak twice.

They laughed as the sound of Ginger's little paws hit the floor when she immediately ran from her bed in Miri's room to find the source of the sound. The little dog wasted no time jumping into Thea's lap and grabbing the toy.

"Oh wow," Miri said dryly as Ginger went to town on the toy, filling the room with what was possibly the worst sound in existence. "Thank you so much."

Thea grinned. "Me and the boys were in Walmart and Jacobi picked that thing up and kept squeezing it in

Jamir's face until his brother just about bit his head off. I figured it might be cute to torture you with."

Ginger jumped off Thea's lap, plopping herself on the ground next to Miri's feet, and continued squeaking. "Well, look at her, I can't take it away from her either."

Thea cackled. "You better not!"

"If you think I'm buying that shit about you coming all the way over here just to give my dog a toy, you are out of your rabbit-ass mind."

"You aren't that far from me."

Miri raised an eyebrow. "Not close enough for all this, though."

"Jesus Christ, girl. I can't get you nice and loose before I come in with the heat?" Thea threw her arms in the air in exasperation.

"Why would you say it like that?! You are so disgusting."

"Disgusting like you and my brother bumping uglies in my laundry room?"

Miri's mouth gaped, a low, choking sound coming from somewhere in the back of her throat. "We . . . we . . ."

"See, unlike y'all two, me and my husband don't have any secrets. He told me how he caught y'all half-naked and sweatin' like my ass in church at the birthday party."

There was no stopping the grimace that overtook Miri's face. She felt guilty as hell, like a fucking degenerate. Was there any coming back from this? If Thea had come to her house today to knock her block off for almost sleeping with her little brother on her damn washing machine, Miri would have to let her get her licks in.

Luckily, it seemed like Thea found it funnier than she did. "Chill, girl. It ain't nothing I haven't done myself. I had Ahmir clean it after so it's all good. Plus, this is nothing compared to you and Leo hunching all over Auntie Roberta's house."

"We were not hunching!" Miri lied boldly out of instinct.

Thea rolled her eyes with a scoff. "Yeah, all right, and I wasn't practically tiptoeing around that place trying my level best not to walk in on y'all."

"We . . ." Miri sighed. "We thought we were being careful."

"As careful as a cat in a henhouse, sure."

They really had been sure. She and Leo had spent what felt like hours mapping out perfect places to have sex. Times when the guardians were away, when they actually had somewhere to themselves, or when they'd have to sneak around and find outside locations. At the time, Miri had felt a certain amount of pride in the fact that she'd outsmarted so many people with her A1 sexual knowledge.

She'd been a fool. Even if a hilarious one at times.

"Well, I'm sorry you had to be reminded of that," she told Thea.

"I'm not saying I'm jumping for joy that I have to kinda bear witness to it, but . . . I'd be lying if I said it wasn't nice to see you two back together."

Miri shook her head. "You know we are not back to-gether, Thea."

"Yeah." The other woman's eyebrows drew in. "Which is something I really can't understand."

"Do you know that he might as well have proposed to me a few days ago?"

"He told me what happened."

Miri couldn't contain the shock on her face. "And you condone it?"

"I don't condone him doing it at a freaking hardware store, but you know how Leo can be," she said, shaking her head. "Focusing too much on the bigger picture that he don't see the details."

"I—" Miri didn't know what to say. It was like her mind had been wiped clean. "I don't want to talk about Leo with you right now."

She knew it sounded ridiculous. She'd spent so long avoiding talking about him when what she'd probably needed most was to talk through all the bullshit. Opening up to anyone about almost anything had always been difficult for her, and when Leo was added to the mix, she got even worse. She felt so . . . protective of the feelings she had for him. Both the good and the bad.

Miri had spent the past couple months talking to people about Leo and their relationship. No matter how reluctant and stubborn she'd been, she had done it.

But what she was feeling now? All the deep hurt and long-awaited elation that swirled around in her belly every time she so much as thought his name, that, she needed to figure out on her own. She wasn't confident that anyone else could truly understand this. Not because they didn't have the capacity to feel it, but because she had no clue how to articulate it.

She was the one that needed to make a decision about what to do next. And she needed to do it only under her own influence.

Thea raised her hands again, this time, in a calm, defensive gesture. "That's fair. That's your right. I'd rather talk about us anyway."

Miri breathed out heavy, thankful that she hadn't been forced to argue her issue. "What do you mean 'us'? Is there an us?"

"There used to be."

Finally, Miri plopped down on the couch, the wind knocked out of her.

"Look." Thea made her "I mean business" face. "I know I'm older than you and I have kids and a husband so I can't run these streets with you all the time, but I miss you, damnit."

"I miss you too, Thea, you know I do."

"Do I?" Thea's jaw clenched.

Miri scooted closer to her sister-in-law, taking her hands. "You're the only sister I've ever had, Thea. You taught me everything growing up, you looked out for me, I idolized you."

"So why did I have to lose you when I lost him? If I was so important." Thea's words were wet and choked and Miri forced herself to keep her eyes on the other woman's face.

The question made Miri want to puke and the answer

didn't do her much better. "Because you were a reminder of him. I didn't know how to be around you without thinking about him."

Thea scoffed. "We had our own thing, though. A relationship that didn't involve him at all. I feel like you didn't even give me a chance to show you that I loved you, with or without Leo around."

"Thea." Miri squeezed her fingers around her sister-in-law's hands, trying to command all of her attention and convey her love for her at the same time. "I love you. But you don't know what it was like for me. Everyone said we were making a mistake by getting married so young and then we went and proved them right. He didn't have to deal with the fallout, I did. All the stares and laughs and people telling me how they knew all along it wouldn't work." Miri tried to shake her tears away. "I was too afraid if I talked to you, I'd have to hear that from you too. Or even worse . . . that you'd take his side."

She watched as Thea's eyes softened, not so much anger resting in them, but deep sadness. "Oh, Miri . . ."

"He's your brother." Her words were choked. "He's your blood, not me. As close as we were, I know that family comes first. I didn't want to give you a chance to have to choose, because I knew it'd be him, and I couldn't handle you rejecting me too."

Thea jumped forward, wrapping Miri up in her arms until Miri's head was on her chest. The older woman smelled like Marc Jacobs perfume and shea butter and all Miri wanted to do was sink into it—so she did.

"There would have been no choice to make." Thea's

words were soft. "I wouldn't have allowed there to be. Blood doesn't mean anything when it comes to family. You're as much my sibling as he is. Always have been, always will be."

Miri looked up at her with wild eyes, suddenly feeling very childlike. "Really?"

Thea gave a wet but genuine laugh. "Yes. You're my sister. Whether my goofy brother is around or not. Which means that if you ever think you're going to shut me out again, I'm beating your ass."

"That sounds fair to me," Miri said, hugging her closer. "I've missed you so much. So much has happened."

"Girl, you're telling me." Thea squeezed her back. "I had my first threesome and couldn't even call to tell you."

That made Miri sit up. "Shut the fuck up."

"Hand to God . . ."

"With Ahmir?"

"Of course."

Miri's eyes widened, the tears drying on her face completely forgotten in favor of getting tea.

"Did you like it?" she asked.

"The only way I'll tell you about it is if you promise to get together with me at least a couple times a month. I don't want to sit up here and do all this crying and carrying on just for us to go back to the way things were."

Miri nodded. "We can have a standing date. One where we don't talk about your brother at all, because all I want to hear about is how you're a swinger now!"

"I didn't say it was all that." Thea rolled her eyes. "At least not yet."

Miri squealed, throwing herself out of Thea's arms and back onto the couch. "I can't believe I missed all this. I'm the worst."

"I won't disagree with you. But just like I told him"—Thea didn't need to clarify who "him" was, they both knew—"you're going to do better or I'm beating asses this time."

Aside from her mama, Thea might have been the only person on the planet who could make Miri back down from a fight in fear. "I've learned my lesson, I promise."

Thea smiled at her, all hesitation gone. "So should I start with the fact that we met the dude at church or . . ."

Four eardrums nearly found themselves burst with the sound of Miri's scream.

25

LEO

"**Uncle** Lee, you're not leaving again, are you?" Jamir, his older nephew, sat next to him on the floor in Thea's living room, drawing on some kind of big white sketch pad. "Me and Cobi like it when you're here. You were never here before."

Leo rubbed a hand over the top of the boy's head, feeling the soft coils. The words were innocent, but they caused guilt to well up in his stomach. It had been two weeks since Miri had run out on him, and outside of making sure she'd managed to get home safe by checking in with Ms. Patrice, he hadn't reached out to her.

He couldn't bring himself to. And not because he didn't want to, either. He did. So badly he damn near had to leave his phone off at all times to keep from dialing her number.

He'd sat on that bench outside Puck's for three hours. The first hour, he'd promised himself that he would wait until she came back. But by the time the second had rolled around, he'd realized that she wasn't going to. He hadn't gotten angry until the third. But he'd driven home heated, and guilty about it. How could he possibly be mad at her for leaving him when he'd done the same to her? Then again, he hadn't left her in public, terrified about his safety. Had he?

His mind was awash with thoughts and feelings and decisions. He hadn't known what to do, so he'd pushed himself into working on the house. His focus had been single-minded and he and the rest of the contractors had practically finished all of the big projects. The only things left to do were the more aesthetic options. Backsplashes and paint colors, all the things that made a building of wood and insulation a home.

Leo still hadn't found it in himself to make those choices. And since Miri obviously wasn't interested, maybe he'd enlist one of his cousins to help.

Everything felt like it was up in the air, seconds away from falling and crashing into him. His marriage, the house, all of it. He found it crazy, though, that even with all that, he hadn't thought about leaving Greenbelt.

When he'd driven back into town that first time, he'd had clear intentions of booking it if Miri didn't want to take him back. Now, he'd connected with a sister he'd missed, a brother-in-law who was cool as hell, and two nephews he hadn't really been able to see grow up. And his baby niece, well, she didn't say much yet, but it was nice to be there for her all the same.

There was no way he could go back to seeing them for a few days once every year. This was his family. And as much as he'd avoided it, Greenbelt was his home.

But it was still small, and the thought of being there while Miri remained was painful. Could he continue seeing her at church or at the store, knowing that he loved her, knowing that he'd fucked it up, and still manage to survive? He didn't have a lot of faith. But he would try.

He'd been a coward before. A child. He hadn't known the first thing about making decisions and being a good partner. And it wasn't like he was all-knowing now either. But at least he knew enough to admit when he was dead wrong.

Whether they'd ended up staying together or not, he shouldn't have left her the way he did. He shouldn't have left his family behind either. He wasn't going to do it again. This time, he was going to stand in his shit, even if it meant being miserable.

"No," he told his nephew. "I'll be here for a long time."

"Until I'm old, like you?" Jamir asked, his eyes so, so young.

"Yeah. And when you're old like me, you're going to be the one taking care of me. Making my lunch and making sure I take a bath every day."

Jamir turned his little nose up, thinking. "That's okay then, you can go back to where you were before."

Leo's laugh was a loud, barking thing that made him jump but didn't faze Jamir, who immediately went right back to coloring.

Hell nah, he wasn't giving this up again.

Not for anything.

That night, Thea, Ahmir, and the kids went to Ahmir's parents' for a family get-together. He'd been invited but had decided that he'd rather have some time to himself in the house. Which essentially meant that he'd watched football until it pissed him off, made some chicken wings, and gotten a little too comfortable free-balling in his basketball shorts.

He damn near fell off the couch and onto his ass when the doorbell rang. People didn't just go around ringing folks' doorbells these days, let alone so late in the evening. Even the nosiest neighbors gave it a rest when the sun went down.

Through the peephole, he could see her. Illuminated under the lightly flickering lamp on the porch, Miri stood in front of the door. Hands wringing, face unreadable. Leo didn't open the door right away. He stood there silently, staring at her through the tiny fish-eye lens.

He was surprised, and part of him wanted to make her sweat a little bit. But he wasn't that much of a changed man, not when it came to Miri. So he unlocked the door, taking a long, deep breath as he pulled it open.

In the yard, the crickets chirped. In the distance, a dog barked incessantly. But on the porch, the loudest sound was their silence. His hands went into the pockets of his shorts, then tucked beneath his arms as he crossed them. Back and forth with his inability to stand still in the face of the buzzing, anxious energy between them.

"I don't know what to say." Miri spoke her words into the night.

"So why'd you come?" Leo was deep in his feelings and couldn't help but make a dig.

"I came to . . . apologize . . . or explain myself. Shit, I don't know. I'm mad at you, but I feel guilty about what I did too."

That shut him up. Because he understood exactly what she was feeling, but multiplied by about a million. He still considered his actions to be, by far, the worst of the two. But his hurt wasn't soothed by logic.

"I shouldn't have left you there like that," she said. "And I'm sorry."

Miri wouldn't even look at him really. Every time their eyes managed to meet, she jerked hers away instantly.

"You're sorry that you left or you're sorry for how you left?"

She huffed. "That's unfair."

Leo's arms crossed again. "You know what, at this point, it's not going to change anything, is it? So what does it even matter?"

"Now you're being ornery."

"Yeah, Miri, I'm being ornery. Maybe because I put all my shit on the table, and instead of letting me down like a grown person, you ran off. Had me thinking your ass was somewhere hurt or dead in a ditch. All when you could have just told me, 'No, Leo, I do not want to be with you.'"

"I'm sure that sounds familiar," she snapped. "Sounds an awful lot like what you did to me. Only you didn't leave me for a couple weeks, you left me for eight mother-fucking years."

"Yeah, and I was wrong for that. I've got no problem acknowledging that. That don't make what you did any less bad though."

"And I'm not saying it does. But surely, you under-stand the position I was in," Miri huffed. "How else was I supposed to respond? It wasn't exactly something that calls for a yes or no answer, not when it comes to us."

"I wasn't looking for a yes or no."

"Yes, you were, Leo." Her teeth were damn near bared. "And don't lie to me. Yes. You. Were. I just don't under-stand how you can come back here and think that every-thing can be fixed because we spent two months together. Two months, mind you, that I could barely stand to look at you. I don't know what this is, but it ain't that."

"You're sitting here acting like I asked you to sign your life over to me." Leo shook his head. "I told you what I wanted for our future, not what I'm demanding from you now."

"I don't understand how you can focus on the future so easily when the past isn't even really in the past." Miri's voice went up a notch.

"Is it ever?" Leo sat down on the porch steps, sud-denly bone-tired. But Miri kept standing. "Is the past ever actually gone or does it follow us around forever? Every decision we make is based off of what happened then. Every little thing you feel about me isn't bad. The parts that still make you smile and put up with me. The part that couldn't wait to have me inside you again. Those are built off the past too."

Miri let out a sigh. "I'm not denyin' that there are good things in our past, I'm just sayin', they can't outweigh the bad things. Not for me."

"And I'm askin' why not."

"Because, Leo." Her tone was fierce. "You married me, then you left me. I was twenty-four years old, naive as all hell, feeling like absolute shit because I thought I'd run my husband off. At first, all that was there was just . . . sadness. I was devastated. I thought I was too weird, not even close to what a 'good southern wife' should have been. I'm bisexual and we ate McDonald's more than I ever cooked for you. I hated cleaning, I never wanted to go to church. I knew more about sex than you. I felt like a freak. By the time I got enough sense to build some confidence, I replaced all that sadness with anger—or I tried to, at least. And even if I'm not angry at you right this minute, all I can think about is feeling inferior and promising myself I'd never let myself get there again. It's like I built up a defense against you."

Leo felt sick, his stomach roiled with nausea. Hearing what his actions had caused in her made him physically ill. So much of his time had been spent thinking that her pain over his leaving had been mostly about . . . well, her missing him, and less about how his actions had exacerbated anxieties that were already there. Maybe he'd done it to keep from imagining that she was in the same type of pain he was in.

"You know what, we're more alike than we ever thought." He released a bitter laugh. "I left because I felt like I was failing you as a husband. My whole life, I was taught that a husband provides—he provides above anything else. Up early, two jobs, making sure shit was straight. When I married you, I thought that if I provided for you and loved you, we'd be all right. But I couldn't ever do that. Nothing was ever enough. Two jobs, barely enough sleep, you still had to work, and we still didn't have enough. The husband I was didn't feel like the husband I was supposed to be, the one I thought you deserved. I figured you'd be better without me than you were with me. So I split."

"I wanted to work," Miri stressed.

He shot her a look and she released the only laugh they'd had that evening.

"Well, I didn't *want* to work, because who does. But, I never had any problem with both of us working to keep ourselves afloat. That's what life is, Leo. We're from Greenbelt, how many housewives do you know?"

"None," he admitted. "But that was always the goal, to be able to have it like that. I wanted to set us up so you could work because you wanted to, not because you had to."

"That's honorable, it is. But . . . what made you think I would ever want to depend on you for money? Or any man, for that matter?"

His head snapped up. "That's what marriage is, depending on your person for stuff."

"Sure." Miri's eyes softened. "But that means all kinds of stuff, not just money. It's up to every person in the relationship to figure out how that kind of stuff works for them. There isn't one set way to be married or to be in a relationship in general. We're all too complicated for that to work."

"I'm not ever going to be the type of husband who works constantly and never sees his family. The big-piece-of-chicken type of dude, that ain't me." The words were said more to himself than they were to her. It was an admittance, a confession. "I'm the type of dude who wants to start a garden. I want to plant tomatoes and peppers and sit on the porch with my woman while we watch them grow."

"I'm not the type of wife to greet you at the door with a roast or pretend like I'm ashamed of my ho phase. I want you, Leo. Mad as you are, you know I do. I wouldn't be here if I didn't. And"—Miri gave a raspy laugh—"I hate tomatoes, but I want to watch the ones you plant grow too. But I can't do that if we're going to keep hurting each other. We're too grown not to realize that we don't have to pretend to be things we aren't."

"A husband who doesn't provide, a wife who doesn't nurture." He laughed. "Our grandparents are rolling in their graves."

"My granny definitely had a whole-ass boyfriend and my grandfather did not seem to care at all, so, I'm willing to bet none of them were as into that traditional heteronormative bullshit as we thought."

She took a few steps forward until her toes touched the bottom of the stairs. Leo stood up, meeting her at the bottom. "Fuck traditional," he said.

"Traditional is miserable." She brought her lips to his and everything in his body loosened.

For the first time in years, he felt complete, content.

He could have sworn he heard the crickets start singing louder for them.

26

MIRI

She felt like there was a live wire under her skin. It wasn't crawling, creepy and itchy, nerve racking enough to make her want to scream. It just made her feel restless, unable to sit still in the passenger seat of Leo's car as he drove.

Their reconciliation, if that's what it had been, hadn't been followed by them jumping into bed together, then running off to Vegas to renew their vows. Instead, they'd made out a little and cried a little more, before Leo had sent her off home, stating that he had something to do before they could "finish up."

That had been nearly two weeks ago. She'd only seen him a couple times since then, but he'd called her every day. And they'd talked, a lot, just like they had when they'd been kids attached to the other end of corded house phones with their feet kicked up in their beds.

This morning he'd come knocking on her mama's door like gangbusters, waking her up out of her sleep and dragging her out of the house with her bonnet still on. It wasn't hard to figure out where he was taking her once they got on the road, which was why she didn't really understand the dramatics.

She could see the differences in Auntie Roberta's house from a block away. The exterior had been re-painted to match the same shade of white it must have been when it was originally built. The new windows had black frames, creating a stark contrast that modernized the entire home.

"Did you add on to the front porch?"

Leo grinned over at her. "You like it? We had plenty of wood left over from the floor and I . . . I know . . ." He sighed, then cursed under his breath. "Fuck it, I put it in because I know I've just always wanted a big porch."

The new driveway wasn't paved yet, so the car shook a bit as they pulled up the gravel.

She stayed silent as he turned off the car, got out, and came around to open her door for her. When he took her hand to help her out of her seat, he didn't let go.

"It's got enough room for one of those porch swings over there." He pointed to the right, where the porch now stretched the entire length of the house. "A wooden awning is going in next, so we can sit out here in the rain."

· Miri stopped at the bottom of the steps. "I'm hearing a lot of 'we' here."

"Yeah." He nodded his head. "I meant what I said at the hardware store. I want the same thing I've wanted all along."

"Which is what again?" she asked, voice shaky. "I feel like my brain never really registered what that was."

"You. Me. Together. In this house."

"In this house?" Miri craned her neck to look at the home in front of them. It was beautiful, maybe more beautiful than any other home she'd ever seen.

She had memories here too, almost as many as she had in the little house she and her mama had shared. The big yard she'd run around countless times, the front door she'd stood in front of, waiting for Leo to be allowed outside. It didn't feel strange and soulless. It felt familiar, comforting.

"In this house," Leo clarified. "I don't know if anywhere else in the world could be more perfect for us than this place."

"And you want to live in it with me?"

"You know I do."

Miri swallowed, her mind immediately wandering back to the thick stack of divorce papers sitting on her dining room table at home. Page after page of hard-to-understand legalese, all culminating in a few signatures that would mean the ultimate end of them.

She'd looked through that stack of papers more times than she could count. Convincing herself that she was so sure of what she wanted. Pretending like her hesitation in signing them had nothing to do with still loving the man in front of her. Desperately, ridiculously.

She thought she'd gotten over the dreams she'd once had for them. The happy, loving marriage, the comfortable home, the security of it all. When he'd left, it had taken her a long time—years—to come to terms with the fact that the only life she'd seen for herself was a complete impossibility.

Now here she was, standing next to the man she'd always wanted, in front of a home more beautiful than she could ever dream up, and she couldn't quite wrap her head around it all.

"I'm going to be honest, Leo. I don't know what that means for us. Are we supposed to stay married? Are we supposed to just . . . pick up where we left off? Because if so, then the answer is no. It's got to be."

"There's no picking up where we left off," he told her. "We were kids then, too young and ignorant to be in a serious relationship, let alone married." He moved to stand in front of her, one of his hands going to the side of her face, his rough thumb stroking her cheekbone. "I want us. But I want us as the people we are now, not those kids."

"Those kids are still in us, though, Leo. That's the problem. Who's to say they're not still the ones making decisions for us."

"They are, kind of." He shrugged. "Me and you have always wanted each other. I don't care if it sounds corny, but I had to leave pieces of myself back here when I left.

There was no way I would have survived so long without you otherwise. Every part of me that was interested in anything even remotely romantic or sexual . . . I left here with you, where they belong."

Miri's brows furrowed. "What do you mean?"

"I mean . . ." He paused, closing his eyes briefly, a pained look appearing on his handsome face. "I mean, I haven't been with anybody since you, anybody but you. Not in any way. Not dates or sex. Hell, I've barely so much as looked at another woman."

"You're lying." Miri shook her head, unable to believe what he was telling her.

That couldn't be true. He had to be telling stories. Had to be.

Leo shook his head. "I'm not saying I didn't think about trying every once in a while when I got real lonely, but goddamn, woman, you're the only one I want. You're the only one I've ever wanted. Nothing compares to what we had, not even fantasies."

Something felt like it'd caught in her throat. Her eyes stung and she had to take a step back, separate herself from him so she could at least try to get ahold of her thoughts.

"That is not my experience," she said. "I've spent all this time trying to find a way around my loneliness, trying to find pleasure, trying to have good sex. I've probably fucked half the eligible people in this town one time or another, and I won't apologize for it."

"I'd never ask you to because I don't care," he chuckled. "We dealt with our shit in different ways and I'd never begrudge you for how you decided to have your fun. I just wanted to let you know that for me, it's always been you. Only you."

Miri felt like she was choking on smoke, her lungs heavy behind her rib cage. Her body was hot too, and not because of the heat. Every fiber of her being wanted to run into his arms, sink into the possibilities. She needed to keep her head on straight so she could make a decision that wouldn't fracture them even further.

She needed to think about herself, sure. But Leo had always been the softer of the two of them. Sweeter and more sensitive, he was following his feelings—just like he always did. And even more than she didn't want to see herself get hurt again, she knew she couldn't handle seeing him hurt even more.

"If we do this." She held up a finger as she saw the smile spread across his face. "If. We have to see a therapist. Together and separately, honestly."

He swallowed, suddenly looking more nervous than she'd seen him look in a long time. "Okay. I can do that."

"And we need to take things slow. We can't just fall back into being a perfectly happy married couple. You need to court me again."

"I'm going to do more than that," he said. "I'm going to make you love me again."

"I never stopped," she said without thinking. She didn't find herself regretting the admission either.

"What about the divorce?"

"Fuck the divorce."

She stepped closer to him, taking his face in between

her hands, long nails clutching his cheeks. "But if you ever, ever think you can walk out on me again without so much as a real goodbye, I will hunt you down and divorce your ass so fast your head will spin."

Leo, the ridiculous ass, just grinned. "Deal."

27

MIRI

Miri let him lead her upstairs by the hand. Making their way through the half-done house, smelling freshly done drywall and inhaling dust, he opened the door to the master bedroom with a caveat.

"This is the only room in the house that's fully done," he said. "Furniture and everything."

Her brows furrowed. "That's weird."

Leo shrugged. "I wanted something to be done for us, some way to show you that I'm trying to see this through this time."

She separated from him, slowly walking around the room. The flooring had the same dark, polished wood as the rest of the house, but the softest-looking bed sat atop a large area rug that stretched out from under it. Her fingers trailed along the white comforter and the pretty little pillows up top.

"Did you choose these?"

His face heated and he rubbed at the back of his neck. "Thea did. She helped me with all of it, honestly. But she said she wanted to keep it neutral so you could do it up how you wanted."

"It's beautiful." The smile on Miri's face was nothing short of lovely as she looked around the space.

Leo moved closer to her. "I'm glad you think so. I . . . I wanted you to be able to actually see yourself here."

"I can see myself in this bed, for sure." She fell back onto it, spreading her arms and legs wide, her limbs still far from hanging off the sides. "Fuuuuck, this bed is amazing."

"The bed was all me." Leo's chest puffed with pride. "Remember that one little vacation we went on? When we stayed at that hotel in Charleston for the weekend?"

Miri closed her eyes, a smile widening her lips. "The Hilton Garden Inn. It had a separate tub and shower, that big ol' TV, and an indoor pool. That was the nicest place I'd ever stayed in."

"I remember the bed the most," Leo said. "You sunk into it—"

"Like a cloud." She cut him off, voice dreamy.

"When we weren't in that pool, we were in that bed. When we went home and got back in our lumpy bed, it was hell. I wanted something different for us this time, so I tried to create a hotel bed. The mattress is real high quality and there's goose-down padding and I got sheets so expensive the price almost gave me hives, but I'm proud of it."

"Where'd you learn how to do all that?"

He walked slowly, cautiously as he went to join her on the bed, sitting on the side, close enough that Miri could feel the heat of his skin on hers. "I do know how to use the internet, you know."

When she caught his eyes, his were playful. It had been so long since she'd really seen them that way, and she wanted to make the look stay. "Sometimes I forget you're not actually an old man, you know."

"Yeah, me too."

They stared at each other for a while, her eyes getting lower with every second. Miri couldn't help herself from trailing her gaze down his face. Over the flat of his nose and his thick lips. His skin was smooth and she reached up to trail her fingers softly along his strong jawline. Warm and soft, he leaned into her touch.

Even sitting there fully clothed, Miri found herself overwhelmed by his fineness. And the way he looked at her . . . God, like she was the only thing in the world worth admiring. It made her feel like a feral thing.

He leaned down until their mouths were mere centimeters apart. "Tell me I did good."

When he spoke, their mouths brushed. His lips were warm and a little wet from his own spit. Just that, the smallest, almost innocent touch was enough to make her wet.

"You did good, baby." Her words were all comfort and confidence. "You did so fucking good."

She turned a bit, wrapping her hands around his neck, pulling him until he was lying beside her. Like always, she led, her lips sure and firm but a little frantic too. They kissed like lovers returned from war. All desperation and relief, like they wanted to crawl inside each other's skin and feel from the inside. And goddamn if that wasn't exactly what Miri wanted.

He ground his hips into her and Miri chuckled into his mouth, a slightly cruel thing that made him shudder with pleasure.

"Should I prove it to you?" she asked.

"Fuck yes."

She pushed him onto his back, swinging one of her legs over his waist to straddle him. He couldn't help but immediately lift his hips up to seek anything even close to warmth and friction.

Her hand went to his face, digging her nails into his skin just enough to make him hiss in pleasure.

"You fucking asshole." Her words were hot as she pressed her mouth against his, nipping his bottom lip.

"Your asshole." He grinned up at her.

"Have I told you how beautiful you are tonight?" His voice came out dark and husky and he could see something in her go liquid at the sound.

"I don't know." She smiled at him behind hooded eyes. "Tell me again just to be sure."

"You're beautiful." There was no doubt or hesitation

in his voice. "I've never seen anything more beautiful than you in this housedress, sitting on my lap like you own it."

Leo and his words seemed to make her feel so desired that the need to show him how much she appreciated it overtook her. "I do own it, should I show you?"

A little growl left his lips as she climbed off of his lap but was quickly quieted when he watched her scoot down between his legs. She rubbed her face on one of his thighs through his jeans and his eyes went wild.

"Should I take you in my mouth, Leo?" His words had escaped him. He let out a groan but that didn't seem good enough for her. She practically growled, "Answer me, Leo. Tell me what you want."

"I want to fuck your mouth," he said once he finally found his voice. "I want you to make me feel good."

"Let me take you out then, let's see what I can do."

Her hands were sure as she took her sweet time undoing his belt. She smiled up at him the entire time, her gaze wild and powerful.

The second she finally got his pants opened and pulled his dick out, she realized how much she'd missed having her hands on him. She started with her tongue. Making him hiss as she ran it over his sensitive head, his thighs quivering under her hands.

She wrapped one of her hands around the base of his thick dick, and she took him in her mouth, creating a suction as she let her spit make him wet and messy.

Leo pulled her bonnet off and pushed a hand into her

dense hair, but instead of pushing her head down, he just gripped lightly at the strands. It wasn't harsh enough to hurt her, but it did encourage her.

"I forgot how good this is," Leo ground out. "I thought I remembered but fuuuuck."

She pulled off of him and ran her tongue on the underside of his length, following the vein that pulsed underneath his skin. Pulling away from him completely when she felt him shudder.

"Fuck my mouth, Leo." She made her demand with no hesitation and he showed none as he followed it.

His hips thrust as much as they could in his position, shallow at first, letting her get used to the feeling of having her face fucked. Instead of using her hands on the stretch of him that wasn't in her mouth, she rested them on his thighs and started moving her head down as he thrusted up.

She moaned once he finally hit the back of her throat and swallowed on him even more. The slap and swallow sounds completely drowned out everything else; they sounded so loud in Leo's ears that he briefly wondered if anyone else could hear them.

The longer Leo fucked her throat, the more worked up she became. Her pussy pulsing, wetting her thighs as they pressed tightly together. The pressure became completely unbearable, but she had no interest in pulling away for her own relief—not yet anyway.

Instead, she reached down, and shoved a hand between her legs. There was no finesse as her fingers roughly pushed between her puffy lips and rubbed at her clit.

"Are you touching yourself?" Leo's voice hadn't lost any of its huskiness, and it only made her wetter.

She still couldn't give him an answer with her mouth full, but he didn't seem to actually need one from her.

"Did me fucking your face get you all wet? I haven't even touched that pussy yet and I bet it's already all wet and dripping."

Miri filled herself with two fingers, and while they weren't nearly enough to completely ease her need, they were enough to make her moan around him.

Leo's thrusts sped up, his dick going deeper, faster. And while he fucked her mouth, she fucked herself. The sensation of being filled twice over had Miri's entire body on fire. Her cunt clutched at her fingers and her lips stretched almost painfully around him.

Before either of them could come, Leo used the hand in her hair to pull her off of him. Breathing hard, hair all askew, she knew she must have looked like a complete mess, but he kissed her anyway—all tongue and unrestrained lust.

Then, he pulled her up a bit, shifted, and laid her down under him. His lips went to her neck immediately, sucking and nipping at her hot, sensitive skin as she writhed, eager to have him touch as much of her as possible. Leo didn't seem to want to give her what she wanted, though—not yet anyway. He kept kissing down her neck and across the skin on her chest that was uncovered by her dress. When he realized that there was no way to free her tits from the clutches of her housedress, he settled for brushing his thumbnails over them through the fabric.

His touch felt amazing, but it seemed like he was specifically avoiding the place she needed him to feel the most. Even as she spread her legs wider and twisted her hips, he paid absolutely no mind to her swollen pussy and worked her up even more.

The whine she released was desperate and needy and she felt no embarrassment over it.

"That's right," he said darkly against the skin of her neck. "That's exactly how I want you. It's my turn to make you beg."

Miri wasn't nearly too proud to do what he wanted, especially not when doing so would get her what she wanted so desperately.

"Please," she pleaded with him. "Please, please fuck me, Leo. I need it."

For all of his talking, he didn't seem to have the will-power to hold off for much longer either. He moved to the side a little more and prompted her to close her legs some so that he could work her panties off. She spread her legs open immediately after and the second she felt the air against her pussy, she shuddered.

He took a second to stroke his dick, looking down at her, seeming calmer by the second, as if not having his hands on her helped him focus enough to get his bearings back. Even his eyes looked a little clearer. Miri wasn't so lucky. She hadn't calmed down at all. In fact, watching him stroke his hand up and down his cock just served to make her even wetter.

By the time Leo moved between her thighs and ran the tip of his length through her folds, she feared that she'd go off the second he got inside of her.

"You need me to beg you some more?" she asked gruffly as he circled her clit before dipping more into her soaked slit. "Or are you going to fuck me the way we both need?"

"Uh-uh," he grunted. "I'm just trying to savor the moment. I don't want to forget anything about this moment. Not how wet you are or how beautiful you are spread wide for me. Definitely not the way your eyes look when you're desperate to be fucked."

His words made her grip his shoulders hard. When she felt his head finally, finally pushing at where she opened up, her acrylics dug into his hot skin and her breaths quickened.

"Fuck."

"Shit."

They moaned out at the same time, both words coming out broken and desperate.

The stretch had Miri arching her back immediately. Leo was thick and long and the way he filled her made her pussy ache in a different way than it had before he'd gotten inside of her.

As his hips moved, they matched the rhythm of the song. He wasn't putting too much force behind his stroke just yet, but it was enough to make her cry out.

Leo kept his forearms on either side of her face, keeping himself steady as he moved in her.

"You feel so good, baby." She loved that even after

all these years, he never had a problem being vocal with her. It spurred her on.

"I've never felt anything as good as you," he said back, pleasing the hell out of her. "Not a single thing."

Miri rocked her hips up into Leo's thrusts and it only made him fuck her harder. There were goosebumps raised on every inch of her skin and every brush of his flesh against hers sent her falling closer and closer to the orgasm she'd been chasing for far too long.

She could smell the heady scent of her sex in the air and hear the wet slap of skin every time his dick left her, and thrusted back in. It was all too much for her to handle. She was overstimulated the same way she'd been when he went down on her, and just like that time in Thea's laundry room, she knew she wasn't going to last much longer.

One moment, her eyes were clamped shut with the overwhelming sensations, and the next they were blown wide as his pelvic bone brushed against her responsive clit.

"There you go, sugar." Leo's voice was ragged. "Fuck me back just like that. Move those hips."

She did exactly as he told her, both of them moving to the same beat even though the song had changed twice over since he'd first fucked into her.

"I'm about to come," she gasped.

He growled into her neck. "I know, I can feel that pussy tightening up around me. Come for me, Miri, let me see you lose yourself."

She took off silently, nails digging deep into the

cheeks of Leo's ass as he fucked her through her orgasm. It was a big one, prolonged by the feeling of him inside of her, the scratch of her dress against her sensitive nipples, even the slightly uncomfortable hardness of the cabana cushion underneath her. Everything combined to make her stomach seize up tight and her pussy flutter even tighter.

It only took a few more thrusts before Leo's hips lost some of their rhythm. A hand found its way back into the thickness of her hair and held on as he came, filling her up with a groan so low and sexy that it made her shiver.

Miri's arms left his ass and wrapped around his back— they stayed that way for a while, his half-hard dick still inside of her as they both shuddered through the aftershocks of their orgasms.

The second he pulled out of her she missed him. So much so that she barely gave him time to catch his breath before she was cuddling close to him again.

His arms went around her at the same time, as if he needed to be as close to her as she needed to be to him. Miri was quiet as she waited for her heart rate to return to a normal speed.

"I can't believe we just had sex in a construction zone," Leo laughed after a while. Miri could feel the vibrations of his words through the ear she had on his chest. "I feel like I should have given you something more romantic than this—at least with some rose petals or something."

"Stop trying to make stuff perfect and focus on the good we've got now." Miri had no intention of moving but she wished she had the energy to get them under the covers. The heat that she'd felt all over her skin had given way to a cool sweat that had her shivering for a completely different reason.

"Yes, ma'am." He ran his nose over her hairline and down her cheek.

Her fingers pinched one of his nipples and he let a fake howl out into the air that had her laughing louder and more genuinely than she had in a while.

"Rest up, boy. Because the second you can go again I'm about to ride you all the way to heaven."

Epilogue

~

MIRI

Four months later

"I cannot believe I let you talk me into this shit," Jade grumbled.

"You are such a baby." Miri laughed, completely unsympathetic. "Acting like I'm your granny dragging you Easter dress shopping. You're on a beautiful island in the middle of the ocean—for free, I might add."

Jade rolled her eyes. "Free doesn't even mean anything to you anymore, you've got more money than God now."

"Not anymore." Miri grinned. "Greenbelt just so happened to get a very large endowment aimed at helping its most vulnerable residents get the money to restore and maintain their homes."

"Hmm . . . I wonder who the generous benefactor could be."

"We'll never know." Miri's shrug was all faux non-chalance. "Anonymity is a bitch, huh?"

The two women were hiking through a thick patch of wooded brush on their resort. And by hiking, they simply meant walking on something that wasn't a concrete sidewalk. There was a small trail cleared and marked with little stones. Even the so-called woods weren't particularly isolated. If she listened hard enough, Miri could hear the music from some kind of lunchtime celebration less than a mile away.

Miri had talked her closest friends and family into joining her and Leo on a once-in-a-lifetime trip to Bora-Bora—all expenses paid, of course. It hadn't taken her much effort to sell it to them, admittedly. She didn't think any of them had ever been out of the country before, let alone a place as spectacular as French Polynesia.

Each couple had their own little bungalow that stood high over water so blue she could hardly believe it was real. Aja and Walker had come along happily, even managing to separate from each other's faces for long enough to have group dinners and excursions. Leo's childhood best friend, Quentin, and his husband, Chuck, had been more than happy to tag along as well. Thea and her husband had left the kids at home for their first real vacation as a couple. Olivia and Jade were there too, of course. Miri had even booked them the honeymoon suite. Largely so that they had more space for some individual seclusion if they wanted, but mostly to troll them. Her mama was there as well, but all she was interested in was sitting in her new bikini on the beach, trying to "get

her cougar on." Miri didn't know if she'd been successful, but she'd definitely seen a few lone figures leaving
Patrice's bungalow in the wee hours of the morning over
the past few days.

Ginger was back home, checked into some bougie
doggy hotel in Beaufort. She'd wanted to bring her little
baby so bad, but the trip was long, and the resort didn't
allow dogs—no matter how cute—so she'd been forced
to leave her only child behind.

When the group had met for breakfast that morning,
Miri and Leo had suggested that they take an excursion
to a nearby waterfall. Aja, the angel, was immediately
on board. The rest of them had been skeptical. Thea had
immediately been suspicious, making a comment about
how she'd just seen a movie where a group of people
went off to a waterfall on a tropical island and all ended
up dead.

Leo had been forced to assure her, with literal Goo-
gled statistics, that they almost certainly wouldn't die at
the waterfall before she'd finally agreed to come. The
rest of the gang had gone a bit early, but Miri had stayed
behind a bit, taking some extra time to get her hair just
right and spend a few minutes with herself.

Jade had waited, not wanting Miri to make the trek
into the jungle by herself. No matter how much she grumbled about the mosquitos or the walk, Miri was happy to
have the company.

She and Leo had staked out the location their first
night on the island at the recommendation of one of the
resort staff. Both had been overcome, every sense taken

by the smell of the forest and the flowing water. They'd made love on a towel, then immediately decided they'd needed to bring their people here. It was a space that needed to be shared.

The jungle was hot and humid, but the massive mosquito presence demanded some type of protection. Miri wore a white bikini with an ankle-length cover-up with twin leg slits. She felt cool and sexy . . . and nervous as hell.

Miri could hear the waterfall before she saw it. It was loud, rushing and bubbling and flowing. A collection of sounds so beautiful even Jade's stank-ass mood was changed.

"Are we getting close?"

"Yeah," Miri answered. "It's right over here."

Her heart started beating faster in her chest, her steps picking up the pace unconsciously.

When they finally came to the clearing with the waterfall, every bit of her anxious energy melted away. Her people were there. In the water, sitting in the sand, canoodling half-hidden behind a large rock. They all looked happier than she'd seen them in a long time. Relaxed and content.

She barely noticed Jade running ahead of her, throwing off her own cover-up and cannonballing right next to where Olivia was floating on her back in the water.

Like two magnets, so different but so closely drawn, Leo turned his head to see her the second she found him. Her feet kept moving her forward and he hopped up from his spot in the sand.

They met in the middle. Leo's arms wrapped around

her waist, drawing her in. Their kiss was warm and familiar, and her belly filled with more fire than it ever had. Her hands went around his waist, fingernails grazing over the short hairs at the nape of his warm neck.

When he pulled his lips away, she whimpered a bit, too overwhelmed to be embarrassed about it.

"This was a good idea," he told her, laying a kiss on her forehead, then her jaw.

"It was, wasn't it?" Miri honestly didn't think they'd ever been this happy in her life.

She and Leo had announced that they were back together almost immediately—it had been impossible to hide, and to be honest, they hadn't really wanted to. They'd spent the past few months trying to figure out how they should commemorate their new beginning.

Miri hadn't wanted to have a second wedding. While her marriage to Leo was something she was learning to love again in new and different ways than before, she hadn't felt like the person she was today wanted the spectacle of a wedding, whether it was in a church or in Aunt Roberta's—or, now their—backyard. Leo had agreed. So, they'd gone through options of commitment ceremonies to elopements to a surprise drive-by wedding ring toss.

The one thing both had ultimately landed on was that, while they loved their friends and family, whatever ceremonial thing they wanted to do didn't need to include them. They'd taken to separating their marriage into two parts—the marriage before and the marriage now. So much of the marriage before had been dictated by other people's influences, whether intentionally bad or not.

They loved their friends and family, but their marriage wasn't for any of them. It was for Miri and Leo to live in and celebrate. So, they'd done this instead. Invited almost everyone they loved most in the world to a tropical island so they could all celebrate each other.

In private, Miri and Leo had remade something close to vows to one another. Feet dangling over the little balcony of their bungalow, the night sky so clear and endless above them it made their smallness comforting.

Miri caught her mother's eye from across the clearing and gave her a giddy smile before she met Leo's eyes again.

"I can't believe this is real." Miri's voice was so soft it nearly got lost in the sound of the water. "All of it. This place, the house back in Greenbelt, you, those green tomatoes out front that keep getting eaten by raccoons. I swear, sometimes I expect to snap my fingers and wake up or something."

Leo heard her, though, like always. "It's not a dream, Miri. It's better than that. It's you and me and everything we didn't know enough to want."

She laughed. "Some real one-in-a-million-type shit."

"One in two hundred and two point five million, actually." He grinned, and when she quirked an eyebrow at him, Leo laughed too. "What? You know I had to look it up."

Miri had never experienced salt-kissed skin before. She'd never spent so long completely relaxed in the sun, letting sea salt bake into her every pore. Even when she and

Leo made their way back to their villa and into the air-conditioning, she couldn't quite bring herself to wash it all off in the shower yet. She surprised herself at Leo's offer to wash together, giving him a sly smile and telling him to find her once he was done instead.

Pouring herself a glass of the complimentary red wine that had been left in the kitchen, she sat on one of the plush couches on the overwater patio.

It was just after dusk, night hadn't quite set in yet, allowing her to still see the horizon.

It was beautiful here, all warm sand and tall trees. The air smelled fresh and salty and the only thing she could hear was the flowing water lapping at the stilts keeping the property up. She couldn't quite figure out why, but something about it reminded her of home. The smells were all different, and so were the sounds, even the way the air touched the skin of your shoulders didn't feel the same. But as she sat there in her robe, face at the sky, eyes closed, pure content in her spirit, it wasn't at all different from how she felt on a summer evening, sitting on their little porch in Mama's rocking chair, just taking a little while away from all the big things. Just feeling the little things.

It was almost thrilling that, when she felt Leo's presence behind her, it didn't at all disrupt these feelings. Except maybe her skin got warmer. And maybe leaning back into his chest was infinitely better than the wooden limbs of the rocking chair.

His hand was still hot-water warm as he stroked it through the top part of her robe, so gently over her sensitive skin, from one shoulder to the other. Not quite around her neck, but warm and secure. The motion made Miri press her thighs together.

"Today was good." His voice was quiet in her ear, but he was close enough that she could feel the words through his chest.

"It was." She nodded gently. "I'm glad we were on the same page about how we wanted to do this. It's not that I don't want everyone to know—"

"It's that this needs to be just us this time," he said. "At least for now."

Miri laughed. "On our new ten-year anniversary I'll give you the wedding of your dreams, I promise."

Leo bit at her ear playfully, and she squirmed happily. "I want you to do one of those little dances down the aisle to me."

"I'll be damned if I'm ever as corny as you."

He hummed. "We'll see about that . . ."

"What's that supposed to mean?" she scoffed, all fake bratty.

"I just feel like I could convince you to do it is all."

She made his arms unravel from around her with one tap and turned her ass to face him on the couch. "That's awfully confident."

Leo's chuckle was deep enough that it made her look down at his chest as if she'd see the source of it inside him.

"I'm not saying you're not the boss." This made her snort. "But we both know how easy I can make you fold."

Miri narrowed her eyes at him. Her first instinct was

to disagree with him, argue for the fun of it. But he was right. Her bite and her bark never did completely hold up with him. Not unless they were having sex, at least. Even then it was shaky at best.

"Speaking of . . ." He grabbed her up by the waist and hoisted her onto his lap. She flailed a bit, still not used to being lifted.

The belt on her robe had loosened as she moved, and by the time she was situated with her thighs across his, it had become all but useless. Briefly, she debated whether she wanted to close it, tie the belt tight around her waist and prolong the teasing.

But then she saw the look in his eyes when he looked at her—her body reacted instantly. Dark brown eyes making her nipples tighten and her pussy run slick. His hands went back to her shoulders, moving the sleeves down her arms until it was resting in the crooks of her elbows, leaving her breasts bare to him.

"If I were to do something like this"—his gentle hands cupped her tits from the bottoms, rubbing his fat thumbs over her nipples—"you'd be nice and receptive to me."

"Hmmm . . ." She tilted her head back a little, pressing her chest into his hands even more. His fingers were so slow as they circled her flesh. Rings of fire and ice that made her shudder. "It might take a little more than that."

She smiled as she felt his breath on her nipple in response and when he nipped at it just the slightest, her hiss was downright filthy.

"How about that?" Leo asked.

"You might be a little bit closer."

His answer to her goading was to reach around, lips still around one of her nipples, and clutch her ass cheeks in his hands. He guided her hips to rock against his. The moan that escaped her lips was too needy to contain.

"Closer like that?" His tone was gruff.

It wasn't long before she got tired of just the feeling of their robes creating friction between her legs.

She wanted more.

"I think we can get closer still."

Her hands worked the cloth out of the way, her voice breaking when his hard, bare dick pressed up against her wet, sensitive flesh. Leo moved his hips off, making his leaking tip brush against her clit.

They moved like that for what felt like an eternity. His hands on her ass, helping her move, while hers wrapped around the back of his neck. Leo's mouth was everywhere it could reach. Licking at her nipples, sucking love bites into her neck.

Her pants were loud into the evening sky, and it wasn't until she opened her eyes again, desperate to see him, that she realized they were out in the open.

"Someone could come out on their patio and see us," she panted, hips never missing a beat. The slick slide of them together was deliciously noisy. They were more than ready for each other, wet and swollen, aching to come together finally. It had been mere hours since they'd last had each other but it might as well have been years.

"I know." He spoke the words into her collarbones. "Any time they wanted to, they could step out and look over and see how hot you are for me. Desperate enough to rub yourself against me all exposed like this."

She probably would have been mortified if someone had actually caught them, but they hadn't seen anyone from the other villas since they'd moved in. The risk felt relatively low, but the reward would be divine.

"Leo," she moaned, the slip-slide becoming too much to bear. "I need you in . . . fuck . . ."

He moved his hips back a little farther, making her gasp when his dick grazed her entrance. "You need me in here, wife?"

Miri held her hips still so that his tip was pressed up against her willing flesh. All it would take was one small press, the smallest of movements, and he'd be exactly where they both wanted him to be—deep inside her.

"Please don't tease me." She laid her forehead in the crook of his neck, her body stilled by his hands.

"It's so fun, though, when else do I get the chance to see you lose it like this than when you're on my dick?"

She contracted her pelvic floor, hoping that the fluttering would drive him wild enough to let up on his delicious little power trip.

When he hissed, a strike of triumph zinged through her.

"How long are you going to torture me?" she gasped.

Leo caught her eyes. His pupils were dilated, making the already dark brown irises even more intense. The look on his face made her insides clench.

"How long are you going to let me?" he asked.

There it was, yet another reminder that while she certainly belonged to him too, Leo was hers to command.

She shifted her hips without another word, both of their moans ringing out into the evening sky as she moved down on him. He was thick and hard and the stretch of him inside her made her eyes roll back.

Miri kept her hips still once he was fully seated, getting used to the feel of him. Every time they came together like this, every piece of the puzzle moved together perfectly. The way their bodies moved, the way their mouths fit together, even the way they sounded. Each element of their lovemaking existed as proof that when they drowned out all the bullshit, they worked so fucking well together.

He moved slow, her hips rocking back and forth gently, gritting her teeth as his dick slid perfectly over her sensitive spots. Leo kept his hands on her ass, and while he didn't try to force her out of her pace, his grip tightened. Fingers digging into her hot flesh, spreading her open.

When she finally did lift up, she did it with her eyes on his. The almost excruciatingly perfect drag up, and the release of her hips that sent her back down into his lap again.

"Goddamn," Leo hissed. "I can feel you dripping down my balls, Miri."

"I've been waiting all day," she panted back. "If we'd been alone at the waterfall I probably would have fucked you in the dirt."

Leo's hips canted up, fucking her back, releasing a guttural moan from his diaphragm. His thrusts weren't frantic, but they forced her to grip at his shoulders. Their teasing had turned rough, and as good as she felt, all she wanted to do was sink into the feeling of it.

Her nipples brushed against his chest, hard little points on hot skin that made her clit sing with every rub.

Their hips slammed, and she could feel the fullness of Leo's balls every time her ass clapped on his lap. The sound of their skin and the slickness of her pussy was as loud as the water below them. Time felt meaningless, minutes, hours, days, years. Nothing mattered but this—them.

Her orgasm built up slowly in her belly, a snake coiling tight, tight, tight in the center until it was so wrapped around itself that her thighs quivered.

When she opened her eyes with a gasp, it was dark out. The only thing that allowed her to see him was the lights from their villa.

God, was he gorgeous. All that smooth brown skin covered in sweat, teeth bared, eyes focused on her. She felt like the only person alive. Like anyone could have walked in and it wouldn't have mattered, because nothing mattered as much as this.

"I'm going to come." Her words were whispered into Leo's ear as she clutched at him, one of her hands stroking the wet flesh around her clit but not directly on it. She was ready, it was there, right fucking there, but she didn't want to let it go yet.

"I've been holding back since the minute I slid inside you," he said. "Trying not to embarrass myself."

"Don't hold it back anymore, baby. Let it go." She bit his earlobe, sucking the supple skin into her mouth. "Come inside me, Leo. Please. I need it."

As if all he needed was a word from her, his body seized, dick throbbing inside her, arms tight around her waist holding her to him. She found herself filled with warmth and satisfaction as he spilled. His orgasm seemed to last awhile, but he never finished fucking as he worked his way through it. And even after coming, he stayed hard.

Extra slick, made messy with him as he pushed his come deeper into his body with his thrusts, Miri came all over him. She wasn't loud, but her vision went stark white and her body clenched nearly to the point of pain. The sensation made its way through her entire body. All warmth and bliss and that had her clenching rapidly around him long after she'd collapsed on his chest.

"We've definitely gotten better at that." She spoke the words into his neck.

Leo didn't say anything for so long that she thought he might have fallen asleep. "It could only be this way with you," he said.

She closed her eyes, sighing as he softened inside her. "I know."

Three months after that

Miri loved her little greenhouse. Aside from the bedroom she shared with Leo, it was probably her favorite place in the house—even if it was technically outside of it.

Admittedly, she used it more for "smoke breaks"

than she did for actual gardening, but Leo had installed some type of fan system to make the heat more bearable and he'd even put in a little love seat. Sometimes she sat out there for hours, blissfully scrolling through her phone. Other times, she enjoyed some of the best naps she'd ever had surrounded by thriving plants and sunlight.

More than once her husband had been forced to come retrieve her from her little space to eat dinner or make it to whatever plans they'd made.

Now, though, Leo was in Beaufort at the hardware store. The boys had convinced him to install a tree house on the property. Considering how they had more land than Ahmir and Thea, and that he loved a good project, Leo had been all for it.

She knew that this would be an all-day task for him; the man could spend hours upon hours just looking at different types of wood. Miri knew she'd have all the time she needed to herself, which was why she'd finally decided to complete a task she'd been putting off for months.

Armed with one of the many shovels they had in the shed, she found a little spot of soft dirt next to her greenhouse and set about doing something she had a lot of experience with—digging a hole.

Ms. Candice had taught her that she didn't need to go any deeper than three feet. It was spring now, and while it may not have been as cold as it was up north, it sure as hell wasn't as hot as an August afternoon. Her face might not have gotten as sweaty, but her body sure felt the effects of the labor.

Maybe this was part of it. Ms. Candice said that her father had taken to burying his money so as not to get flashy with it. There must have been something to this particular extreme. The digging took hours. It made your back ache and your shoulders tense. Shovels were heavy and even the softest of dirt was hard to move. Burying was hard on the body—and digging up wasn't at all any easier.

There was a sacrifice involved in both actions. A certain sense of extremes. Whatever you put down there would be hard to get to, you had to want it to go after it. Really fucking want it.

The pain had nothing on the time, either. Dirt flying into the eyes, skin covered in grime for hours and hours. There was a time, after those first few pushes of the shovel, when it was easy to give up—turn away with the realization that this was probably a ridiculous thing to do. And if you didn't follow that urge, it wasn't long before quitting became an impossibility.

Toward the end, it became a game of pure spite and endurance. Which was why Miri stared down into the hole she'd spent five hours digging and refused to resist the urge to spit. She was in desperate need of a shower and a massage and a good, hot meal. But before she could do that, she took another lesson from Ms. Candice's rule book, and picked her shoebox up from where she'd laid it.

It was a sturdy box, made with the cardboard that

wasn't so easily bent. But she'd still tied it closed with a red ribbon that Leo had secured around one of her Christmas gifts that year.

Pulling at the bow, she flipped it open. Instead of money, the only thing that lay inside was her divorce papers. The same ones she'd gotten from her lawyer what felt like a lifetime ago.

The papers were off-white and crinkled and she could spot what looked like a coffee stain on the middle. They looked like they'd been through hell. Or, alternatively, held at the bottom of her purse for months— which they very much had been.

She'd spent months trying to figure out what to do with them. Throwing them in the trash felt too inconsequential. Shredding them felt too extreme. Briefly, she'd considered burning them. Jade had convinced her to set up a scene. Light some candles, play her favorite sad-girl playlist, and take a lighter to them like she was in a deleted scene from *Waiting to Exhale*. That hadn't felt right either.

It wasn't like she wanted to keep hold of them in fear, like she was second-guessing her decision to stay with Leo. That wasn't it at all. But getting rid of them completely felt like throwing away a part of their story.

Miri didn't think she was supposed to have so many feelings about a stack of papers she hadn't even used. But fuck it. People had way weirder things buried in their backyards than this. At least it wasn't a body or a bloodied hacksaw.

She ran her fingers over the crinkled papers. Not unfolding them, not interested in reading over the words she must have gone through a hundred times, but remembering the feeling of them in her hands.

She didn't want to ever have to touch them again. She didn't want to have to read through those difficult-to-understand, harder-to-emotionally-grasp words.

They'd started this up again with the full intention of seeing it through, and so far, it was working tremendously. So much so that sometimes she found herself viewing their past as farther away than it actually was.

Leo was working on renovating the nail shop, which meant that Miri was seeing certain clients in a little spare room in the house. Almost every day of the week, she took him a sack lunch. Sauntered up to him while he was covered in sawdust and sweat, and pressed a little lunch box into his hands like she'd been doing it forever.

They spent every night together, and any time she woke up out of her sleep to go to the bathroom or get a glass of water, his eyes blinked open too.

They were attached at the hip so close that it would have been embarrassing if it didn't feel so incredible.

But as good as things were, as good as she hoped they'd continue to be, the past was still there, and it made everything about the present possible.

It was bizarre to view divorce papers as a good-luck charm—but she'd never shied away from bizarre.

Miri had won something she hadn't allowed herself to even consider—and she wasn't talking about the money.

These were hers to do with as she pleased. And what

she wanted was to tie the red ribbon tight around the box, press these memories into South Carolina soil, and let the earth reclaim them so that she could fully reclaim her love.

And so she did.

Acknowledgments

I want to start by, as always, thanking my mother. I would not exist without you and this book would not exist without you either. For all the groceries we had to put back and for everything we couldn't have. We made it happen—finally.

My sister Angel, who is my biggest cheerleader and the best person I know.

My sister Ashley, who shares with me a love of reading that is unmatched.

My grandparents, Granny and Poppy, who are both gone now but who raised me and loved me even when I complained about the fact that we never had anything "good" to snack on in the house.

I want to thank my agent, Kim Lionetti, for believing

in this book even before she met it. You're a Rock Star and there's no one else I'd rather be doing this with.

Vicki Lame, what can I even say except thank you? Thank you for your patience and your insight. Thank you for being the best editor an overly sensitive writer could ask for. I always feel most proud when I write something that makes you feel those Big Feelings you love so much.

I want to thank Vanessa Aguirre, for so graciously putting up with my late emails. Kerri Resnick, for being my favorite cover designer ever. Marissa, Brant, and Meghan, for making sure *Play to Win* has a chance to succeed out in the world. This goes for everyone else at St. Martin's Griffin who has had even a finger in the production of this book.

To my "Andy Chat" babes. Nat, Cici, Demi, Soph, and Lauren. Y'all are all over this book.

To any person who I absolutely didn't forget but have neither the time nor words to express everything I feel.

To me, again, for getting through it proudly, even when I thought I'd never actually get to the last page of it.

Thank you. I love you.

About the Author

Madison Van Zile

JODIE SLAUGHTER is the author of *Bet on It* and *Play to Win*. She is a twentysomething romance author who spends most of her days hunched over a laptop, making fictional characters kiss. She loves love, so she writes romance novels full of heart, passion, and heat. When she isn't putting steamy scenes or declarations of devotion on the page, she can normally be found being generally hilarious on Twitter, dreaming about brisket, or consuming way too much television. She lives in Kentucky.